LIGHT IN THE GLOAMING

A Novel

J.B. SIMMONS

Jonathan,

Congrats on winning the giveaway!
You're going to love the book — may
it fill you with light.
Can't wait to hear what you
think! — J.B. Simmons

jbsimmons.light@gmail.com

ISBN 978-1492263173

For Lindsay

Chapter 1

The Will to Live

**"For the state of innocence,
the paradisiacal condition,
is that of the brute.
Paradise is a park,
where only brutes,
not men, can remain."**

I was betrayed and banished to a society of nothing. We have no law but survival, and the only thing holding us together is the wall around us. It rises as high as twenty men, without seams or cracks and with enough grayness to swallow you if you stare too long.

My resolve to escape had been slipping away before I met a man named Lucian. Like the rest of us, Lucian was cast down into the Gloaming alongside a dozen other poor souls and a bushel of scrap food. His welcome was a horde of men charging at him and the crumbs that fell beside him. He faced the onslaught like a seasoned sea captain staring down storm clouds on the horizon. I admired his calm.

He chanced upon a small loaf of bread when he fell. Such luxuries are rare in the trash that normally feeds us, but he held it casually. Some gaunt shape turned immediately toward the edible treasure. Teeth bared, the man growled and leaped at Lucian, who dodged the attack and swung his elbow into the man's head.

As the assailant crumpled to the ground, other men caught sight of the loaf. They ran at Lucian from every side. Just before they reached him, Lucian heaved his bread high into the dank air. The men's famished eyes followed the golden blur upwards. Lucian seized the distraction to do the only smart thing.

He ran. Finding a gap in the crude free-for-all, he charged out of the city's center and into an alley.

I had witnessed this while lurking on the fringes of the fight, and something about Lucian beckoned me to follow. Outside the central falling ground, narrow streets weave through shells of buildings. Some are one-story abandoned warehouses, but most reach up thirty or forty feet. Only the tallest building reaches half way to the ceiling. They are all made of gray stone blocks, topped with black slate roofs. Despite once solid construction, holes litter the structures. Inside, anything worthy of interest has been picked over a hundred times.

Lucian had picked a tight alley for his retreat. He should have known that the darker the path, the greater the danger. I chose a broader road and sprinted to the small square where Lucian's alley would lead. I hugged the crumbling wall of a low building and looked for movement. It was a desolate square, with a broken fountain trickling over bones.

I turned up the alley, wading into quiet darkness underneath high buildings on both sides. I tensed as my eyes searched ahead. Before me, on the ground, was a twisted, facedown body. I bent down and prodded the head to the side with my foot. I heard a slight splash the instant I realized it was not Lucian.

I spun too late and took a glancing blow to the cheek, enough to knock me into the wall. Lucian's uncertain glare fixed on me. His hesitation was enough of an opening. Here most men fight with their fists, but not me. I pulled a short iron pole from my tattered pants just as Lucian lunged. The blunt weapon crashed into his right temple. He went down limply beside the man he had taken out. Their blood puddled together, and it was deathly silent.

For the first time in many fallings in the Gloaming, I felt compelled to help. Instead of abandoning Lucian for dead, I

2

dragged his body down the alley. We had to cross the open square with the fountain, but I sensed no one around. I stayed low and moved fast. We slipped into an unassuming warehouse where I often hid.

Once inside, I checked for organic shadows. Finding none, I pried open a dusty metal gate on the floor with my pole, and slid Lucian down into the pitch-black cellar.

We battle over places to sleep as fiercely as we kill for food. As I sat over Lucian, I questioned my decision. It would be safer to cast him out on the square. He would not survive there in this weakened state. Or maybe I could abandon him here. Nothing good would ever come of this god-forsaken place.

I quieted the thought, cracked open the cellar gate to let a little light in, and studied the man. Blood had matted over his right temple and ear, but he was breathing regularly. Even in the dark of the basement, I could see that he was not like most that fall in the Gloaming.

He looked strangely familiar, though I did not remember seeing his face before. Perhaps he had been the son of a noble. His countenance weighed in favor of nobility. I raised one of his eyelids and saw a piercing blue eye. While lean and delicate, his frame suggested plenty of practice with the sword. He had to be strong to have survived to this point. He certainly had not weathered as many days of decay as I had before falling here.

It was hard to judge his age. His face was unwrinkled, framed by light brown hair and somehow radiant. My skin was chalk to his bronze. I wondered how long it would take for his tone to corrode like mine, but seeing his vitality brought a glimmer of hope.

I began trying to restore him. In my hideout, I kept a few morsels of food, and the fountain outside made water accessible. I thought it would be enough to sustain us a few days. I settled into a corner, where I had built a bed of ragged cloth scavenged from abandoned bodies. Sleep came upon me more easily than I had expected.

My dreams were surprisingly bright, like a raindrop of light splashing into a sea of darkness. I was on my back. The ground was covered in something lush and green—grass. A bright light shone onto my face. Clouds drifted high above. A gorgeous woman was lying at my side, reclined like a queen. She had long brown curls, and her laughter was like honey. I felt her hand in my hand. The feeling was warm and soft as the name Lorien came to my lips.

Darkness suddenly slid in front of the light, and the woman disappeared. I awoke sensing the shadow. Lucian was looming over me.

As I coiled, clenching my blunt weapon, I saw the confusion in his eyes. Wavering, he managed to say, "Where am I?"

It was an obvious first question with a tragic answer. How could I tell him what horrors I had seen? With my tongue dormant for so long, I was reluctant to unleash it. The sound of his voice was music to my word-deprived ears.

I answered with silence. Instead of words, I began to rise to my feet, lifting my pole as a warning. He clenched his fists as I stood.

"Who are you?" He asked and took a step back, outside the range of my weapon.

"One question at a time," I attempted. My voice was harsher than I had wanted. "We will get to the questions of where and who, but you should be asking why." My answer sparked fierceness in his eyes; the same that I had seen when he first dropped in the Gloaming.

"I know why I am here," he said bluntly. "I committed crimes against Prince Tryst, something to do with not respecting his laws. Laws that no free man could obey. He ordered that all boys between seven and twelve years old, and every firstborn son who reaches seven in the future, be handed over for a life of service in his new army. He calls it the Lycurgus. Well, he commanded me to give away my seven-year-old lad. What father would abide by that?"

He did not continue in words, but he wore a sad story on his face. His expression reminded me of why I had saved him. I could see that his mind had sharpened his spirit, caging the beast until its prey was in sight. It was clear that he had not been beaten down before he fell to this place.

"Where were you yesterday?" I asked.

His eyes opened wider at the question. "Why do you ask?"

"Please, tell me who you are and how you got here." The word "please" played nicely on my lips. It brought a tiny grin to my face. Facial muscles strained at the now-foreign effort. He seemed to relax in response.

"My name is Lucian." He paused. "That is enough for now. Yesterday I knelt before Tryst, expecting to be named a knight. He questioned my obedience because of certain things I had done, like hiding my little boy. Perhaps I reacted too strongly against him. It did not end well."

"Next thing I knew, I had a bag over my head and my hands were tied behind my back. I was dragged out and down more stairs than I could count. Someone then ordered me to stand and pushed me forward at sword point. Just as I stepped over an edge, the man behind me cut the rope binding my hands. I lost my footing and began sliding down. It felt like a smooth tube of metal. There was nothing to grab as I slid down hundreds of feet. As the slide began to flatten out, and as I was slowing down, the tube ended in mid-air. I fell a short distance onto what smelled like decaying trash and sounded like moaning men."

"Before I could make sense of any of it, the floor beneath us fell away. Everyone and everything in the pile crashed down into this place. That is when a bunch of starved-looking men ran at me and tried to kill me, so I ran. It is fuzzy after that, but seems like you knocked me out and brought me here."

He rubbed his temple gingerly. "And what about you? Why and how did you get here?" His voice sounded curious and somehow innocent.

"My tale is similar in some ways, Lucian. Unlike you, I was imprisoned in a hanging cage for a long time before I was cast down into that long shoot. What I was before that does not matter anymore."

"What you were before the cage matters. Who are you?" He tried to study my face, and I was thankful for the dim shadows. "I think I have seen you before," he said.

"No," I shook my head. "Let's just say I am a man trying to survive here. I have been here a long time, and it is good to be talking to you now. You can call me Damon."

He pretended to accept the answer. "Damon, you have my thanks for bringing me here alive. It is good to meet you."

Lucian put his hand out. I looked at it, confused for a moment, before realizing he meant to shake my hand. He seemed sincere, but his healthy body made him dangerous. We could unite for now, I decided, because his anger pointed in the same direction as mine, and because I still had the weapon.

I reached out and clasped his hand. Human touch. I breathed more easily, and he smiled in return.

"I understand your issues with Tryst's reign," I said. "You have to harness those memories. The anger can fuel your fight for survival, but it can also fester and lead to your death here."

"So Tryst has hurt you as well?" Suspicion laced his voice. I offered no answer, and a moment later he had an easier question. "How long have you been here?"

I held out my right arm, the one without the weapon, to show him my tally. Two parallel lines of shallow white scars stretched from my wrist to my bicep. I had started a third line at my wrist—it was up to seven marks.

"This is how you track time?" His expression slid to pity and fear. "How much time for each scar?"

"I do not know." This is where hope comes to die, I thought but did not say. My mind filled with what I had done to earn the scars. But the words froze on my lips. He was too fresh to understand the Gloaming. He would learn, just as I had. "The light never changes here. I carve a mark on my arm every time I survive a trip to the central square, where the scraps of food and men drop."

"Well there must be a way out," he declared.

I felt a surge of some foreign feeling at his demand. It rose up from my empty belly and escaped from my parched lips as laughter. Its source was cynical, but the sensation of humor was sweet.

"I will not stay here." He growled the words like a threat and looked ready to charge out of our hiding place. He was not accustomed to failure, it seemed.

"I have tried escaping. I have tried again, and again. What will we do? Jump over the wall? Dig under it? There is a hope-consuming stone ceiling above us. The only light seeps in from the slits at the top of the wall. Trust me, there is no way out."

"We will find a way," he proclaimed.

His vigor and persistence was as admirable as a child's quest to slay a dragon. I did not want to beat down his bright spirit, remembering that when I had first arrived, I too had expected to escape and exact my revenge. Time here had destroyed that expectation and left only bitterness, emptiness, and an unfulfilled thirst for justice.

I decided to describe the brutal city, but to leave out the sins that I had committed to stay alive. Giving words to evil acts would not help anything, and being with Lucian urged me toward something good.

"Let me tell you more about this city, Lucian. I call it the Gloaming. Everything devolves into chaos down here, like in some torrid swamp of man's worst. You cannot help but lose track of time, because there is no hint of sun or moon."

"You fell at the center of the city, a perfect square. It pulses like the heart of a beast whose skin is the wall around us. Men who survive the first fall disperse into the city from there, only to return when they are starved. All of us have to go back there for the food that seems to fall at regular intervals—bones, half-eaten loaves, rotten fruit, or whatever rubbish. I count the time between each fall as if it were a day, and I reward myself for surviving each day with a deep scratch into my arm."

"My tally of scars is at ninety-seven. I started this tally after the seventh falling, because I had begun to lose track of all time and dimension. The scars are my badges of honor, and they could mean weeks, months, or a year. I hope it has not been longer. Now my arm is running out of space. I do not know of anyone who has survived as long here as I have. But then, I do not really know anyone here."

"In a way, life begins with the fall. Before then, I was locked in a tiny, floating cage for days. I had no food, but thoughts of revenge sustained me. I received water only from rare blasting sprays into my cage. Before my life faded someone opened the cage's door, inviting a leap into the unknown, which leads to here. I think most men suffer something similar before they are cast down, judging from their pathetic state when they land."

"If the hanging solitude begins the obliteration, what follows might be even worse. The men here attack newcomers as if they were viruses, while trying to steal away some piece of newly fallen food. The fittest survive that first critical moment, and they become a part of this world. Life then becomes brutish and simple, a slavish need for sustenance. I learned from early years in an orphanage that boys will sin freely if they lack restraints, so imagine the evil here when grown men have neither restraints nor food. It is amazing how quickly virtues succumb to hunger. The scarcity makes that a reality for all of us. More and more men arrive with the same appetite, but the amount of falling food never increases."

"My guess is that dozens die every few days. No one survives without killing, but our population remains constant, because of the forlorn souls who drop with the food. They drop from the black pipe that stretches up into the ceiling above us, like a road to memories of the brighter city lost to us above."

"You are a rare example to have avoided the cages. I think many of these men were murderers and thieves sent to rot here. Others were Tryst's opponents, but I think he has avoided sending men who I would know. No one talks much about his past, which soon becomes irrelevant unless it equips you to survive. My past is probably the only reason why I am still breathing. I believe you have that same kind of will. I sensed it when I first saw you. Perhaps the two of us could help each other stay sane. Surviving down here with the mind intact is no easy task."

I sat back after those words, my mouth dry. Only then did I notice that Lucian's mouth was hanging open, stunned. I turned my face away, but I had already revealed too much.

"I think I know who you were," he stammered, "but what have you become down here?"

"Survival has become my reality." I ignored his first comment. "And fury at being here made me willing to do anything to survive. I have fallen a long way."

"This place is breaking you." He paused uneasily. "There must be a way out of here. Could we signal for help from outside? Many remain loyal to you, but they have no idea you are alive."

I shook my head, but no words came.

"I know who you are."

"No, you do not." My voice was firm, as if the words could change reality. "You think you know who I was, but that man is gone."

"I know who you are." Lucian kneeled before me. "You are my prince, Andor Vale, and I live to serve you."

Chapter 2

Crowning a Prince

**"A living thing seeks above all
to discharge its strength—
life itself is will to power;
self-preservation is only one of the
indirect and most frequent results."**

The banquet had more food than the hundreds gathered could eat. There were baked turkeys, lamb shanks with mint jellies, and fresh cut salmon fillets as long as a man's leg. At the center of the feast was a wobbling tower of cake, dripping chocolate as servants hurriedly passed slices through the grand hall. The guests gobbled it down, but their anxious gazes never ventured far from the newly crowned Prince of Valemidas.

Tryst sat at the head of the hall, with two beautiful women beside him. He gave the most prized position on his right to his only full sister, Ravien. She was like the prince mirrored as a woman, with a high brow and precise features. She could have been his twin if not for being born a year before him. Many now mistook her as an ornament to the prince, like a dark orchid blooming in his shadow. She looked the part, but her ambitions exceeded her brother's.

On the prince's left was his younger half-sister, Lorien. She wore the trained smile of a young queen. She had the prince's strong features, with softer lips and eyes. Amber curls framed her regal face. Her long black gown graced the ground and dipped to show a royal pendant at her chest. The gown suggested that a slip of the fine silk off her shoulder would leave her naked before the banquet hall. She might have worn it because she felt like she was hanging on by less than the fabric was. She wore no other jewelry or color. Let them take the lack of coverage as a sign of honesty and sincerity, she thought. Little of that existed elsewhere in this hall.

More than a few guests saw Lorien as an ominous presence. She was like a funeral pyre that remained unburned, a reminder of the prince who had disappeared just months ago, the prince she had loved. She wondered whether her half-brother honored her for her loss, with a hope that she would change, or whether he kept her as a prisoner because of her anger and opposition to her own blood. Certainly no one could be watched more closely than a guest of honor.

Before she could settle on any answers, the servants pounded the huge gongs in the four corners of the hall. The sound echoed off the marble floors and columns, muting everything else until Tryst stood. Applause erupted for the new prince, who held his arms out to receive the praise. Lorien could not deny the power of his figure. It was wrong for him to be in that position, she thought, no matter how naturally he filled it.

Lorien pulled her eyes away and glanced across the room. The vast space of the palace's main hall always took her breath away. The glow of chandeliered candles lit the tall columns and the guests' faces. All of them were transfixed by Tryst.

The full high court was in attendance—the patriarchs of the fifty noble houses. Those patriarchs had held the power, by majority, to nominate someone else after Tryst betrayed Andor. But they had bent to Tryst's will and put him to a vote of the people, where his charisma had carried the day.

If only someone had evidence of what he had done to Andor, the people might have turned against Tryst. Instead, they had elected him to be prince for life, as was the Valemidas custom. Now he could be removed only by death, disappearance, or a vote against him by forty-five of the fifty white-haired nobles. With the nobles' ancient grudges and constantly shifting factions, Lorien knew that was not going to happen, especially not with House Talnor, one of the strongest, in Tryst's camp.

Tryst had given the patriarchs positions of honor tonight, but not as much honor as they had wanted. They and their guests sat clustered at round tables near the prince's head table. At his table, Tryst had invited his newly sworn knights to flank him and his sisters. Prominent knights and merchants filled out the rest of the crowd.

Lorien continued surveying the guests until she noticed a small, foreign man lurking in the corner nearest to Tryst. Her fists clenched as she recognized him as Ramzi. He stood out as a Sunan with a small symbol tattooed on his right temple, close to his exotic eyes. He was watching Tryst intently, nodding like a puppet master whose head rises and falls as his puppet dances.

He was the advisor who had fueled her brother's rise. Over the years he had taught Tryst about the march of history towards an ideal. The ideal for Ramzi was a fanatic devotion to a god who would reward him in the afterlife for imposing order. It seemed that neither Ramzi nor his god cared in the slightest if the men leading the march of history trampled over every human being in their path.

She forced the evil advisor out of her mind.

Her focus had to be on Tryst. She found it hard to believe that she shared a father with the man. He was lean and tall, but by no means the tallest man in the room. His height was perhaps his only aspect that did not dwarf others. Whatever he lacked in size, he made up for in angles. It was if every line of his body directed the eye upward to the steep angles of his face. From the sharp point of his chin to his wide cheekbones, his face was like an elongated acorn, eerily well-suited to holding a crown. His posture was earned in action, more play than real battle, yet it demanded respect.

Unlike most princes in history, Tryst had not changed his appearance with his rise to power. Lorien might have admired the independence, but instead she counted it as another drop in the pool of his arrogance. As always, he wore tight-fitting charcoal trousers and a high-collared white shirt. The stark style was punctuated by ornate silver bracers on his lower arms and by the silver plating that hid almost all the black of his boots.

His attire contrasted with the city around him. In Valemidas, the great capital, everything had color, and this banquet was the height of that radiant style. Servants wore rainbow-striped tunics to be sure they did not fail to include the colors of any of the five most powerful noble houses. The ladies wore shimmering reds and purples and greens and blues. The patriarchs followed suit in their own distinct colors and patterns.

In the middle of that kaleidoscope, Tryst stood in his black and white and silver. He wore his only colors in two ancient relics, a diadem and a sword that passed down to every Prince of Valemidas. The diadem was made of a light, strong metal. It clung to his brow perfectly but was mostly hidden by his black curls. There was a massive diamond set at the front of the diadem. Next to Tryst's blue eyes, any other jewel would be a pittance. But this brilliant stone fueled his glare and matched it. It was like a third eye with the same color of pale blue.

The other relic was a sword known as Zarathus. Made of the same hard metal as the crown, the sword was said to have been forged for Valemidas' founder. It passed from prince to prince, and power followed in its wake. At Tryst's side, it looked darker than Lorien remembered, as if the sword had taken on a different personality than when it was in Andor's hands. The rubies in the hilt molded to Tryst's fingers, giving him perfect control over the long blade.

Tryst stood poised with these two relics declaring his position. He continued to hold out his hands like he was consuming the hall's uproar—as naturally as his guests had consumed the feast.

He slightly lifted his head, letting the light of a thousand candles dance across his face. The cheers roared on. What felt like a frozen eternity to Lorien was perhaps a minute. As the applause began to fade, Tryst stepped onto the table and thrust Zarathus into the air above him. The crowd cheered again.

Lorien shuddered in disgust at what her brother had become. He had conspired from the side of Andor, as one of his highest knights, to steal the throne. No one knew quite what or how it happened, but one day Andor was suddenly gone and Tryst was in his place. Despite endless searching and questioning, no one had uncovered any proof of what had happened. Andor's body had not been found, and most assumed he had been killed.

Tryst would not speak of it, except to repeat that it was a tragedy that Andor was gone. And now, more people were disappearing, children were taken from their parents, and the city's list of crimes grew longer by the day. It seemed dangerous to say anything against Tryst.

She kept her face blank as she looked up at her brother basking in the moment. He would accept nothing less than this position of prince, especially with Ramzi whispering into his ear about his destiny for power. That still did not explain how he convinced some of the most powerful nobles to help him. Tryst was shrewd enough to know that controlling them would open the path to the throne. Maybe he and Ramzi had used threats or promises about stopping the disappearances among the noble houses.

That was far from true for the regular people of Valemidas. Many had gone missing soon after Tryst took control. Those that would not bear Tryst's heavy yoke suffered the consequences. Some had fought back when the best young boys were taken from their homes for a life of military training. The resistance had waned after those who fought the loudest were not seen again.

There were rumors about Ramzi administering a dungeon worse than death, but Lorien had not been able to learn more about it. Every rumor of Ramzi seemed cloaked in smoke and myth, the way the devious man liked it.

If the people could not rid themselves of Ramzi and Tryst, then the nobles would have to do it. They were the ones who had upheld tradition over the generations. If enough of the houses united their private guards, maybe under the command of Sir Justus Davosman, they might have enough power to withstand Tryst. Not for long, though, because his forces were growing stronger by the day.

Everyone had failed from the beginning with Tryst. After his and her father had died and left Tryst a parentless teen, only Ravien and Ramzi seemed to have any influence over him. Others praised him, blinded by his talents. Even when he rose to Andor's council of knights, no one suspected this.

Looking out upon the banquet from her seat of honor, Lorien stared truth in the face. This was Tryst's coronation and Andor was gone. But she would not give up the fight. She had nothing to lose, she told herself as she fought back tears. Her life was nothing without the prince she loved, except to bring justice to the prince she detested.

Chapter 3

The Stab of Survival

**"Two are better than one, because
they have a good reward for their toil.
For if they fall, one will lift up his fellow.
But woe to him who is alone when he falls
and has not another to lift him up."**

Time passed quickly as Lucian and I worked on a plan for escape in the dark cellar. I was thankful for the company, even though we ate through my stockpile of three potatoes and a carrot in short order. He was more vulnerable to his stomach's demands, not being accustomed to real hunger. I had explained to him that we were more likely to die fighting for food than from starvation, but he remained undeterred.

"If we team up, we can handle anything up there. I am healthy, and your skills in battle are legendary." He touched the wound on his head. "I've seen enough to believe it, my prince."

The title did not fit me as it once had. "We cannot risk it yet. We have a while before the next falling, I can feel it."

"Let's just have a look around. Isn't it safer outside the central square?" He was not going to disobey, but he was restless.

"Nowhere is safe, not at any time. You have to align your stomach with the rhythm of this city. Endure the initial flickers of hunger until a deeper pain follows. You feel your body beginning to break down, with no energy to think or act. Then, when your body trembles at the pain and yearning, you leave for the Gloaming's central square, starving and fierce. You end that brutal hunger cycle focused on nothing but food."

"So you suggest letting this pain build more?" Lucian wrenched. "I am here to serve, but I can hardly take this." It had probably been a day since we had eaten.

"You must take it, but perhaps we can go out for a brief stretch." There was some truth to our strength in numbers, and the next falling would come soon enough.

Lucian wanted to know the perimeter of the city, so I led us there. The path that ringed the city was empty and tranquil. It felt good to use my legs.

I ran my hand along the cool wall as we walked together. It was unnatural and oppressing, with sheer gray stone reaching to the ceiling. Going over the wall was not an option. We had no tools, so breaking through was hopeless. Some men had tried to dig below it. I had seen holes in the ground that went down over ten feet. They were pressed against the wall, sometimes with a pile of bones at the bottom. The diggers probably lost the sustenance to maintain the effort.

Claustrophobia pressed down on me as Lucian floated ideas for escape. Ladders. Holes. I explained why all the possibilities would fail, but I whispered my only remaining hope: "Lucian, the last, desperate option is the box above the main square."

He responded brightly. "You say the square is the beginning and end of life here, so it must be the way to get out of this hell. We could build up the pile of bones and debris under the box. Then you could stand on my shoulders and jump for it."

"That would be suicide, Lucian. I might reach the box, but it would be sealed shut. For it to work, the box would have to be open, which means men would be falling and fighting for food all around. We would not survive."

"More bones could be found around this place." Lucian suggested. "We could form a mountain with them. We could add any other materials we find. Maybe then we could pry open the box with your pole."

"I have seen men fail at this many times," I explained. "The falling ground is a lethal place for such work. Someone will think we have food, or new men will fall. We will be attacked. No one lingers there unless he seeks death."

"Who could possibly care if we were carrying bones around that empty place?"

I admired Lucian's straightforward question. He seemed to be a practical man, without guile. He was no noble's son.

"I have learned this the hard way. The square looks empty and unassuming, but everyone who roams carelessly there meets a dire end. Men succumb to senseless violence here, driven by their fear and their stomachs."

"But we would work in silence, when no food is falling."

"It is the Gloaming," I insisted. "You cannot stay in one spot. All we can do is dash through the square for a morsel of food. Perhaps in a hidden corner of this place, we could gather bones, but there in the center, a blink might be enough of a pause to result in ruin."

"It cannot always be so dangerous. Surely everyone sleeps."

"Yes, but not at the same time. Have you seen any change in the environment during your stay?"

"I guess not. It has been dark and gray the whole time."

"It is always dark and gray. It is like a constant ominous storm, marked only by the lightning strikes of decaying matter from the box."

"There must be safer times to be there. It should not take us long to gather things to stand on. We can do this together. We have to try something. Here you are decaying, but you know Tryst has to be stopped. It is worth the risk."

Hearing Tryst's name brought all the hate and bitterness back. "Put that life behind you. It cannot be recovered."

"You can recover, and you can change things. I know that we are not meant for this. We have to get you back to Valemidas."

My mind drifted out of the Gloaming, to distant memories of my city. I struggled to find the words to respond. I wanted more than anything to be back, but I was afraid that I could no longer help anything in my fallen state. "I am not what I once was, Lucian. You said so yourself."

"What I know, my prince, is that the people loved you. And they will love you again. You saved me, and you called me friend. I have seen warmth returning to you already. Even now you would be better than Tryst for the throne. It is rightfully yours, and getting you out of here will be just the begin—"

Ringing was all I heard after that.

Something pounded into my temple, and I went down hard.

Lost in conversation, we had been caught off guard. My head spun, but I could still see. I struggled to my feet.

A blur of iron swung towards Lucian, who crumbled to the ground.

A man rounded on me. Cornered could equal dead.

I could not get the ringing out of my head, nor could I find my weapon. There were three of them closing on me. The first dove at me recklessly. He was skin and bones and incredibly fast. I pressed my back against the wall, slipped to the right of his attack, and used his momentum to slam his head into the stone.

Just as I did, one of the other men kicked my legs out from under me. I fought to stand, but he was on top of me in an instant. His left hand closed around my throat, squeezing. He pulled his right fist back, ready to punch with a fiendish rage.

As my hand touched the metal pole on the ground at my side, calmness entered my pounding head. I was bigger, better, but gasping. I could not breathe.

Suddenly air flooded into my lungs. The man's body flew to the side, and I seized the moment to swing my pole down at him. His pallor splattered in color. He looked like he had soaked in this place; like me, he must have been here forever.

I sprang to my feet and saw that the three attackers were all down, motionless. Lucian wavered before me, his eyes dim. He had a metal barb plunged into his neck.

I fell to my knees as he did. His life was spilling down his chest. I caught his body as it collapsed, and I laid it down gently alongside the others.

There was no sound, no pulse, when I pressed my ear over his heart. A great weight held my head there while tears filled my eyes and I began to weep. My body shook and my voice broke as it roared out. I mourned for Lucian and more—the sorrows of this horrid existence, and what it had done to him, to me, and to everyone else down here.

After some time, I was able to lift my head and kneel beside his body. I bent down and pulled my hand over his face to close his still eyes.

As I thought of his final moments, thankfulness began to overcome my anguish. Even in the starved and rotten Gloaming, Lucian had brought selflessness into the chaos, putting my life before his own. His last thought had probably been of saving me.

I had counted survival as my best accomplishment, but it counted for nothing on its own. Memories of my earliest days here flooded my thoughts. I had succumbed to carnal instincts in the beginning, angry and starving, and not just for food.

I remembered once walking to the central square with my sanity withering under desperation and rage. There had been dozens of men falling and fighting all around. I had raised my weapon as I walked, challenging them all. Their famished eyes had circled me, and men had charged into my fury. I could still see the face of the first man who had dashed at me. His face had met my metal pole with a smash. Masses had jumped at me, and my violence had exploded against them. I had attacked over and over, trying to obliterate everything around me. The screams had been brutal as I shattered the bones and souls of any man within reach. None of them had been armed, or well-trained. They were probably simple criminals, where I was the fallen prince. It was some cruel ironic justice.

Those sins had left me hollow, hungrier than before. There was no freedom, only self-loathing and a callous devotion to survival. That had been the first of many such horrors, all inflicted by me. I had done, time after time, what I most did not want to do.

Being with Lucian exposed the demon that I had become, and the thought of his sacrifice revived hope in something greater than myself. Losing him led to despair, which led to emptiness, which led to an overwhelming desire for forgiveness. I yearned for anything that would relieve me of my regret and sorrow.

In that broken and dark moment, kneeling over Lucian, a glorious light flashed in my mind. It burned away the final fragments of my prideful shell, so that I no longer blocked the light from reaching me. It was a light of truth and goodness, a source of life. As Lucian had died for my sake, so must I be willing to do the same for others. An old priest had once said words like that to me. It had meant nothing then, but now layers of reborn reason enmeshed my mind. Living free required an embrace of the possibility of death. Survival would no longer be my tyrant, not even in the Gloaming. Lucian had shattered those chains.

With a final nod of thanks, I turned away from him and walked resolutely to the center of the Gloaming. I thought of the suicide plan of leaping to the box that hung there. Where I had always been looking for strategies to survive during a falling, I now remembered how sometimes a man would fight against gravity. He would cling to the box, dangling above the fight below. Eventually his strength would give out and he would drop to meet the frenzied pace of the falling ground.

As I had told Lucian, it was death to stand on the mound of bones to await the fall, but death no longer concerned me. Men would often stand or fight below the box before a falling. Few of them got out alive, but between them reaching up to catch falling food and the occasional hanging body above, the distance between the box and the ground might shrink for an instant.

With my quickness, if everything aligned, I could have a momentary window to escape. A falling body could be like rungs on a ladder, reaching up to the box. The box would have its black metal flaps open. I knew that if I could gain upward momentum, I would reach whatever those dangling men had held. If not, I would surely die. So be it.

As I arrived at the mouth of an alley looking onto the grim square, I marveled that no one had attacked me while I mourned over Lucian and came this far along open streets. Having given up my fear of death, maybe I looked insane, covered in blood and dirt, striding confidently. I would have stayed away from a man like that.

I noticed men lurking at the mouths of the other alleys leading into the square. They bore the marks of Gloaming veterans, preparing for an imminent falling. They crouched in the shadows and tried to look in every direction at once. I heard a yell and a brief fight, and silence settled again. We were all jockeying for the first position to dart into the square, and if you did not watch your back, another man would sneak up and kill for your spot.

These were my comrades. There was a hateful respect in the air, as if our fallen souls united below the black box, because we all knew that it was a mortal competition for who would get food and get out alive. Many would die, and not just the new men who fell.

The black pipe from the ceiling trembled, beginning its violent shake. The noise of the Gloaming rose. It was a grinding mechanical groan. The air quivered under the weight of it, sending a wind across the sea of bones and mud and over all of us.

I gathered some bloodstained dust from around my bare feet and spread it across my face. I breathed in the stench of decay and let my own sigh of horror join the chorus. The sound of a huge thud in the box drew my eyes.

That was the sign for the charge. I raised my pole and exploded out of the alley. The ground was firm and I covered it in long strides. As the gates of the black box began to creak open, I saw the man opposite me charging. We locked stares, like bulls prepared to gore, until he swerved. Something about me made him decide against the challenge.

My legs propelled me faster, hitting a full sprint as the black metal doors above gave way. Without the box's floor, nothing kept the trash from falling.

I sprang up the mound of bones. Just as I crested it, I shifted towards a man running up the pile to my left. I jumped as high as possible, and my feet connected on the man's shoulders. I immediately leapt again, propelling myself off of him and into the air.

I dropped my pole mid-leap and grabbed the foot of a man who was hanging above me. Chaos swam below as I climbed up his body. I clawed and pulled and rose while he kicked at me violently.

With my hand clutching the man's shoulder, I saw his hand slipping from a rounded clasp of the metal door. He could not hold both of our weight, and his grip released just as I yanked myself up and snatched the clasp. Our eyes met as he fell, screaming in horror. He landed on his back and was swarmed by the men below.

I did not look down again. As the floor gates began to swing shut, I hurled myself into the box. An instant later the gates sealed me in silent darkness.

Breathing deeply, I felt around until I found a thin pipe stretching upward. I began to climb, pressing against the pipe's sides.

My mind reeled. I was lost before I was willing to die, and now thanks to Lucian and a fateful leap, the forgotten feeling of hope flooded me. No matter how long and uncertain the journey would be, my soul was lighter, escaping the darkness below me.

Chapter 4

The Mind of a Prince

**"He who fights with monsters should look to it
that he himself does not become a monster.
And when you gaze long into an abyss,
the abyss also gazes into you."**

I am Tryst, the Prince of Valemidas at last. I was born for this coronation night, to deliver this speech. I will show these people true greatness and inspiration. Ramzi says legends of the past will be shadows of what I will do for my people. They will all forget about Andor soon enough. No one rivals me.

Some of these nobles applaud me now, too cunning or cowardly to show open resistance. I will weed out my opponents. They were born into their positions. They did not earn their delightful nobility, not as I have earned this. They notice the faces that are missing here tonight. The wise ones know enough to support me, so that their faces will not be missed at the next banquet. That banquet will be soon, because a greater victory is coming. Every nation will bow to me.

These people will learn the extent of my power, and they will love me for it. Lorien dares to avert her eyes from me, but her love was always distant. With Andor gone, surely she will draw closer to family. She should know that I protect my own blood, even half blood. Ravien understands. Now both of them can have everything they want. Let these nobles be baffled by my darker sister and her attire. Let them think her an assassin. It is close enough to the truth.

Starting tonight, there can be no more dissent or distrust. I will not allow it. The path of love for the prince has been tried, and it has failed. The people will respect me in a way they never respected Andor. He was too soft, bending his will to them. I will make the people bend to my will, and eventually overthrow these worthless nobles and their class. Once they are gone, I will be a prince without restraints. I will become the first ever King of Valemidas. But let the nobles savor my moment now, while they still can.

"Nobles and friends, my guests, welcome!"

Yes, see me smiling and gracious. Drink deep of my words.

"If there is anyone who doubts that Valemidas is a place where all things are possible; who still wonders if the dream of our ancestors is alive; who still questions the power of our city, tonight is your answer. I am your answer."

"It is the answer told by the masses gathered outside this royal palace. It is the answer told by all of you gathered to celebrate with me now. Noble, merchant, and peasant—all Valemidans send a message to our continent that we are united under my rule. It is the answer of me putting my hands on the arc of history and bending it toward the hope of a better day."

"I want to thank you nobles for your support. The structure of our city is built on the traditions of your nobility. It is built on the legacy of you nominating a prince born outside nobility, to be approved by a majority of the people. I thank you that, once my predecessor was gone, you picked me to lead. I thank the people who then elected me. I also want to thank my sisters, Ravien and Lorien. When we were young, training with your noble sons and daughters, we never thought to rise to this station."

Ravien will enjoy these lies.

"It was thanks to the privilege of growing up with this great generation of future nobles that we were able to make it here tonight. What was then our privilege has become our city's advantage. Take Jacodin Talnor. I grew up beside him, and now

I lead him with the benefit of that experience. These traditions of Valemidas bear fruit."

The buffoon of a noble's son is all smiles now, thinking me earnest as I point him out before the crowd. What irony that he should think himself comparable to me. At least his father Ryn will appreciate the flattery. Jacodin is too spoiled to share Ryn's ambition and success.

"But none of you picked me because of the past. You did it because you understand the enormity of the task that lies ahead. For even as we celebrate tonight, we know the challenges that tomorrow will bring are the greatest of our lifetime. There are enemies amassing in the mountains of the west, disappearances in our midst, crimes on our streets, unpaid debts to the Sunan people, and deep uncertainties about our future."

"The road ahead will be long. Our climb will be steep. We may not get there in one year, but I am certain now that we will get there. I will protect Valemidas. You will protect Valemidas under my leadership."

"My first days as prince will break those who oppose our vision for this city. I will set order in place and restore our wealth and grandeur. We will all pay a little, but the rewards will be spread and paid in time. Everyone will cooperate."

Ulysses just winced at that, my own knight. He knows what that cooperation will mean in the midst of war. I must remember to have Sebastian monitor Ulysses' every move, for he will still feel the tug of loyalty to Andor. I must get Andor out of my mind, and out of everyone's mind. Memories of him are too fresh in this room.

"Our army will have a new name, and new demands. It is no longer a mere group of knights and soldiers, it is the Lycurgus. To serve, men must swear to me and to the laws of the Lycurgus. They are strong now, but they pale in comparison to what is to come. The Lycurgus will begin with our firstborn boys. They will be raised pure, fierce, and disciplined, and none will resist their focused fury under my command."

And I will crush anyone who tries to hold back his firstborn. They have seen the examples, like Lucian. He opposed me on this, and then he disappeared just before his knighting. Perhaps I could direct Father Yates to incorporate a firstborn rite as part of his religious teaching; the people seem to need some opiate for this duty.

"While these young boys train, I will lead our men out to conquer the growing threats beyond our walls. We leave in a week to destroy the Icarians. To allow that sedition to fester, even though it would be quelled if it pressed us, would encourage enemies throughout the continent and beyond. We will march through our countryside and gather support for our military and our city. They will relish the opportunity to give to our mission and to serve under me."

"After we defeat our enemies in the mountains, we will bring our forces back to Valemidas. But not for long. This entire continent will be ours. Every last town council and sheepherder will bend the knee and pay tribute to Valemidas and to your prince."

Ah, the first gasps from my guests. So conquest is their soft mark, their cowardice. How far, already, they had let me push. These pathetic nobles should read enough into my words to know their plight. At least a few lean forward with thinly veiled ambition, like Sir Justus Davosman. Even he, the adoptive father of Andor, will bow to me and help my mission in time. I will take special delight in that.

"Valemidas is the light to this land. This is our time—our time to extend our reign to every city. There will be no more free cities. Every city will be governed by us, Valemidas, the greatest free city. Expect a better Valemidas. Expect more than ever before, under my reign."

I raise my arms to end with flourish and begin the cheers. Yes, I was born for this, in a way Andor never could be. Shower the praise on me now, nobles. We will all remember this night as the beginning of your end. The world will never be the same.

"Thank you all! I will lead us to victory, here and everywhere, now and forever!"

The applause rains down and puddles at my feet.

*　　　　　*　　　　　*

27

"I think the speech played very well, my prince." Ramzi's words, as usual, followed praise with politics. "I am glad I added that line about spreading our presence. The more ambitious nobles will understand the message. Sir Ryn Talnor, for example, is probably already plotting about which surrounding city-state he might send his family to rule over. He supported your rise in exchange for that promise. I have my doubts, though, about Sir Davosman. His loyalty will be hard to buy."

Tryst was leaning over a balcony in his chambers, gazing at the dim flickering lights of the city below him. The masses were gathering in the central square of Valemidas for a celebration of the coronation. At his advisor's last remark, Tryst glanced back at him, eyes amused, before turning to look over the city again.

"Ramzi," he said into the night, "you worry too much about the support of these nobles. I already have what I needed from them. I am the Prince of Valemidas. We are creating the Lycurgus as an unparalleled force under my command. History has never seen the like, even if we are modeling it after some ancient philosopher-king. The point is that the nobles could not stop me if they wanted to, and my power will only grow as the boys in the Lycurgus train."

"Of course, my prince." Ramzi bowed low.

He bowed a lot, each time to hide a negative thought. This time he wondered if the prince had ever not been arrogant. But there were worse flaws, particularly for his purposes. It meant the prince would not question if his growing powers came from dark forces, instead of from himself and his throne. Ramzi believed his god would reward his faith and his sacrifices of men to the Gloaming by granting favor to this minion.

"I suggest," Ramzi began, "that we will find it easier to dismantle the nobles later, if we have their support in the coming days. The Lycurgus needs time to grow loyal and strong. It would be beneficial to have each noble house send a few of its best knights to aid in the battles. And, if we are going to truly tilt the balance of power back to you and the people, our task will be much easier if the nobles do not expect it until it is too late. One of our allies could be the merchants guild because—"

"How much longer, Ramzi?" Tryst interrupted.

They had hashed through this many times before, and Ramzi knew it was best to keep Tryst in his good mood. "Not long at all. It has been a long and great day. I have just two more issues that I think are worthy of your attention now."

"Fine. Speak up, and be quick about it. Every minute you take now is a minute that I miss my people's celebration outside." Tryst turned to face his advisor, his arms crossed.

"Understood." Quick, slippery words came easily to Ramzi. "The first issue will let you sleep easier on the march to war. As you know, the prince typically appoints someone to handle the administrative leadership in Valemidas while he is away. These are the issues I have been boring you with most days—things like paying our builders, deciding disputes between the nobles, and regulating the people. I would be glad to send you daily reports, so that you can handle these matters. But you will have more important things on your mind as the leader of the Lycurgus. If you sign and seal an approval of me as your acting minister here, I can save you the trouble."

Tryst did not answer immediately. Ramzi knew the prince did not care about these details, but the lingering silence disturbed him. Had he played his hand too strongly? Since he took the throne, Tryst had become less compliant, less predictable. Ramzi held his tongue, trying to hide his anxiety.

"I will be gone only a month or so. I doubt much will happen here." The prince's voice sounded distracted and unconcerned, as he tapped his fingers idly. It comforted Ramzi to hear the usual contempt in his prince's voice.

"What should I do if you disappoint me?"

The question took Ramzi aback. He thought he had won more trust than this. He forced his words to take the form of obedient deference. "My prince, I will not disappoint. You know me well enough to know that. But if I did, you could do whatever you wished. As always, I remain subject to your direction."

"Fine. You may play minister in my absence. You will be monitored, of course. This is an important assignment. If you fail me, you will live a while in the dungeons that you manage."

Ramzi swallowed his indignation and fear. "As you wish, my prince." He whistled and two of his clerks scurried in from the waiting room outside, carrying a large parchment with small, delicate handwriting. Ramzi signaled for them to hold it out to Tryst.

"The prince has agreed to appoint me Minister of Valemidas, to handle the city's administration in his absence. My prince, please sign and seal here." Ramzi pointed to a line at the bottom of the document.

"You have never been shy for power, have you Ramzi?" Tryst signed it without waiting for an answer. "If you had my strength, I might fear you."

Tryst waved the clerks out of the room with the flick of his wrist. "But you and I know that you could never make it this far without me."

"You speak the truth, my prince." Ramzi stifled a smirk at the irony of his prince's ignorance. He also held down his surging excitement; there was still treacherous water to cross. He would celebrate this victory when appropriate. For now, he summoned courage and a calm voice.

"There is one final thing to discuss," Ramzi began. "Sebastian has reported to me that two guards in the lowest chamber of our dungeons were found bound and gagged. This is the chamber with the cages that hang over the Gloaming. The guards were not harmed, and they had no information on who had assaulted them. Strangely, a sweep through the dungeon and prison cells revealed that no one had escaped."

"And?" Tryst seemed impatient. The sound of the people's celebratory music had begun to fill the room. "What do you make of this?"

"Oh I am sure it is nothing, my prince." Ramzi prayed the words would slip by without much notice. "Perhaps it was a failed attempt at a rescue by someone outside. There were four guards in that chamber, so two of them were not harmed, and they did not hear any disturbance. We can double the guard, in case someone tries something again."

Ramzi hesitated before saying more. He wanted to pin as much of this as he could on Sebastian, the prince's chief spy. He had never trusted the man. Although they were both from Sunan, their purposes never seemed to align.

Sebastian had come to Valemidas without explanation as a teen. Ramzi had tread carefully after seeing Sebastian's Sunan tattoo, as it included the mark of royal blood—a pyramid the size of a thumbnail by his left eye. Sebastian had risen quickly among the spies, first serving Andor and now Tryst. Ramzi was more consistent. He advised only Tryst, who he identified from the start as a proper vessel of power. His consistency meant that his loyalty would not be doubted until it was too late.

"I should add, my prince, that Sebastian speculates that there could have been an escape from the Gloaming. I told Sebastian that was ridiculous. The Gloaming is inescapable. Still, Sebastian insisted that I tell you his theory." As much as he hated to obey the spy, if Ramzi did not put his spin on this story now, then Sebastian's later report could spell more trouble.

"Very interesting, Ramzi." The prince stepped closer and locked eyes with Ramzi. His stare made Ramzi step back. "If that is all, you may go now."

"What do you think happened down there?" The question slipped out of Ramzi's mouth before he had weighed it. He was baffled at the report, and he feared Tryst's fascination with the Gloaming. The prince did not answer quickly, and Ramzi's mind wandered.

Only a handful knew that the place existed, much less that Tryst had ordered Andor to be banished there, over Ramzi's objection. The only place for a deposed prince, Ramzi had believed, was the grave. Tryst had said one thing in response to Ramzi on the issue: the Gloaming was worse than the grave, because it degraded the soul to utter despair and depravity.

For once, Tryst had been right. If the little that Ramzi had since learned about the underground city was true, the horrors of the place were being funneled into power through Zarathus. The nature of the connection remained a mystery, except that it was somehow spiritual. That gave Ramzi faith that his god would use the sacrifice of Andor to the Gloaming. A force of light turned into a force of dark, a force that would lead to Ramzi's ascendancy.

"You are probably correct," Tryst said at last. "No one escapes the Gloaming." He was smiling, sincere and sinister. "I would like to speak with Sebastian tonight, though. Tell him to come to me after I return from the celebration. Have a hot meal and a pretty maid waiting for me, too. I may be overcharged, since I expect quite a night down there with the masses."

"Yes, my prince." Ramzi struggled to find a way to exit on better terms. "Please do take care out there. As much as the people love you, there will be opponents who could attack. Nothing you cannot handle, of course."

"Of course," Tryst said dismissively as he turned to face the city. "Farewell, Ramzi."

Ramzi bowed low and fled the room. He told himself that he deserved this victory. Tryst would not have made it this far without him. In return, the prince owed him power. Ramzi licked his lips at the thought of ruling Valemidas.

The people would be controlled, in the name of the prince. Once controlled, the people would destroy the nobles. Once the nobles were gone, nothing would stop his dominion and shaping of the world's history, as long as he could hold Tryst's reins.

Chapter 5

The Enemy of a Prince

**"It was iron and wheat that
civilized mankind
and caused it to be lost."**

"Something about this night feels wrong." The watchman said to his replacement.

Most night watches in the mountains passed without incident. Maybe a rare wolf howl or a passing hare would interrupt the quiet, but even those moments were muffled by snow. It was still understood among the Icarian rangers that there was constant danger. They garrisoned tiny watchtowers, looking down on the valleys below.

This night, it was not just the cold that made the watchman shiver.

"I feel it too. Unnatural like. The night smells and tastes normal, but my senses tell me that something is shifting."

The men caught eyes for the first time; they shook off the dread in a quick handshake. Nothing beat the comfort of a comrade in this solitary duty.

"Get to the city and find your wife's warmth. I have it from here, and I will heed your advice. It is a night to stay alert." The replacement smiled and patted the left breast-pocket of his heavy wool coat. "I brought coffee with a nip of something special. Whatever is lingering out there will not catch me unawares."

"Good man. Thank you for the reprieve." The tired watchman turned, almost forgetting the ritual words.

He turned back and found his comrade's eyes again. "May our city's warmth keep you this night. Our fate rests in your eyes and ears. Watch for Icaria, watch until Icaria calls you back."

They clasped forearms and the replacement answered quietly, "Until Icaria calls me back."

Without another word the watchman scrambled down the precipitous crag, towards home. He silently cursed the few rocks that scattered below his feet. He had been on duty a day and a night, but that was no excuse for such careless noise.

Something evil truly was at play. It was as if an unseen scheme had been set against his people. He felt that it was nothing a watchman would see. Just as the mountains hid the storms until the moment they struck, this approaching danger would be secret until it was too late.

The night's darkness was giving way to morning when he caught the first glimpse of Icaria. The bridge to the city was thin, long, and swaying high above a chasm. An open valley led to the bridge. It was the site of farms but no homes.

Across the bridge, his people's homes clustered on a small peak. The city was like a natural extension of the rock, its lean buildings like a bundle of spears. The peak was an island amidst the surrounding ravines. Every time the watchman crossed the bridge into the city, he left the world for a safe and secure place. He believed that, with this position, no one could conquer Icaria.

The guards nodded a silent welcome as he passed. Just inside the tall gate, he heard the soft bell announcing dawn. Chime, chime, chime, chime. The fourth ring meant a morning meeting. All who could attend would, even a cold watchman returning from the night.

He sighed and pulled out his small silver flask. It had been a gift from his father, who had served and died on the watch, like his father before him. The watchman finished off the last sip and greeted the little fire it stoked in his empty belly. Seeing his leader, the Summit, would be a welcome reassurance of stability and strength.

He began climbing the winding stairs to Icaria's great hall. Hundreds had already gathered when he entered. Most lived near the hall, saving them from the five-hundred-step climb that was taxing the watchman's weary legs. The night of standing and climbing had drained his energy. Leaning against a stone pillar ten times his height, he breathed slowly and watched the rest of his city amass. Almost five thousand all together, they were wrapped in heavy furs that replaced the just-removed blanket of peaceful sleep.

The Icarians looked up at their leader, standing at the tip of a ledge of natural stone that loomed above. They waited for his guidance in total trust. The Summit could not be blamed for mistakes made by the Icarian betrayer.

"Morning arises, Icarians." He spoke from the edge of his perched point. They answered in unison, craning their necks upward, "Day awaits, our Summit." Forty feet above, he could survey all his people.

The watchman knew what this meeting would entail. The Icarians had long been seeking a softer home. At last they had discovered the force to acquire it. They believed a warmer and greener land would be more suitable to their collective culture. The watchman felt a deep sadness as he looked on their faces. Their gentleness, bred in the harsh climate, always gave him joy. Like a bear protecting her cub, they were ruthless against outside threats but tender towards each other. Only in this climate could that character persist. They were wrong to have wanted the easy life of lowlanders.

"Icarians," the Summit began his speech. "Here in the mountains, made strong by the cold, we developed the greatest weapon known to man. We have the seed of amazing power, the power of explosions never seen before. We mined it from the minerals buried deep within our mountains. But, tossed out on the barren rock, the seed died before it could take a breath. If we had kept it hidden in our caves, it would have grown to something invincible."

"Now it will not to grow in our hands. We let ambition in the form of a stranger's promise of wealth and power steal our senses. Sebastian boasted great things to us. We were all seduced by his smooth words. How were we supposed to resist the bargain of easy conquest, of easier lives? He told us that we deserved it. Progress, he said, that's what we needed. Our power gave us the right to all those green lands, starting with Benevia, where softer people had been frolicking for generations."

"Yet, betraying our way and our faith, an Icarian acted without our vote. He told the stranger the story of our secret science, in exchange for his promise of wealth and power. That Icarian paid with his life, but we too failed. When one of us acts, we all act. It is our way. We also failed by letting Sebastian escape our mountains. No one before had left these mountains against our will. Two of the rangers who pursued him were never seen again. Maybe the hope of a softer life had already weakened us, allowing this to happen."

"Now we will be the ones attacked. Have you shared my troubling dreams the past two nights? Have they been haunted by what we learned in the recent report from Valemidas? Our impatient ambition has forecasted our death. This is a tragedy."

"Seeds of greatness must be given time to grow if they are to last." The Summit cast out a handful of the dark powder over the crowd and shouted. "But these seeds will not last!"

"Our enemy knows us as its enemy." His voice grew calm. "And now Valemidas will march against us. There are too many signs for it not to be truth." The Icarians sat in silence as the word truth echoed in the hall.

"We still have a choice," he continued. "We vote today on our destiny. As is my right, given by you, I have selected the options. There are only three, our elder council has agreed. Discuss, question me, question our council, and choose the course best for us."

"This will be a full Icarian vote. All who have survived their rite of passage must take a position. Once votes are cast, we follow the prevailing option. This is our pure rule, our freedom. As always, you may choose not to vote. If you do, you must leave this night and never again join our city."

"Consider these options well, my fellow Icarians. First, we stay in this citadel of stone. We will arm and prepare for the certain siege. Like wolverines, we will take many attackers down with us. Valemidas might send twenty times our number. We might end here."

"Second option, we retreat tomorrow. We will pack what is necessary and move north and west. Out of the mountains, to the edge of the sea, into colder territory. From there, we would have further votes. Perhaps we build boats and float towards the unknown, or perhaps we settle in harsher, frozen lands."

"Third option, we attack. We all move out of the mountains and execute our former plan early. We take our great, fledgling weapons with us and press as far as we can. Perhaps we will have more votes. Perhaps we will take more land. The only certainty is that we will face the Valemidans. The recent report told of a strong and harsh new prince, leading a powerful army. In the open field, they will flex their strength and render our mountain skills less valuable."

"You are a wise people. I trust you will seek the unfolding of these destinies. We will choose our path and run hard on it. That is the only way we exist. Advance, Icarians. Bind our freedom to each other and climb higher." The Summit bowed, cuing the Icarian's response.

"Climb higher, our Summit," the watchman heard himself chanting twice, along with those around him. He pulled his eyes down from the ledge and felt like a vice was crushing him on all sides. The weight of the mountains showed in his people's steadfast but conflicted faces. Maybe they were hardened enough to handle that weight. The Icarians wasted no time before beginning the debate.

The watchman leaned back against the pillar, exhausted. He had felt something was wrong but had not dreamed it would be this. As surely as the snow falls, he thought, they would fight to the bloody end.

Chapter 6

The Power of a Prince

**"Those who become rulers
through strength of purpose,
acquire their kingdoms with difficulty,
but they hold onto them with ease."**

About a mile west of the prince's palace, in the outskirts of the sprawling city of Valemidas, there was a wooden bench that offered a perfect view. Two brothers sat there. They found the bench ideal for observing the coronation festivities. It was far enough away to allow a safe perspective, and it was comfortable in a traditional sort of way. Hewn from some gnarled oak, the bench's planks were smooth with hundreds of years of use. It was outside the Morning Crest, one of the oldest taverns of Valemidas, built on the hill that eastbound travelers crested before entering the city.

The Crest was built as much by words and tales as it was by stone and wood. Nobles despised it for being too humbly welcoming, too organic, and too cheap. The travelers and thinkers and traders loved it. Every night it was full and different.

Jon and Wren had begun the evening inside. They had found themselves explaining the city's elaborate system of nobility to a farmer from the foothills of the Icarian mountains. The fifty noble houses permeated the culture of Valemidas. The leader of each house was elected for life by the other noble patriarchs. The election cursed them to a life spent aggrandizing power—multiplying supporters in their houses, gathering artists and scholars. The nobles would do anything to be important. The more important they were, the more likely their children or others from their house would be elected as nobles if one of the fifty died. The contest for influence and power never ended. The farmer had found it all rather odd and amusing.

After the brothers had bid adieu to the stranger, they retreated with their ales to the old bench outside. They heard the warm clamor of voices inside and the bustle of the city spread out before them. A few minutes passed before either brother spoke a word.

"Are you enjoying this?" Jon pointed toward the prince's palace while glancing back at his brother. They could hear the distant pounding of drums. The beat sounded like a song that had long been one of Wren's favorites.

"No," Wren said flatly. He had been in a sour mood ever since Tryst's coup, and efforts to cheer him up had been futile. Jon was not giving up, though.

"Too bad, because I thought I heard some dragon roaring down and swallowing our new prince."

"Is that so?" A little grin spread across Wren's face. "Maybe you are right," he said. "I hope he does not get soot on his beautiful face. Prince indeed. He sure looks the part, all handsome and dashing, but he has no right to the throne. Worst of all, most of the nobles seem to love him, so we have no hope of ridding ourselves of him. Bring on the dragons, I say."

"He's just another prince, Wren. Besides, our city needs help—one more attack or one more bad harvest, and we might not have anything left to sell in our store. Maybe Tryst will not be so bad." Jon knew as he said it that he did not believe it.

"That is nonsense. You should finish that ale. Maybe you will find wisdom in it."

"I am taking my time with this fine drink—unlike your vile brews, this can be sipped."

"Good one, little brother. Let's see your wit help you when Tryst decides he needs to raise the taxes on merchants again—"

Wren trailed off as he heard the sound of yells near the palace. "Do you hear that? It is no celebration sound."

"Sounds like someone is trying to spoil your favorite prince's night." Jon figured that Wren would take this seriously enough for both of them.

"We have to check it out," Wren stood, "that is close to our store. I will beat you there." He drained the last of his mug, dropped a coin on the bench, and began sprinting down into Valemidas.

Jon marveled at how his brother could turn everything into a competition. He finished his ale and let his brother have a head start. A minute later, Jon had closed the gap and was at Wren's side as they raced through the city's gate.

The city streets were empty, so they covered the distance quickly. The brothers had spent most of their childhood chasing each other around Valemidas. They hurdled carts and baskets, ducking through alleys and sprinting whenever they found open spaces. As they drew closer to the palace—and their beloved store—the sound of the celebration grew.

Jon paused to let Wren catch up at the end of a musty alley. The alley turned onto the Path of Princes, the broad road leading to the palace stairs. Blindly sprinting into the busy road was dangerous on a normal afternoon, and even in his rush of adrenalin, Jon was aware enough to stop for a moment here. He tried to catch his breath.

Wren caught up a few moments later. "Che...cheater!" He panted and leaned over a large barrel for support. "You know... for our races we banned...that one alley long ago. It is too nasty and crooked...with nothing but brothels."

"This is an emergency," Jon grinned down, "and I would have beaten you anyway." Wren attempted to stand straight, pretending to breathe regularly.

The brothers both peeked around the corner and down the Path of Princes, which opened onto a vast plaza below the stairs to the palace. It was a stunning expanse, like a wide clearing in the middle of a dense forest. The plaza was made of huge slabs of stone that had supported centuries of footsteps. Nothing permanent was allowed to stand in the square except for an ancient tree that rose straight up from the center. It took eight men locking arms to reach around the trunk. The highest branches towered nearly as high as the palace perched on the crag of stone east of the plaza.

Tonight, the plaza looked as if it could not hold another person. Jon and Wren had never seen the space even close to filled. The crowd churned, the sea of bodies undulated, with no single form distinguishable. There were shouts of joy and strife joining together, most heated around the great tree. The royal band played from the palace stairs above, flooding the space with the rhythm of drums. Despite the celebratory and excited notes in the air, it all seemed wrong to the brothers.

"There are tens of thousands. It looks like everyone in Valemidas is here. We should just go to our store the back way."

"Come on," Wren answered, "let's wade into this. I think the loudest yells are coming from near the palace steps." The more serious of the two, Wren never shrunk back from trouble.

Jon nodded. "Fine, someone needs to watch your back if you pick any fights."

The brothers rounded the corner and blended into the crowd. They inched forward like worms in plowed soil. Keeping low, avoiding all eye contact, Jon followed Wren as they made their way to the tree. When they were close to its trunk, movement above on the palace steps brought them to a halt.

A solitary, dark figure stood alone near the top—Tryst. The stairs to the palace were immense, two hundred in all, and between every fifty steps there was a large flat platform. The prince began to descend and paused at the highest of those platforms, where the royal band was stationed. The prince raised his arms and the music ceased.

Every face in the square turned to look up at him. In that moment of focused attention, the prince charged down the next set of stairs. The band followed his descent with a dense symphony on the drums and horns, proclaiming the prince's arrival. The crowd's cheers and yells joined the music.

Wren pulled his eyes away and saw fearful respect and adoration mixed in the people's faces. He also noticed for the first time that at least thirty large casks ringed the trunk of the giant tree. Men and women huddled around the barrels, which each had a streaming tap. The liquid was dark and smelled delicious and strong. The people pressed in and filled their mugs; some of them stuck their heads directly under the flow, taking a long swallow and bowing away so that another could fill the spot. The ground was soaked.

"What are they drinking?" Wren asked to no one in particular.

"The new prince's own ale," a woman's voice shouted from beside him. "Go for it, boy, the stuff's amazing."

Wren turned and saw a small young woman, with plain brown eyes and hair. Her simple white tunic was drenched and nearly falling open. She had a wild, unnerving smile on her face.

Wren shook his head and laughed. "You must have had a lot of the drink, my lady. Is it really worth that kind of excitement?"

In an instant, the woman's face flipped from ecstasy to rage. She screamed and swiped at his face. "Quit your mocking, pretty boy!"

He easily ducked her flailing arms. She seemed to forget about him a second later, as she stumbled towards one of the streaming barrels.

Wren muttered in surprise and looked around for Jon. He saw that Tryst had paused again on the lowest platform of the stairs. He figured Jon might have gone that way, caught up with the crowd that was surging up the stairs to get a closer look at the prince.

He pushed that direction and was making his way up the stairs when he first glanced Jon. His brother was locked in heated conversation with a merchant named Catskill.

"What are you two talking about?" Wren interrupted.

"Good question," Jon said in frustration. "I saw our friend Catskill moving suspiciously close to the prince, and I have been trying to figure out what he is planning to do. You know he is far from a supporter of this new regime."

Catskill simply nodded in response. He was a slight, wily man, losing his short, brown hair. Nothing about him stood out, an attribute the merchant had long used to his advantage.

Wren saw some of the dark drink dripping from the corner of Catskill's mouth. "What are you hiding?"

"Good to see you, too, Wren," he said, "but as I was telling your brother, it would be best if you both went back to your store, and now."

The brothers did not move, and he demanded again, "I said *now*. Go!"

Catskill turned away quickly and moved up the stairs toward Tryst. Jon and Wren stood their ground anxiously. They exchanged a look of confusion, and nodded to confirm that neither was willing to leave until they saw what happened.

The prince was greeting the crowd that now surrounded him. He stepped down the stairs gracefully, saluting the men and touching the faces of the women. They seemed in awe of their new prince's willingness to be this close. It had long been an irony of the prince's position that he was chosen from the common people but, once chosen, he stayed out of their reach. This was not the first tradition that Tryst was breaking.

When the prince made his way to just above Catskill, the brothers saw the merchant pull back his fine cloak and raise a small, loaded crossbow. He pointed it at the prince.

Just before he pulled the trigger, someone in the crowd gasped. Tryst ducked and drew his sword, Zarathus. He plunged the blade into Catskill as the bolt sailed above its target.

The prince then swung at another man who had moved to help Catskill. As that second man fell, an older man was pulling out his sword to try to stop Tryst. The prince swatted away his blade, swept his feet out from under him, and stabbed down into his torso. No one else remained standing within a ten-foot radius.

"This is our celebration! Does anyone else dare challenge me?" Tryst asked with an eerie smile, with his sword held high.

The crowd around him cowered back further. But, after he sheathed his sword and began moving down the stairs again, newcomers continued surging up to greet him, seemingly unaware of the slaughter that had happened just above.

The brothers were in shock. Tryst or someone loyal to him may have seen them talking to Catskill. They stepped quickly down the stairs, against the flow of people on their way up. When they reached the bottom, they ran through the masses, knocking over drinks and people and leaving angry faces in their wake. They reached their store at the edge of the plaza and slammed shut the massive wooden door behind them.

"What happened back there?" Wren said between heavy breaths and fell exhausted onto the floor.

"I sensed that Catskill had some dangerous plan in mind." Jon sat beside him. "But he was never the type to risk his life, much less in an assassination attempt. He had been drinking whatever the prince was serving in those barrels, and I could not get a straight answer from him. I would have stopped him if I had known." He shook his head sadly, "I had no idea it could lead to a bloodbath in the blink of an eye."

Wren shuddered and stared at the ground. "Our prince sure has a way of making an entrance. I doubt there will be more attempts against him tonight, and if so, it would be some drink-induced fumbling attack. This proves again that Tryst believes the people should either be caressed or crushed. In the midst of tonight's chaos, some of the caressed may never learn of those he crushed."

The brothers sat in quiet for a few moments until a woman's voice boomed into the room. "Where have you two been? You are soaked in sweat! Come, you must wash off. I have a meal ready."

As usual, Wren was the first to answer. "Mother, you must know what's going on out there. We were lucky to make it back alive. Tryst killed Catskill and two innocent men. Now this wild coronation celebration rages on. The prince is tearing up our city."

"Have hope, my boys. These princes come and go. Speaking of which, I have something very important to show you." With that, Selia wheeled around towards the kitchen.

Their mother had a way of leaving conversations with her last word lingering. It gave her a sense of control. Since losing her youthful beauty and the power it had given her, she was always looking for ways to preserve her influence. It was not easy for a widow. She talked to every person who crossed her path, and her open way of speaking was disarming. She tended to begin conversations with some sort of thanks or praise. Some people thought her clueless; they found out the truth sooner or later.

Jon and Wren took their mother's departure as a chance to rest in quiet and compose themselves. There was little they could do about Tryst tonight, and they both found comfort in the order of their store, the Invisible Hand. This was their flagship, the first of five trade shops, and it was a symbol for them. Like an old box full of toys and trinkets from their childhood, the store was ripe with sentimentality. But unlike such a treasure trove, the store was open to customers every day.

The Invisible Hand turned more profit than any other shop in Valemidas. It was one of the last great general stores, thriving on the gold of nobles and free commerce. Huge wooden ceiling beams arched above the main room, and the floors were broad planks accustomed to the feet of the wealthy. The store would have seemed cavernous if not for the thousands of items filling the space. Exotic foods, spices and soaps infused the room with a decadent fragrance.

The two brothers made the perfect merchant team. Wren was all numbers and analysis. It was not work for him; it was a calling. But his ability to acquire wealth caused problems. No one liked dealing with shrewd merchants, even when they were honest. He did not rub his skill or his profits in everyone's face, but did not hide it either. To make matters worse, everyone in the merchant world had their own bodyguards and brutes.

That's where Jon came in. He was not much bigger than Wren, but he was the more charismatic and the physical force of the two. Instead of studying, Jon spent his childhood afternoons playing at war. Gifted with amazing agility at birth, Jon had grown to be unstoppable in battle without really striving for it.

J.B. SIMMONS

At seventeen, he became the youngest ever to win the royal melee—an annual bout with over a thousand knights and sellswords from the entire country. Despite his success, none of Jon's victories made him want power or real battle. He preferred to carouse around town spreading smiles, while Wren memorized trade numbers. People respected and tolerated Wren, but everyone loved Jon.

Jon had trained against Tryst when they were young, and now he could not help but think of the prince's weaknesses. "What a strange, unfair fight." Jon said to his brother. "I would like to see how Tryst would fare one-on-one with me again. Not that I would actually challenge him," a slight smile touched Jon's eyes, "but I do not remember him being invincible."

"I think there are safer ways to depose a prince," Wren said as he looked out the window, studying the plaza. "It is clear that the drink in those barrels was spiked. Without their normal restraint, men like Catskill would come out to attack. I fear that Tryst will wipe out more challengers tonight. Why did Tryst do this? The masses have never posed much of a threat to the prince. The nobles must be involved somehow."

Turning back, Wren looked tired and stiff in the candlelight of the store. "Besides, I would not want either of us to face Tryst in the open field. We have not sparred with him since we were teens, and he has gained muscle and Zarathus in the meantime. What I just saw out there was more speed than I have ever seen in you."

Jon shrugged off the comment, answering with a wry grin that spoke his disagreement. He was modest, except when it came to fighting. "Why, I could—"

"Are you two still pining after your new prince?" Selia stormed in. "Remember? I requested your presence in the kitchen. There's something you need to see."

Jon and Wren exchanged a look, confirming that neither knew what "something" she was talking about, and they followed after her. They both understood that subtlety was their mother's only way of hiding significance. If it had not been important, she would have told them all about it when they first arrived.

The brothers scrubbed off their hands and sat down on tall stools around a square chopping-block table in the kitchen. Selia seemed to be cooking a feast, far more than they could eat by themselves.

"Now, you two seem very concerned about what was happening out there in the square. It's going to be fine. In fact, I heard just this morning from my friend Violet that the prince would be welcoming challengers tonight. Of course there would be a few. And I heard from my friend Rosalyn that...."

"Are you listening?" Selia folded her arms and tapped her foot, feigning disappointment.

"What is this *something* that you are hiding?" Wren asked. "Have you invited guests? You seem to be preparing enough food for a prince's banquet."

Selia laughed and pointed to the floor. "I suggest that you open the door to the cellar now."

Wren was the first on his feet. He and Jon pulled back a colorful rug from near the back of the kitchen, revealing a small, thick iron door to the cellar. The cellar's footprint was as big as the whole Invisible Hand, and it was used to hold the store's most valuable antiquities. Only Wren, Jon, and Selia had a key to the door.

Lifting the door required the two brothers' strength. Wren had no time to wonder how his mother could have opened the door on her own. Jon had already darted into the darkness and lit the small torch at the bottom of the ladder down into the room.

"It cannot be!" Jon stammered, then was speechless.

As Wren descended into the room, he saw Jon facing a dark figure in the nearest corner. The light from the torch barely reached that far. Wren tensed and walked towards them.

"It is me, Jon."

Jon leaned against the wall as if to assure himself of the reality of the moment. Wren knew the voice.

"You're back?" Wren said with awe and disbelief. He had never expected to see Andor again.

The man looked terrible. He was deathly thin, with scars all over his arms. His face was hollowed and framed by long, ragged hair and a wiry beard. His hair was lighter than before, almost white. Wren hardly recognized him, which made it harder to believe he was real, and not some ghost. But the eyes told the truth. They had the same dark brown luster, dotted with tiny flecks that glittered like gold.

"Now, now, my boys," Selia began, "I told you there was something that you needed to see. All that fuss about Tryst was unnecessary. Things will be set aright. We will be out from under his tyranny."

"Tryst will pay for what he has done." Their prince leaned forward, allowing more of the torchlight to catch the angles of his face. Jon and Wren couldn't help but notice his frailty. They doubted he could even stand. Yet, as he rose to his feet, they coiled back in instinct. His movement had a fierce edge they had never seen in him before.

"Our prince arrived this morning," Selia explained. "I fed him and have been trying to send word to you to come to the store. Come, let's get out of the cellar. The food should be ready."

Without waiting for an answer, she turned and climbed the ladder. Jon and Wren offered to support their prince. He declined with a motion of his hand and limped on ahead. Always the leader, both Jon and Wren thought, as they followed him up and out of the darkness.

Selia was already spooning out the rich lamb stew. She had also drawn the curtains of the kitchen windows. It was a rebellion dinner, as they huddled around the table. Now two princes were in the city—one too many.

"Are you still fully with me, Jon and Wren? I need you." His voice was coarse but sincere.

The brothers both nodded. "Of course," Wren said, surprised to see relief on Andor's face. "We are with you as we always have been."

"Good, very good. I cannot tell you how glad I am to be with friends like you. I cannot do this alone."

Andor paused, as if unsure of whether to say more. The brothers could hardly believe how gaunt he looked.

"I have Father Yates with me, too," Andor continued quietly. "And others will follow, even those close to Tryst. I went to Yates first, in the Cathedral. No one is suspicious of a beggar in that place, because Yates never turns them away. So, in the early dawn, dressed in rags, I think I made it undetected. Yates gave me food and talked with me about light and dark, good and evil, and forgiveness. I told him details about my imprisonment that I will spare you two from hearing for now. He said that several months had passed for me in the dark and despair. He told me that my soul seemed hungrier than my body."

Andor hesitated again. "But enough of that. Father Yates says I'll recover. The old priest is going to use his privileged position to stay close to Tryst and send messages to me. There is much I need to learn."

Their prince motioned for another serving of stew and sipped a glass of red table wine. He sighed and leaned back in his chair. It sounded like each of his words drained him.

"I want to hear more," Wren said eagerly, "but there is much to tell you as well. War is afoot, and Tryst and Ramzi have imposed a strict order in the name of defending against our enemies. Men from the mountains have united under some fanatic. Rumor is that he plans to march on the lower lands, killing everyone in his path. Tryst has declared that, within a week, he will lead the army out to battle this threat in the mountains."

"That is an old story under a new name," Andor responded. "Valemidas has never needed a tyrant to prevail against our foes." Light seemed to glare out of their prince's eyes. Maybe it was just a reflection of the torch. "We are free citizens. Our men fight by choice, and they are worth dozens of our opponents."

"Yes, but no one can stand up to Tryst right now," Jon said. "He has amassed amazing strength, and the people have made their decision to elect and coronate him for life."

"That is why we cannot linger long. Can you leave the city with me tomorrow?"

"You have our full support, but," Wren added, "you do not look ready to leave tomorrow. You will stand out until you rest—and eat a lot. Maybe you could stay hidden here and rest a few days? And why would we need to leave Valemidas? Men here will rally behind you if you declare your return, and your right to the throne."

When Andor did not respond, Wren turned and picked something up on the opposite wall. Turning again, he set a small mirror in front of Andor.

Andor's eyes opened wide, as if seeing himself for the first time. He sat still for a minute, staring at his reflection.

"Thank you, Wren," Andor finally said. He leaned back in his chair and set down the looking glass. "It is a wise suggestion. I will stay here and recover a few days."

"Excellent," Wren said. "You will be safe here. We can begin to rally your supporters."

"Not yet, Wren. I need more time to plan. This is a treacherous game. I think we will enlist in this usurper's army, learn more about his weak spots. I can hide in the ranks as an infantryman. You two can try to get closer to Tryst. Swear fealty to him, become his knights. Jon, my guess is he will want to keep you particularly close. He always respected your skills in battle. And Wren, no matter how much he dislikes you, he will welcome you for your nose for gold and for your brother's prowess. Tryst must have a way to fund his extravagant march, and I doubt he has paid our city's long-growing debt to the Sunans. Maybe we can join the army from a town outside Valemidas. Let's avoid the higher risks of the city. My appearance might also benefit from a journey in the countryside."

Andor seemed to breathe easier at the thought. "You will deliver letters for me?"

"Yes, my Prince, to anyone," Jon said without hesitation. "I know Valemidas better than ever, and I still have access to the palace. But I still want to know more about what happened to you."

Andor did not respond, and an awkward silence filled the room until Selia spoke. "Very well, my prince and my boys, it is settled. There will be more time to talk, but we all need rest. I have a bed made up in our guestroom." She motioned for Andor to come.

He stayed seated. "A bed sounds delightful," he said. "Jon, will you take writing supplies up to my room, and some soap and a sharp blade? Wren, check your trading book numbers, because I must to talk to you about the gold that we'll need. And Selia, would you be so kind to pour another bowl?" A small, sincere smile touched his face. "It feels like a lifetime since I've had something so warm and delicious."

Jon and Selia sprang into action, happy to hear Andor issuing orders and to obey him. Wren stayed to keep him company and discuss his plan.

Andor's presence changed everything. Even though there was an unmistakable darkness weighing on him, he was the best hope against Tryst. The two of them could not co-exist now, and Andor was the only rightful prince.

Chapter 7

Softness in the Night

"Now, for the love of Love and her soft hours,
Let's not confound the time with conference harsh:
There's not a minute of our lives should stretch
Without some pleasures now.
What sport tonight?"

Wren could not sleep, and it was not just because of the prince's return. Although his mind was sharp, his body felt soft. It was like a dull sunset, when the sun fades away without glory.

He remembered training as a younger man, running miles every day and losing sweat and blood in constant competition. His hands had been harder. Walking had been crisp, like a uniformed march always poised to turn and strike. After days of slamming padded blades against his friends, he could tap into his comrades' existence. He knew where their bruises were and who they wanted to soothe them.

Sitting now, running numbers on his stock of gold, Wren the merchant knew little of others. He knew little of his body. He just understood the trade; his thoughts ran over the profits that would be streaming in if he bought low on iron now and sold his excess grain. The numbers were hard, but the resulting profits only added to his body's softness. Delicious feasts, lace cuffs, fine leather shoes—those were his hard-earned marks of inner crumbling.

His merchant companions praised his advances and his shiny façade. They would say something like: "You were such a brash young man, Wren, driven to conquer and no fun to be around. You are such a pleasure now, welcoming and rich in disposition. Blah, money, blah." That kind of empty flattery made Wren think of something Father Yates had once said. "Do not lay up for yourselves treasures on earth, where moth and rust destroy and where thieves break in and steal."

It all made Wren want to run from this life. He wanted to be hard again, to show those merchants what it felt like to suffer the assault of his blade. Maybe, like a young knight rising in the ranks to remove the padding of his sword, Wren would combat the formidable enemy of wealth and society. If the pad on a blade could be removed, so could his softness. The longer the parasite of comfort clung to him, the more dangerous it became. Removed of the comforts, he would be a danger again. Otherwise, Wren thought, he would be no help to Andor at all. What is the point of a sword if it is always padded?

He rose from his bed and went silently down the stairs. It was not uncommon for him to awake in the night and work, but this night was the beginning of something different. He would be leaving with Andor and Jon soon. He felt unprepared, uncertain.

Cracking open the back door to the alley behind the shop, Wren slipped out into the night. The air was crisp, seemingly cleansed of its earlier foulness. A few low clouds dotted the sky, and the moon filled the tight passage with pale light. Wren walked along the building's wall. The end of the alley opened on a small road that led to the main plaza. He turned his head around the corner and studied the scene.

The bacchanalia was complete and its consequences were obvious. Bodies were scattered on the ground, concentrated around the central tree. Wren crouched and darted from mound to mound. Most of the people were alive, breathing irregularly as they fought unconsciously to rid their bodies of the toxins consumed during the festival. It was a stale reminder of the night's excesses.

Tryst and his royal band were nowhere to be seen. The bloodied bodies had been left on the stairs where Tryst had struck them down. The deceased should have been given more respect, taking their bodies away for burial or a pyre. That was not Wren's calling this night. He still felt a desire to fight, to lash out against the softness inside him and his city. So he left the plaza, looking for trouble.

He wandered the city's streets for at least an hour. There were a few lights in windows, and he smelled the first scents of bread baking for the morning. Dawn would be coming soon, but now the city was mostly dark and quiet. Weary but desperate for action, Wren decided he would make one last stop before returning home.

Walking along the road that hugged Valemidas' outer wall, Wren made his way to the front gate. Beside that gate, Wren knew, he would find the Sojourner's Inn. The owner, Randall Kay, was a friend. He had been a merchant, and a fair trader with Wren. Randall had always liked drinking more than trading, so he set up this little place near the gate. He had told Wren of his vision. It would be a simple inn with a simple tavern—a place meant for travelers to visit when they first arrived in the city. He would be the middleman between them and Valemidas, which often confounded its visitors by sheer size.

Business had been great for Randall under Andor's short reign. Travel had been open and frequent. Since losing Andor, the city's gates stayed closed more often than not. There was danger in the midst of the changing princes, and Tryst tried to hold greater control.

Still, tonight Wren heard a large crowd as he approached the Sojourner's Inn. He paused outside a window and looked in.

Set off against the opaque night, the tavern had a warm glow. Its main room was a small rectangle, with fires burning brightly in hearths at both ends. Four long wooden tables, lined with benches, covered much of the floor. In the corners, there were rich leather couches around low tables. The space was surprisingly full. It was as if every activity of the night had been drawn out of hiding and into the Inn.

Wren did not see his friend Randall, who was surely asleep at this hour. Two of the innkeep's guards were standing at the two doors to the tavern, and at least five serving maids were racing about. They filled tankards with ale while dodging groping hands. Randall had a strict rule that was fitting for visitors to the city if not for soldiers. The maids dressed simply but provocatively, with white bodices fastened tightly over skirts that did not reach the knee. They were to be admired, but the patrons could not touch. Bandying words was encouraged, as long as it never became serious. Contact was forbidden. Randall would always say, "Take your ales and have a peek, but if you touch, it's the door you seek."

It took only a few moments for Wren to see that doors would be sought tonight. They probably already had. The men were mostly soldiers who seemed to have come straight from the night's debauchery. They were rowdy and lustful, making this the perfect company for dispelling softness. Wren would have a target on his chest, with his linen attire and aristocratic grin.

He walked into the Sojourner's Inn stridently. The noise of the place shot out of the door as soon as Wren opened it. The guard welcomed him with a curious glance. It was a strange time of night for someone to be arriving, much less a wealthy merchant. Wren paid him no heed and found a seat at one of the benches, wedged beside two particularly boisterous men. From their plain brown uniforms and crude language, Wren marked them as the lowest of infantrymen. A minute of observation confirmed his suspicions.

They were cussing and yelling about their conquests. The whole room was full of stories, and most of them sounded at least a shade off the truth. Conquests in distant lands and princesses saved. Wren found it amusing at first. The mood was unsettling, though, because these men lacked leadership and direction. The night of heavy drinking, starting with the corrupted stuff in the main square, only made it worse. Now the maids were suffering the brunt of their rowdiness. Even though Randall paid the girls handsomely, Wren planned to make one of these brutes apologize for the rudeness.

Wren downed his first drink in minutes and listened to the crude conversations around him. The two men he was wedged beside may have been the worst.

"Dustin, take a look at this one," the lout to Wren's left garbled. "I'd like to get my hands on her." Wren followed his glance to an attractive tavern maid who was leaning over the bar to the kitchen. She turned with six massive tankards clutched to her chest.

"Nah, Tuco, you oughta be lookin' somewhere else. That one's mine." Dustin was barely keeping his head off the table, but he managed to give his mate a clumsy punch to the arm.

"Quit that, Dustin. I reckon next time you touch me it'll be trouble." Tuco responded in slow motion, drawling out words. "Besides, with a body like that, this woman has enough for both of us. Watch this."

Tuco tried to stand and wobbled. Wren could not contain his laughter at the man's poor balance and judgment.

"What'er you laughin' at, fancy boy?" Dustin demanded.

Wren grinned wider and pointed at the approaching maid. "Dustin, right? I mean no offense. I am just admiring my next catch." His voice dripped with sarcasm.

"Boy, I'm gonna—" Dustin started but was cut short by Tuco, whose eyes were locked on the serving maid who had reached the table. "Oh lord, she, uh, heats me like the summer sun," he kept his eyes locked somewhere below her chin and above her waist. "My princess is here, bringin' me drinks. It don't get no better."

She leaned over Wren's right shoulder, obviously amused by the compliment. "Gentlemen, it looks like you are close to empty. I have a little more special brew for you, if you still want some." She wore a devilish smile, as if daring them to touch. Catching Wren's non-glazed eyes made her tense a bit. It seemed she was used to handling the drunk ones but stayed more wary of others.

"I need all the special brew you got." Dustin's attempt at some kind of composed flirtation was pathetically hilarious. Wren almost fell off the bench laughing.

"Why thank you!" She answered. "It only gets better by the tankard for the hopeless," she said as she spun, tossed her hair and was off to the next tease. The men shared a dull glance, but anger began to build at the insult. Apparently an insult from the woman sharpened their senses.

Tuco lumbered up, arrested by her spell and losing restraint. Once on his feet, he moved with surprising speed and pinned her to the wall. He began groping desperately.

Seizing the good cause for action, Wren jumped to his feet but fell flat on his face before he could stop the assault. Glancing back, he saw Dustin looming over him, fuming and bright red in the face. He had been tripped.

"Cheap move," Wren growled from the ground.

Dustin pulled his leg back to kick. Wren was almost to his knees but knew that he would not dodge the boot coming at his face. Shifting to block the worst of the dead-on blow, he saw a black blur swipe out Dustin's back leg and send him tumbling to the floor.

Wren rose to his feet and turned to protect the maid. One of the Inn's guards had ripped Tuco off of her and slammed him onto the ground. Some of the soldiers had left their seats and were approaching in an unstable circle. It seemed they were willing to fight for each other this night.

Time froze for Wren. Every trained fighting instinct surged out of dormancy. He counted ten soldiers, weapons drawn, with only three people facing them—Wren, the guard, and a hooded figure in black. The other guard was outside the circle, ready to help. The maids were fleeing the room. Other soldiers were around, but seemed to be staying away from the fight.

"To my sides," commanded the dark figure who had helped Wren. He and the guard slid into position quickly. Wren tried to focus on the assailants but was distracted by the lady issuing orders. It had to be a woman, he judged from her voice and slim stature. She had two long blades drawn, longer than was allowed under recent regulations in Valemidas. It all seemed familiar— the tone of authority, the long black cloak, the close-drawn hood, the refined stance—but he had not yet seen her face.

Before the puzzle came together, he was ducking to dodge a tankard thrown at his head.

Crouching, Wren pulled a dagger from his belt and threw it into the shoulder of the soldier in front of him. He charged towards the soldiers to that man's right, opening his left flank and entrusting it to the woman in black.

The soldiers were moving slow, drunkenly. Wren dove into them low, taking out their legs and staying under their weak stabs. He sliced at the calves of two men and rose as they fell. He connected a knee to the head of one falling man and moved to face another. The man swung his dagger wildly, nicking Wren's shoulder. Before Wren could counter, the man's eyes went wide in shock and he fell forward. Two hilts carved into ravens stuck out of his back.

"Ravien!" Wren shouted before he could think. He locked eyes with her and briefly forgot where he was. He forced his mind back to the room. The fighting had stopped, with several men on the ground around them. The last of the soldiers were fleeing out the door. Of course, thought Wren, no one in his right mind would stay and fight the prince's sister. She was glaring at him.

"You did pretty well, Wren," she said softly, "but you seemed a little slow. What's a merchant doing out this late?" She seemed more interested in her question than in the answer, because she put her finger over his lips and whispered "shhh."

She then began taking the identification tags from the soldiers. Those tags were another new requirement under Tryst. A few soldiers were groaning in pain, a few seemed unconscious or dead, including Dustin. No one resisted Ravien.

As always, the princess wore snug black boots. They flared out at the knee, revealing bare skin up to her black skirt. Wren could not keep his eyes away.

The two Inn guards were also watching her. They had found a spot on the bench where they rested. Only their eyes moved, following Ravien. As they stared at her, three of the tavern maids were tending to their wounds. One of the guards was bleeding heavily from the forehead and the side.

Ravien, after collecting the tags, stepped to the injured guard and cupped his head in her thin hands. She locked eyes with him and whispered something that Wren could not hear. Rising from him, she pressed something into the hand of the maid standing at his side. The other woman blushed, smiled broadly and said, "oh no, well, maybe, oh, thank you!" Whatever Ravien had said and given, Wren guessed that it had left the man a better chance of living and the maid a better chance of ending up with the man.

The prince's sister then faced Wren again. Her eyes were so dark, like midnight pools reflecting the Inn's light. "Follow me," she said without any question about whether he would obey. With that, she disappeared out the door.

Wren followed and found her sprinting to the right as soon as he was outside. He took off as fast he could. The quick pace knocked all thoughts and breath out of him.

He gained ground on every straightaway, but she stayed out of reach. She made her turns too quickly, and left Wren guessing a few times about which way she had gone. Whenever he lost sight of her, she would appear for an instant and then be around the next corner. It was as if she measured the distance between them, keeping it exactly far enough to avoid losing Wren or letting him catch her.

After maybe ten minutes of pursuit, Wren was exhausted. Lack of sleep and battle fatigue wore on him as much as the run. He had always been a runner, but that history did not make up for years sitting at a desk.

Just when he decided to make a final push, closing the gap to a mere ten paces, Ravien ducked into the door of an anonymous building on a dark alley. Perfect, thought Wren, because Ravien proved herself to be so unskilled indoors. He saw again the recent memory of his attacker falling with two daggers sticking out of his back, and Ravien looming behind him.

Wren opened the door slowly. The hinge was silent, as was the room inside. It was musky, with cobwebs hanging from the low ceilings. Wren wondered how long it would take someone to find him dead in this abandoned place.

He froze for a moment at the potential truth of that thought. She really could be trying to kill him. Wren had known Ravien for a long time. Everyone who grew up around Tryst knew his sister. They had been inseparable as kids. People whispered, often loudly, that she was the reason Tryst had not married. He would never meet someone who could equal his sister, they said. Wren had his doubts, but he had not spoken to Tryst in years.

Ravien was loyal to her brother and her intentions were unclear, but Wren believed she had played no part in the coup. She cared too much about a free Valemidas, and about Lorien, to help depose Andor. Either way, he felt helpless to resist her call now. He took another step, then another. When a temptress like that beckoned, who was he to leave her waiting?

Once inside the building, the only place to go was up. A narrow stairway on the far side of the room led to the second floor. Wren went up and found the second floor to be almost an exact copy of the first floor. He climbed four more flights of stairs. Each floor was the same. Wren knew that Ravien could not catch him off guard in an empty room.

The sixth and uppermost floor was also like the five below it. The only difference was that this room had a door opposite the stairs. It stood open to the night. Wren stepped lightly through the door and surveyed his surroundings. He was on a small and flat roof, with no railing between it and the sixty-foot fall to the ground below. There was no sign of Ravien here, and Wren thought that perhaps she had vanished.

Then to his right, where there had been nothing a second before, he saw a silhouette standing at the top of a high arched roof. Without pause, Wren sprinted towards the figure. Adrenalin propelled his jump from the first building to the second, covering six feet with nothing below. He did not look down and charged on.

The second jump, to the arched roof, was even longer. It also dropped further, and Wren landed hard against the slate tiles. Looking across the gap he had just leapt, he was feeling pretty good about himself. But when he turned an instant later, the silhouette was gone. He ran up to the peak of the roof and tensed at the quiet solitude. Not again, Wren thought. She has to be—

"Silence." The voice was a seductive whisper, unlike the dagger pressed to his throat. All Wren could think was that it was impossible. She had slipped him from behind, and now she had him pinned.

"As I said, Wren, you feel a little slow." Her right hand moved down against his stomach; she patted the small extra layer of fat. "You used to be rock solid and so sharp. It is a shame what your wealthy merchant's life has done to you. You will have no chance taking down my brother in that shape." She breathed the words into his ear.

Wren fought hard to stay calm, torn between fear and something like desire. "I wouldn't dare try such a thing, Ravien. Tryst is the prince and he has my loyalty."

"Don't waste my time with lies." She jerked him closer and drew blood with the dagger. "I saw you and Jon in the square tonight. I also know who is in your shop right now." There was not an inch of space between their bodies.

Her words sent Wren's mind spinning. Maybe she was going to kill him. How could she possibly know about Andor? Feeling desperate, he kept silent and considered his chances of fighting back. As long as she was alive with that knowledge, everything was in jeopardy.

"Do not think of killing me, Wren. It wouldn't do any good, because I planted the secret with someone who will survive me. Besides, my dear little bird, you would not want to hurt me." She pressed even closer, her lips grazing his cheek. "I can help you, and you have always wanted me." She shifted to the left and bit down lightly on his ear.

Wren felt the change in position and the subtle relaxing of Ravien's grip. In one flash of movement, he leaned his head away from the blade, grabbed her tight forearm and slung her forward over his shoulder. She slammed onto the roof, landing on her back, still clutching onto Wren and the dagger. The momentum of the throw knocked Wren down to a knee, and the two struggled on the slanted roof for position and control.

Ravien was strong and lightning fast, but Wren overpowered her. Her legs were locked around his waist, but he was on top and had her shoulders and arms pinned down.

Wren gloated for a moment at the position, smiling down at his captive princess. They were at the edge of the arched roof, and her head was hanging off the end, long black hair flowing towards the ground six stories below. Her eyes raged up at him, dark embers threatening to consume him.

"Ravien my dear," his voice was half serious, half mocking, "you have always been a dangerous woman. Maybe I do want you, but you know too much. What do you propose I do with you?"

She responded with a grin, as if she were the one in control of the situation. "I propose that you question everything you know about me. Question my loyalties and my desires. I am a sister to the prince but also to Lorien. If you displease me in the slightest, there is no doubt that Tryst will learn of your plans. We both know what that would mean. But if you please me," she rocked her legs, swaying both of them precariously over the ledge, "and that's a big if, then your plot might have a chance."

Wren shrugged innocently and thought of distracting her. "What kind of plot are you talking about? Everything I want is right here." With that he plunged and kissed her deeply. For a moment it felt like she was returning the passion, but a sharp pain forced him to pull back. She had bitten his lower lip and drawn blood. Again.

"I can believe that," Ravien breathed out, failing to hide her grin. She lowered her voice to the quietest of whispers that Wren could barely hear, "but it is not so much you, as Andor, who concerns me."

"Now!" Her yell pierced the intimate moment. He froze as a sharp point pressed into the back of his neck. Apparently he could not hear anything coming this night. He looked into Ravien's eyes, trying to make out the reflection of who was behind him.

She returned his deep gaze and spoke delicately. "Wren, be silent and stay completely still." He loved the sound of his name as it rolled off her lips. "I know you and Jon are planning something with him." She let that hang in the air; Wren fought to keep his face blank. "I will be joining the Lycurgus on this march, and will stay close to my brother. If you try to harm him, it will not end well. But some of our interests may be aligned."

Wren could no longer suppress his look of surprise, and Ravien seized on it. "Remember, question everything you assume about me. Now you know that I am not alone." The unknown blade pressed harder into the back of Wren's neck, driving his face closer to Ravien's. "We will communicate with you, and you must obey our requests. If you do not, you have no chance. You might succeed, although not in the way you expect, if you please me."

She leaned closer and gave him a light kiss. "If you please me."

Suddenly everything went dark, as the person behind him tied a cloth over his eyes. He felt a blade at his throat again, forcing him to stand blindly. He felt Ravien escape from below him. An instant later, her voice was beside his right ear. "Stay blind and count to fifty. Then you may return home and get what little sleep you can. It would not please me if you count too quickly. Dawn is coming."

Wren obeyed the command to the letter. He thought through Ravien's words, looking for hidden meanings. How did she know? Who was she working with? No matter how he approached it, they were in trouble. She had the position and the information to ruin everything.

At the count of fifty he pulled off the blindfold, which smelled of lavender. There was no one to be seen.

The view over the city was amazing in the early pre-dawn. He could make out the spires of the prince's palace to his left, and the walls of Valemidas wrapped around the sleeping city. It was peaceful now, but the effects of Tryst's reign, and Ramzi's oppressive rules, were rippling through the city. Wren shuddered at what would happen to the peace under a lifetime of Tryst.

Andor's plot had to succeed. As Wren made his way back to his shop, he prepared to tell Andor and Jon what he had learned. It would not be easy, because he would have to explain how he ended up on a rooftop with Tryst's sister. He climbed into bed for an hour of sleep and found himself dreaming of a dark and beautiful woman.

Chapter 8

The Power of Words

**"The delight which arises
from the modifications of pain
confesses the stock from whence it sprung,
in its solid, strong, and severe nature."**

Lorien was feeling crushed within the tower walls. She stood before the mirror in her dressing chamber, looking luminescent in the morning light. She was like a candle flame rising up from the cold stone floors.

Over the past months she had hardly left her rooms. The measure of time had been difficult. After losing Andor, every day grinded by in the same bleak misery. Like many in Valemidas, she missed him as a prince, but she alone felt empty without him in her world. They had planned to marry. They had planned to have children. They had planned to rule Valemidas and its kingdom, together. Andor had promised as much to her, and if not for her traitor half-brother, she would be making final preparations as a bride.

Instead, she felt ready to crumble. Mourning overcame her. The tears would have filled buckets—buckets labeled devastation, fear, and anger. As the days passed, she plunged deeper towards the cause of her pain.

The night before, when Tryst had been coronated, she had channeled her emotions into ambition. His speech before the nobles had been bad, but what followed was even worse. Lorien had heard accounts of his murders on the stairs of the palace. Rumors said that a dozen men had died at Tryst's hands, and that his opponents had been drugged by some drink to keep challenging him. The atrocious display would only confirm the people's terrified respect for their prince.

It disgusted Lorien. She knew that Tryst and Ramzi would use that fear to shackle the people with even more onerous laws. She would fight them by whatever means she could, because she knew that Andor would have wanted it. Otherwise, she might as well be banished on some island to waste away in solitude.

Before she could fight, though, she needed to recover, to regain her composure. The dark circles under her eyes were her battle wounds. Staring into the mirror, her lips turned up at the thought. At least it was an improvement from the first few weeks, when she had given up. Her own hand had not resolved to take her life, but she could not bring herself to drink, eat, or sleep.

With her brother sitting as the prince, she was a princess by right. That meant she had a duty to protect her people. A wrecked princess would be little help against the overwhelming force of Tryst. She could try to use her status against him. A change of scenery would be a good start. Today, she told herself, she would get outside to the city and maybe even beyond.

Tryst would of course have her watched, wherever she went. He had picked all of her serving maids and guards as soon as he had stolen the throne. They reported to him and had little loyalty towards Lorien, although they had begun showing sympathy.

She looked over the wardrobe that her maids had brought for her to choose from today. The huge oak armoire was full of dresses, most of them black. Lorien appreciated that the maids had come to respect her mood. She ran her fingers along one simple, elegant riding dress. It was made of fine wool, with a full neck and a teardrop-shaped exposure at the back. Like most of her recent attire, it was well suited to a funeral on a rainy day. Scanning the rest of the options, Lorien decided that none of them would work. Her clothes needed to match her task, if she was to escape her downward cycle of despair.

Calling to the maid sitting outside the room, Lorien tried to picture herself from before, as if she was about to join Andor on an adventure. She could sense his presence in a way that had been lost to her for many days.

Her maid appeared before her. She was small, with innocent eyes and straight dark hair. Lorien wondered whether Tryst had hand-selected each servant to pick the ones he thought Lorien would come to trust. He should have known better.

Lorien forced herself to smile as she spoke. "Cheril, bring me other options, perhaps in green and brown, and suited for riding. I will need riding boots." The maid nodded politely and turned to go. Lorien added, "and nothing black."

She felt better already. Stripping out of her gown, she gazed at her body as if seeing it for the first time in months. She was shocked at her thinness. As the daughter of a knight, she had always had a healthy amount of lean muscle on her frame. Her mother had often disapproved of her physical activities, but they had been a part of who she was. Now, her skin was stretched thin over her bones. Her ribs could be counted, her shoulders were sharp, and her frame made her small breasts look large. Pulling up her hair, Lorien could see a pulse along her thin neck. It was startling how her body had diminished. If she did not start eating more, she really would waste away.

Her maid returned with an armful of clothes. "Thank you, Cheril. I see that the porridge you brought has become cold. Send for another hot breakfast, with eggs this time."

Cheril failed to hide her surprise at the request. Of course, Lorien thought, the servants would have noticed, and reported, that she was not eating. She decided that next time she saw Tryst she would tell him that his coronation speech had lifted her spirits. Her smug brother would believe it, too.

The selection of riding garments was inspiring. Lorien found what Andor would have wanted her to wear. It started with the leather boots, which rose to her knees and had bright silver buckles at the top. She picked a dark green riding dress, which had small, buttoned pockets at the chest and on the arms. The pockets would help hide her frailty. To avoid exposing her pale thighs, she found a pair of knit leggings. A light brown cloak completed the look of an adventurer. She decided against a hat. It would be good for the people in the city to recognize her today.

Shortly after she was dressed, the food arrived. She plotted her day as she slowly ate the rich breakfast. The meal raised her spirits so much that she considered ordering more, but she decided her body should be eased back into its more normal routine.

She did not bother to tell anyone she was leaving. A retinue would follow her whether or not she asked. Her confidence rose as she left her quarters. It had been too long for a princess of Valemidas to stay sheltered.

The prince's palace sat perched above the city, with walls rising up from the steep, rocky hillside. Among the spires of the palace, the tallest were two slender towers set on either side of the central keep. The palace was built in recent eras of peace, with opulence growing on top of the fortified castle that had long protected the city. The only entrance was along the grand stairs to the northwest of the palace.

Lorien had been holed up high in the southeastern tower, which meant a brisk walk to reach the stairs leading to the city. She decided to walk the long way along the inside of the wall, rather than cutting through the central keep and risking seeing her brother.

The grounds of the palace were not as she remembered them, even though the paths and gardens retained the same elegant beauty. The difference was in the people. Just months ago, Lorien would have seen knights sparring and laughing during breaks. She would have seen nobles milling around, plotting certainly, but with at least an air of cordiality. She would have seen children.

Today there was no laughter. Nobles and children were nowhere to be seen. It was as if Tryst had banished playfulness from the palace. Soldiers abounded, but they looked stiff. They marched in twos, backs straight with discipline. She did not see any sparring, although a few lines of men practiced spear thrusts under the barking commands of knights whom Lorien did not recognize. Making matters worse, she was trailed by an unapologetic, unsmiling group of six guards.

It was far too pretty a day for the lack of gaiety. Yesterday had been nothing but heavy spring rain. Lorien had hardly noticed it, but now she appreciated the changing season. The young buds on trees seemed ready to burst. The grass still glistened from the morning dew. Under the clear blue sky, the moisture might give way to the first flowers this very day. Lorien focused on the natural surroundings, and away from the soldiers and the followers. She could not handle more thoughts of war, or of anything negative. This was a day to be uplifted. She needed to recover.

The prince's stables sat along the wall, just inside the gateway to the palace. As she approached, she was surprised to recognize the stableboy outside, Telemachus. He had been Andor's squire. He was also the son of Ulysses, who was among the few of Andor's sworn men that Tryst had kept on his own Knight's Council. A knight of Ulysses' caliber was not easily replaced. Tryst probably believed his loyalty to be to his position on the Council, not to the person of the prince. She hoped her brother was mistaken.

Lorien smiled as she walked towards the stable. "Tel, it is good to see you," she said.

The young man bowed low. His dark hair was shaggy as always. "My princess, it is an honor," he mumbled sincerely while staring at the ground.

She reached down and lifted his head gently by the chin. She and Andor might have had a son who would have looked like this. "Come now, you look as if you see death walking. Please saddle up Juniper. I am going for a ride."

He hung his head for a moment again. "You look wonderful, my Lady. It's just that, well, I have not seen you in a long time. Many of us have been worried about you." He looked up, excitement lighting his eyes. "But here you are, and it is a great day for a ride. Juniper has missed you. She is such a beautiful mare. I say she is the finest we have. She will be thrilled

70

to get out of these stables." He turned and hurried into the building.

"Thank you, Tel," she called after him. Yes, she thought, Juniper and I will both be thrilled to get outside of these walls.

Lorien leaned against the stable while Tel did his work. She breathed deeply, trying to will her strength to return. As she waited, she gazed up at the central keep. It was centered perfectly within the palace, twice as wide as the towers at its sides. Lorien, Tryst, and Ravien had spent many days exploring the imposing keep as a child. Their father was one of the greatest knights of his day, which afforded his children access to most of the palace's grounds. Those were memories of better days, but now she felt a chill at the thought of Tryst in the building. He had removed the bright pennants that used to flow out of the windows. It was like he wanted his palace to absorb all the surrounding light of the city. Lorien sighed and looked back down.

Tryst stood before her.

"You frown, dear sister. What troubles you?" The words carried only a faint hint of sincerity. He looked pleased to have caught her off guard.

Lorien put on the same practiced smile she had worn to his coronation. "You surprised me, Tryst, that's all," she replied. "It is a beautiful day, and I am going out for a ride."

"Now that is a surprise. You have not left the palace in months." Tryst held out his arm. "Come, let's walk together before you go."

Lorien took his arm and tried to relax. It would not do for Tryst to sense her anger. She would play the obedient sister and let him guide the conversation.

Tryst led her away from the stable, heading towards the palace's open gate. They reached the gate before either of them had said another word. Lorien found it strange that her brother would abide by the silence. They stood facing the city sprawled out below them.

"You have been worrying me, Lorien." Tryst finally said, as he gazed over the city. "I hear that you have not been eating."

He paused, and continued in a lower voice that none of the nearby guards could hear. "You did a poor job hiding your frustration at my coronation. This has been a time to celebrate the rise of your brother as prince. You are now the princess that you always wanted to be. I know what you have lost, but what more do you want from me?"

Staring at her and awaiting a reply, Tryst had anger and concern blended in his expression. His eyes were shadowed under his furrowed brow, contrasting starkly with the radiant blue diamond on his crown.

Lorien was taken aback by his openness. Her lips pressed together as she sought calmness. Of course he is concerned, she thought. I am his vulnerability—he cannot rid himself of his sister, yet his sister loved the prince he deposed. She had to find some use for that.

"Time." Lorien said. "All I need from you is some time. You know well that there have been changes in our lives. It is taking me time to adjust to everything." The words came out easily because they were true. "Just look at me today, out for an adventure."

Tryst glanced down at her body, letting his eyes linger. She had never liked the way he looked at her. "Nice dress, even if it shows too much of your legs. And I am glad to see you back in your boots." He finally returned his stare to her eyes. "Still, Lorien, you look terrible, like a ghost of your former self. Try to get some sun today, and find something to eat."

Lorien could not suppress a little laugh. Tryst's eyes opened wider.

"For a moment I thought you would forbid me to leave," Lorien said. "It is good to see that my patronizing brother still cares for me."

From the look on his face, Lorien sensed that some sort of battle was waging in his mind. She guessed that his stiff pride felt slighted, but that he was also amused.

"You are my sister," Tryst said in a low voice. "Your royal home is here, and I cannot abide you shuffling around in misery for the rest of my reign. I hope your ride today helps." The warmth left his face, and his voice rose. "You will be protected closely by guards whenever you leave the palace. I am adding two more men, to ensure your safety. They have strict orders to tie you up and drag you back here at the first sign of danger." His words carried no tone of joking.

So he did not trust her. She ignored his demeaning comments and replied: "Your guards can follow me today, although I doubt very much that I will need them in the future."

"I will not play these games," Tryst whispered as he came within inches of Lorien's face. "You will be guarded as long as I command it. You are nothing without me. But with me, you have a home here. You are in the prince's family. You are—"

"Princess Lorien!" She turned and was thrilled to see Tel being dragged towards her by Juniper. The beautiful red mare neighed and nudged her shoulder. Lorien ran her hands along the horse's face, which was speckled with bright white marks.

Tel stood up straight, dusted himself off, then bowed to the ground before Lorien and Tryst. "I am sorry to interrupt, my Prince. Juniper here, well, she has been in that stable for far too long. As soon as she caught sight of the princess, she took off. I could not hold her back."

Tryst stared down at Tel coldly. "You are a disappointment. I find it hard to believe that you were ever a prince's squire." The boy looked up with pain and failure written on his face. Tryst did not relent. "Ulysses will not be happy to hear this. Get back to the stable where you belong."

The boy sprinted away, as if fleeing for his life.

Tryst turned to go, but turned back in a swirl of black and clasped Lorien's face between his hands. "Farewell, my beautiful Lorien. You have a privileged position. Take care not to lose it."

Lorien met his locked gaze evenly. "The same goes for you, Tryst. Farewell." She pulled herself out of his grip and leapt onto Juniper's back.

Tryst stormed off without another word. Once he was far enough away, Lorien let out a sigh of relief. Her body was taxed just from mounting Juniper, and her mind raced through the implications of the conversation. First, she thought, I must thank

Tel. With the slightest pull on the reins, Juniper turned and cantered towards the stable. Tel had his face against the wall, but he turned as Lorien approached. Tears filled his eyes.

"Tel, you wonderful lad," she said brightly from the saddle. "I owe you my thanks for retrieving Juniper and saving me back there." He looked confused. "You see, our Prince was trying to control where I went today, but I wanted to move freely. Now I can, thanks to you."

Amidst his confusion, the boy blushed and bowed. "Thank you very much, my Lady."

Lorien smiled as she rode away. She realized that Tel would be the perfect way to reach Ulysses. That crafty veteran could be a great help, if only he retained some loyalty to Andor's allies and some distaste for Tryst. Surely he would. She wondered whether Tryst would ever learn that kindness was the best way to get what you wanted.

As she rode through the gates, Lorien felt a weight lifting off her shoulders. It felt right to be riding Juniper, even if she was trailed closely by eight of her brother's guards. Her mare pranced down the stairs leading out of the palace and into the city. At least her horse could feel that all was as it should be with the world.

The view as Lorien descended the stairs was just as moving as she remembered it. Valemidas had grown organically over generations, which meant that every twisting road had known hundreds of stories and names. Other than the Path of Princes, which was a straight line northwest from the stairs of the palace to the city's main gate, no road or alley stayed straight for more than twenty steps. Even natives of Valemidas got lost in parts of the city. A merchant from the dock quarters would have difficulty in the low hills that filled the nobles' southwest quarters. A noble from those quarters would not find his way—nor would he want to—near the soldier's barracks, taverns, and other seedy establishments that surrounded the main gate of the city.

Visitors to the city had no chance without a guide. Although getting lost was half the fun, the many guides had long ago formed a guild, with the sole mission of helping people get from one place to another, safely.

Natives and visitors alike could appreciate, without a guide, the stunning colors of Valemidas. Near the city there were deep quarries of white stone and slate. Over time, that steady supply had resulted in almost every building being built of bright white walls and steeply pitched, slate gray roofs. Against that simple yet luxurious backdrop, the thousands of merchants and craftsmen of the city had developed their own colorful pennants, which they proudly flew from their rooftops and windows.

Lorien found herself inspired by the consistency and individuality of every building. They had strong foundations and ornate decorations, both of which seeped into the city's culture. The community had followed generations of custom, but the individuals retained a liberating distinctness.

Now, Tryst wanted to destroy the colors, the distinctness. Sadness swept over her at the thought. Her brother had always favored simple, strict uniformity. He would impose his tastes on his city, and spread those tastes to the entire continent. He would not be happy until every man was a soldier in black, and Ramzi would have every woman stay indoors.

Lorien began seeing the consequences of Tryst's reign as soon as she reached the bottom of the palace stairs and rode across the broad square at their base. Juniper had her head held high, heralding the princess's visit to the city. The people seemed to be in no mood for welcoming a royal. They shuffled their feet and went about their business.

The pattern of the city's movements seemed strange. Lorien had always loved being caught up in the excited feel of the central square, with its people stirring beneath the elegant white limbs of the great tree that loomed in the square's center. Before, hundreds of merchant stands had created a haphazard maze that channeled the shouts of wares and sales. Today the square was well-ordered and nearly empty. Lorien guessed that only a fourth of the merchant stands remained—maybe fifty in total. They formed neat lines that occupied a small corner of the square. That corner was quiet, with maybe a couple dozen shoppers milling around. It was as if trade had forgotten to awake from its winter hibernation.

Lorien rode toward the white tree without anyone approaching her. She remembered the history she had learned as a child about the tree. About ten generations ago, the prince of Valemidas controlled the continent surrounding Valemidas but yearned for more conquest. He had sailed with his greatest knights to Sunan, the nearest nation to the east, a land renowned for its fierce desert and fiercer warriors. At that time the Sunans had less wealth and less strength individually, but their masses were more disciplined and unified.

The opposing forces had been such an equal match that neither had been willing to surrender, not until both had suffered enormous losses. In an offer of peace, the Sunan ruler had offered a large white seed as the seal of a promise to allow the Valemidans to retreat safely. In return, the prince had promised to never attack again, and he had sent his only son to Sunan as his guarantee.

For many years, a small ship would arrive in Valemidas each spring from the east, bearing a note of peace and a letter for the prince from his son. The prince would send a message in return, stating that the tree was strong, as was the peace. The ships and messages had stopped years ago. Now it was just a story that grandparents had passed down. Even trade between the nations had trickled to nothing, as Valemidas had borrowed more and more gold from the Sunans without repayment. Some doomsayers had been warning for too long that it meant war was nigh.

Whatever the truth of that story, the Valemidans loved the tree. It was massive and graceful, at least twice the height of any other tree around Valemidas. The smooth white bark seemed to match the surrounding buildings of the city, and particularly the slender towers of the palace. Each spring, the tree would bear luscious green leaves, which turned fire red and fell in the fall. Lorien thought that the tree was most beautiful in the winter, when its bare limbs sliced through the sky. The people always yearned to see the leaves grow again after the snows melted. But for two years, no leaf had sprouted. The people of Valemidas were distraught and fearful of what the barrenness might mean.

Lorien's musings about the tree's past were cut short by her closer view of its trunk. The tree had been desecrated, with scars carved into the pure white bark. Lorien took them in with shock as she rode around the tree. They were lists of laws, burned black into the white. Each letter was the size of Lorien's hand. "Commands of the Prince" was engraved largely at the top.

Every declaration was like a punch to the gut. First, all boys between seven and twelve years old, and every firstborn son who reaches seven in the future, must be enlisted for life in the Lycurgus. Second, everyone who enters Valemidas must be assigned an identification number, and at all times must carry a card with the number and the Prince's seal. Third, all merchants, tradesmen, innkeepers, sailors, and other workers of the city must register their businesses with the Prince, who has the discretion to deny the license for such work. Fourth, all citizens of Valemidas must record, report, and pay a tax of one-third of their annual income, with avoidance punished by imprisonment. Fifth—

Lorien quit, not even half way down the list. She tore away from the tree, pushing Juniper to a near gallop. She felt disgusted on behalf of the people. They had lived by custom, which bound more deeply than a prince ever could. The laws had always been simple baselines. Do not murder. Do not steal. Do not do other bad things that directly hurt people. But this was an unprecedented intrusion. No wonder so many merchants were gone today, Lorien fumed.

She rode Juniper hard out of the square. She held tight to the mare's neck, and her legs clutched to its sides. Adrenalin rushed as her muscles were drawn tight and wind whipped past her. She felt alive, like she could fight this. It had been only a few months. Her brother had not yet broken the will of the people. She would fight on their behalf, because she enjoyed a position of honor and respect that they would never have under Tryst.

Lorien was half a mile from the main gate of the city before she slowed and noticed another oddity. Only half of the Path of

Princes was being used, the right side. She alone was on the left side of the road, other than the guards who had followed her. The other side was crammed with people inching forward, held in tightly by soldiers who lined the road's median. Everyone was moving in the same direction—towards the gate. Many of them stared at her, with confused looks on their face. It reminded Lorien of Tel's face, because there was the same stupor of bewilderment toward her apparent disobedience.

She rode gently into the masses, summoning a smile. Seeing the people thawed some of the coldness that had been growing in her while hidden away in a tower. Her smile seemed to be contagious. It made her feel like a beacon, but she was drawing her energy from those around her. They fed off of each other.

Some of the people began to shout. "The Princess returns!" "Talk sense to your brother!" "Help us!" The voices clashed into each other. The situation seemed to be spiraling out of control, as the closest people started grabbing at her desperately.

Lorien raised her arms and surveyed the faces around her. They were not angry, but they were afraid, and tense. That did not bode well with her so-called protective guards approaching. She turned to see them forcing their way through the crowd. She felt sure they would try to push the people away from her, in the name of safety.

This was not the time for her to run or put up a fight. It would not do for Tryst to grow more watchful of her now. She waived her goodbye and nudged Juniper to turn back, but paused when she saw a familiar face hidden in the shadows of a hood.

It was Jon. She remembered that he had been a friend of Andor's—an honest and strong man, through and through, Andor had once said.

Without a word, Jon reached up and grabbed Lorien's hand. He ducked away an instant later, disappearing into the crowd.

A few of the guards noticed the exchange.

"Stop that man!" One of them yelled as they closed the distance to Lorien, formed a ring around her, and sent off a couple pursuers. She forced herself to stay calm and give no hint of the carefully folded letter that Jon had placed in her hand. From what she knew, Jon would have no trouble fending for himself.

Her mind raced as she pushed Juniper into a quick canter towards the palace. Why would Jon give her a letter? Had he been waiting for her? Why had he been so furtive?

Lorien tried to quiet her thoughts as she rode up the stairs and leapt from the horse outside the stable. She walked as quickly as a dignified princess could towards her chamber.

Once there, she slammed the door behind her and ripped open the delicate parchment.

Her heart melted at the script. Andor's meticulous writing was unmistakable.

Lorien,

I live, as this writing attests. Your love sustained me.

The past few months have been like death for me. I doubt that they have been much better for you. If you receive this, then you have earned my thanks for not following me into the dark. I have returned and found sanctuary. In time, Yates tells me, I will recover. He and others are already helping me, but it will be a long road back.

As much as it pains me, we cannot see each other now. Your brother is watching you too closely. If he were to discover my return before I gather strength, it would be the real end of me, and maybe even you. I cannot put you at that risk. We have enough risk ahead of us.

It will all be worth it when we are together again. You have my all, as you always did. My next movements will be against Tryst, but you must know that I act for you and for Valemidas. Contact Selia once Tryst departs the city. She has my trust.

Burn this note but hold fast to these words of promise. When you hear from me again, you will be asked to marry me. You will be asked to join me forever. I will be yours, and I will make sure that I am never pulled from your arms again. If for nothing else, I believe I have been brought back from death because our love is too great a thing to cease existence.

Eternally yours,

Andor

Lorien read the letter again. And again. She read it more times than she could count. Night was falling outside her window before she beckoned a servant to request food and a roaring fire.

It took great willpower to place the letter, the tangible proof of Andor's life, into the blaze. But long after the embers burned through the paper, Lorien could see his words. He pierced through the last of her darkness, and she would do everything in her power to be with him again.

Chapter 9

Retreat to the Forest

"Deliver me from a city
built on the site of a more ancient city,
whose materials are ruins,
whose gardens cemeteries.
The soil is blanched and accursed there,
and before that becomes necessary
the earth itself will be destroyed.
With such reminiscences
I repeopled the woods."

It was the perfect day to hunt a prince. The spring morning boasted a pristine blue sky dotted with dustings of clouds. Between the brisk wind and the warmth of the sun, my skin felt more alive than I could remember. This was my first daylight since the escape.

Jon and Wren had convinced me that I needed the bulk of a long overcoat to look better-fed. They had also been emphatic that I cover myself head to toe in garb befitting their bodyguard. They had been all the more demanding of disguise after Wren's encounter with Ravien and Jon's escape after delivering my note to Lorien. The thought of Lorien filled me with joy and fear, fear of what Tryst would do to her if he learned about me.

I ran my hand along my cheek and felt the pretentious scar that Selia had painted there, as if anyone would see it through the grubby and dented helm they had given me. Instead of my sword, I had to carry a simple club and look like I wanted to use it. Worst of all, the brothers made me walk behind them and their horses, dragging along their beleaguered and saddle-bagged mule, Yorst. To complete the part, I thought of what I had become in the Gloaming. If anything would make me look like a vile, ignorant ruffian not to be messed with, that thought would.

Everyone had taken to the streets to enjoy the weather, and at least in the trade district, Jon and Wren seemed to have become local celebrities at some point. Little kids were running up to say hello, and their parents were never far behind. The brothers were loving it, seemingly oblivious to the danger all the attention was posing to me and to them. I never heard anything specific enough to give me an idea of what was so special. The guys were likeable enough, but what had they done to deserve this attention? Maybe they had accumulated more wealth than I had guessed since we had lost touch. I could not ask, so I just trailed them and looked mean.

The uproar faded when we reached the Path of Princes, the broad road that leads out of Valemidas. It is the only straight street to be found in the city, and it carries elegance in the form of its huge paving stones and oaks lining the center.

We were nobodies to the hundreds of travelers who packed the Path of Princes. Few local commoners used the main thoroughfare. They kept to their own neighborhoods and alleys, leaving flamboyance and treachery for the largest vein of the city. Here, there was chaotic freshness and novelty. Perhaps that was why Jon and Wren chose the route—no one would notice a couple merchants on their horses, trailed by a bodyguard and a donkey—but that turned out to be a rather bad idea.

We had just caught our first sight of the main gate when anxiety gripped me. Normally, hundreds were entering and exiting the city on any given day. But now almost all the people stayed on the left side of the road, overcrowded and inching into the city. It was as if no one was allowed to leave the city today, but that was our goal. The brothers might have noticed, but they kept on trotting, whistling as if everything were fine.

On the other side of the Path, carriages were crashing into each other, horses were tangled, pedestrians were trampled. Under my reign and long before it, no rules limited when one side of the Path could be used, no matter which direction travelers went. People went where there was space on the street. Now the flow seemed artificial and imposed.

I did not like going against the grain, at least not now. I could hide behind conformity, but could not bear drawing attention. In the Gloaming, standing out meant death. Yet here I was dependent on two childhood friends, now merchants, who might as well have had targets painted on their chests. I yearned to turn back, but we were already too far along. I just plodded along after them, feeling like the stupidly valiant bodyguard I was pretending to be.

We steadily drew closer to the gate while I tried to look for danger in all directions at once. The breeze had stopped and the sun was beginning to bear down. I had become a cave dweller, unaccustomed to the daylight. The cumbersome coat and helm intensified the stale heat. As I pushed myself forward, step by heavy step, sweat began to pour.

I glanced ahead and could see the faces of the guards beneath the wall. They were grim and their eyes seemed locked onto us, in complete contempt of the hordes on the other side of the road. It was like walking into a trap. Then, as my frantic gaze shifted to those hordes, I saw someone I had never wanted to see again.

Ramzi.

I would have recognized him anywhere, with his shaved head and thick beard. He was standing in the oak-lined median, staring at the travelers who entered Valemidas. A troop of five men in heavy dark armor surrounded him. He wore a heavy purple robe and leaned on a gnarled, black staff a head taller than he was. If he was trying to look like some sorcerer to terrify the people, he was sure to succeed. His sinister glare and the tattoo of tiny stars by his eye made sure of that, even when he wore normal attire.

The sight of him brought all my anger rushing back into my mind. He was the true source of this evil, the one who had corrupted Tryst from the beginning. He deserved to die a painful death. But I fought against that urge. To fight him now, even if we won, would mean losing the battle against Tryst. I needed more time to prepare, to gather my supporters.

I forced my eyes to look at the ground. Ramzi's attention was on the other side of the road, so I thought we would be able to slip by without notice. As we plodded forward, though, the pounding of my heart was joined by the pounding of horses galloping from behind us. I looked back and saw four riders approaching quickly. I glanced forward and saw Ramzi's stare turn to the riders, and then to us.

In that moment, my enemies were collapsing on us just as the men had collapsed on Lucian and me. The sun was blazing, and the bucket on my head was getting smaller. My honed survival sense screamed. I could not go down like this. I had to cause a distraction before Ramzi had a chance to figure out who we were, if he had not already. He had begun walking in our direction with urgency. He was twenty feet away when the riders drew even to us.

I turned and swung my club at the front legs of one of the horses. It tumbled forward and the rider spilled to the ground. The air filled with dust and screaming and furor.

I just glimpsed the brothers' surprised faces as I leapt onto Yorst and charged towards the gate, as fast as the mule could go. I swerved past Ramzi and his guards, while hurling my club at Ramzi. It cracked into his shoulder, and the pained but otherwise blank look on his face suggested that he had not recognized me. His guards gathered close to protect him, rather than trying to pursue me.

I risked a look back and saw the brothers riding out of the cloud of dust. Jon had blood on his lance, and no riders followed. Two guards were charging at us on foot, spears lifted to block our advance, while others rushed to close the city gate. A quick glance to my left showed stillness. Where there had been a crowd rambling into the city, there were now astonished faces watching the fight.

In a matter of moments, Jon and Wren had passed me and pulled ahead. They were going to hit the two running gate guards at almost full speed. Their cloaks were flying. As Jon raised his huge lance overhead, in perfect form, the two men chose life over courage and dove to the side. Yorst and I rode through the gap before the guards were back on their feet.

I saw other guards frantically cranking the wheel that closed the city's gate. It had been lowered two-thirds of the way down and was about ten feet from the ground. I thought of giving up on Yorst and sprinting on my own legs, but it seemed too late. I had a split second to consider what I would do when I was caught before a host of Tryst's guards. It was not going to end well if they stopped me—the former, decrowned prince, returned from death and trying to flee the city on a mule.

Then came an act of brilliance. The brothers could have charged out without me, but they halted under the gate. In the moment of pause before the guards attacked, with travelers forming a circle around the action, Wren reached into a bag at his side and pulled out a handful of glimmering gold coins. Each one could feed a person for a month. He held the riches high for all to see and flung them at the guards.

The surrounding crowd—guards and travelers alike—dove to the ground. While all heads followed the gold, Jon began flinging daggers at the few guards who stood their ground and tried to crank the gate down.

Between the gold and the daggers, the gate slowed enough and everyone lost track of me. Still moving at Yorst's grand pace, I trotted around the people scrambling for gold and out of the city. The first thing I saw on the other side was the brothers' shocked faces.

"What was that?" Jon asked.

"What were you thinking?" Wren demanded at the same time. "I thought we were not going to pick a fight until we gathered some support. That was three versus twenty or more."

His sharp tone was not one used often with a prince, or with a friend.

"Ramzi was there. I could not risk him seeing us." It was true, but I tried not to reveal how I had panicked, or how the Gloaming still affected me. "The fight was a great risk too, and it worked thanks to you. No more talk, we must go."

They looked past me, back towards the gate, and they grimaced. I turned and saw archers on the wall above drawing their bows, and guards charging toward us on much faster horses than mine.

Jon and Wren rode past me, at the danger again. With just the two horses and Yorst, we had no chance of outpacing them. The brothers would have to divert the pursuers.

I spurred my mule to flee due west, away from the wall. A mile of open fields separated us from the dark forest of the Hibernia Glade. Staying on the road was out of the question. Not only was it packed with rank-and-file travelers entering the city, all staring at us, but also I had to take the straightest path to the trees. It was my only hope, because everything else to the west of the city was rolling plains, for nearly forty miles. I needed a labyrinth, where I was trained to survive.

Yorst reached his quickest pace yet, but it was not fast enough. The archers started letting arrows fly within seconds. The brothers had fanned out, splitting to either side of me. I looked back and saw arrows darken the sky above me. I knew these archers had spent years of practice hitting marks just as small as me from just that range.

My next move was all reaction, instinct taking over. I slipped off of Yorst's back and tried to yank him to a stop. He charged on, dragging me on the ground below him. One second passed before the arrows struck.

The mule screamed. A dozen arrows stabbed the ground around me. None were far off, and several had met Yorst before the ground. I hated to hear his awful shriek but I had to survive. I jerked to my feet as the poor mule collapsed.

Looking up, I saw another salvo released from the ramparts. Without pause I ran with everything I had, varying my path to lose the arrows.

The archers were good, but they could not predict my movements. I did not look back and did not slow in the slightest when an arrow sliced the air just above my head. The next thing I knew, I was crashing to the ground from a blow to the right side of my head, and my left leg was screaming in pain. At least a dozen arrows stuck out of the ground behind me.

I staggered to my feet and slid off my helm. It had deflected an arrow and saved me, leaving ringing in my ears. My leg was cursing me, but I sprinted all the same. The arrow must have sliced my thigh but not struck directly. I risked a glance over my shoulder and saw another flying set of arrows and, for the first time, a small group of soldiers charging towards me on horseback. Jon was riding in pace with them, fighting to slow their advance, and Wren was further ahead. It seemed that I had become the most important target.

Hope surged as the forest drew closer and the next set of arrows came up short. I was out of range. The riders were closing on me, but I knew I could beat them to the front line of trees. My body was quick and my feet light, fueled by the escape.

Entering the forest felt like entering a cave. My pursuers would have no chance in this dense territory.

The wood was ancient and alive. It stretched in a thin line from Valemidas, on the north bank of the Tyne River, covering a rectangle of roughly twenty miles by three miles. Some of the trees were almost ten feet across. They reached up for what seemed like a mile. Along the forest ground were velvet beds of moss, interrupted by roots that reached out of the dirt for air. A few gnarled plants dotted the gaps between the trees and caught the dappled light that cascaded down from the canopy above. I had dreamed about this kind of place while everything died around me in the Gloaming. I could feel it healing the decay inside me, left from months of nothing but black and gray.

The nobles called it the Hibernia Glade and had preserved it for centuries as an elite hunting ground. Jon, Wren, and I had spent many days adventuring in the forest as youths—me by adopted right, them by coin. I headed towards the place where I thought they would most likely rendezvous.

Each of my glances back showed quiet forest, but I could still hear the men far behind me in the woods. The best part of their noise was that there were no barks. They must not have had time to bring the city's hounds. There would be no tracking me—at least, not yet.

My body began to lose energy, and my leg needed attention. I slowed my run, careful to avoid making tracks. It was hard to do with my leg dripping blood, but the Gloaming had given me plenty of practice with leaving no trail. I pressed my hand over the wound and kept moving. Within a few minutes, the sounds around me had died. My breathing was like a bass drum playing the rhythm to the ringing in my head.

I continued my stride, but every step brought more pain. My thoughts began to outpace my movements. Surely they would not send more guards. For all they knew, I was a petty thief…of course Jon and Wren would know where to meet me, we had played this game before…the destination would not change just because the hiding was life-or-death serious this time. I thought again of the strange, regulated flow of people on the Path of Princes, and Ramzi's oversight of the order. Never had there been such rigidity on the streets of Valemidas. The people had certainly not looked happy back there. A smile came to my face as I remembered my club slamming into Ramzi. That should have given the people something to cheer about.

I covered more ground and thoughts until I finally heard the Tyne River and saw it flowing through the trees. It was narrowing here, but flowing at a languid pace. I followed alongside it, heading upriver and enjoying the sound of the rolling water amidst the forest. Perhaps a hundred miles north, it sprang out of rocky cliffs and thundered down from the mountains. Yet here, just before Valemidas, it began opening into a vast bay that was often as flat as glass. It was a picture of serenity beside the bustling city, and of turmoil among the desolate and calm mountains.

The wound in my leg had forced me to a limping walk when I finally glimpsed my destination. Ahead was a massive tree trunk lying on its side. I thought of how excited the brothers and I had been when we first discovered this place as boys. The tree was old and covered in mushrooms as big as a man's shield. It was nothing out of the ordinary for a forest like this. But at its upturned roots there was a small crater, and the bottom of the crater had a tiny hole, a few feet across and sealed by a rotting wooden door.

It was just as I remembered it. The door was nearly invisible to anyone walking by without seeking it. We had hidden it years ago with large pieces of bark, and moss had since grown to obscure it completely. I slid down into the crater and began to feel around the door. I felt an edge and lifted gently, making sure the moss stayed in place, and then lowered myself into the earthen cavern.

It was almost pitch black inside, but all I had to do was follow the right wall. I blindly hobbled about twenty feet, guided by my hand sliding over the damp earth. I then slid down to sit on the cool, soft ground. My leg was relieved, almost numb from how I had pushed it. My head still throbbed, but I thanked that helmet for keeping me alive, or at least for letting me keep my right ear. Yorst deserved credit too, may he rest in peace.

I tried to focus my thoughts on the brothers. Of course they would find me. This was the most obvious and safe place for us to meet. They had been on horseback, so they were sure to arrive soon. They could handle those guards. Our escape was just a beginning, a taste of the threats ahead. I had made it alive. I had survived the Gloaming. The brothers would find me. My leg was on fire. My mind was restless. It drifted to dreams in the darkness.

The dreams brought a vision of dim shapes. I was hanging, and my arms were aching. Hands were grabbing at my legs as I clutched some thin bar above me. I knew I would die if I fell. The hands would kill me, I saw nothing but hands. Out of the sea of hands a face appeared. It was a noble face, reminding me of myself, but more severe. It was sharp and dark, full of remorse and sorrow. Ignoring the surrounding hands, fighting through them, I reached down to rescue the face, the person with the face, but it was too far away. A hand caught hold of mine and jerked me down. I swung at it wildly and connected with something solid. The impact to my fist sent shivers up my arm, but I was free. The face was lost.

I awoke to the sound of yelling and groaning. "Nice punch!" A small flame lit the burrow, and Wren was smirking above me. Jon was a step back, holding his face.

"We are, um, here to rescue you…" Jon stammered. Looking down at my hand, I realized that I must have punched him in the midst of my dream.

"My apologies, Jon. I was dreaming, and meant to knock something away. They were trying to kill me."

"You hit me right in the face, and hard." Jon made a small grin. He would be fine, except maybe a black eye. I laughed, trying to hide my concern about the dream.

"What took you two so long? You were on horseback." I rose to my feet. My leg did not seem to be bleeding, but it ached badly. The room spun at the effort, so I kept my hand pressed onto the wall. Wren helped me up.

"And you had Yorst. Where is he? Your leg looks awful. Sit back down."

I remained standing. "Yorst saved me, shielding the arrows. I had to leave him behind. I think that helmet saved me too. The archers were pretty good. Why would they focus that kind of attack on someone who looks like a simple thief?"

"You made quite the scene back there." Wren was doing the talking. Jon began to pull out some bandages from his bags. "Valemidas is not like it was before. There are more rules, and there is a lot less tolerance for breaking them. It was risky to be the only ones leaving the city, if that even would have been allowed. But you broke all order when you saw Ramzi and started attacking guards."

Jon knelt down to my leg and began peeling away the stained cloth of my trousers around the wound. It looked like the arrow had sliced deep into my thigh.

Jon talked while he cleaned the cut and set the bandages. "We were lucky to escape without more damage. Wren and I confused them enough by splitting up, and our horses are as fast as they come. I look forward to hearing your ballad about it when this is all done—two merchant brothers galloping on their steeds, outracing hordes of guards, and generally saving the day." He looked up with a wide grin. "You owe us."

"Yes, my debt to you grows with my gratefulness. Perhaps I can pay it back someday by helping heal our city. I imagine that ridiculous rule about the lanes of the Path of Princes is just the beginning. Ramzi found his perfect tyrant in Tryst."

"You are right about that," Wren answered. "It is not good, and much has changed in the short time that you were gone. There is a law for everything now. The city is strict and regimented, much like Tryst's newly donned military, the Lycurgus. I can see why the soldiers and knights in the Lycurgus need to be that way, but not the civilians. Our preparation for war gives Tryst an excuse to build up an army around him for the sake of defending us. Of course, he'll then have an army for the next conquest—it might as well become perpetual war."

Jon had finished his work. My leg ached from whatever he had done. He looked up at me with some hesitation. "Your leg will hurt, but it will heal. We have time to rest here now. Please tell us more. Other than mentioning this Gloaming place, you still have not told us what happened all that time you were gone, but we can see that it weighs heavily on you. We would also like to know more about your plans, so that we can do more to help you."

They both stared hard at me, as if trying to read me. I did owe them more of an explanation, especially after what they had done to save me.

"I imagine it is dusk out there now." They nodded. "Then we stay here tonight. It will be just the three of us, like when we were kids. You tied the horses far enough away from here?"

"Yes, but…" They both said at the same time. Wren continued. "Yes, the horses are tied to a tree by a steep bank on the Tyne. We lost the men following us, but we think they will send more. Like I said, there is little tolerance for disorder. Even a suggestion of disruption is stamped out, and we caused quite the uproar. Ramzi will not let this rest, even if he did not recognize you. I do not know whether anyone recognized us. The whole thing was suspicious. If they send the dogs, we are in trouble."

"On the other hand," Jon chimed in, "Ramzi is leading a festival at the Valemidas Cathedral tonight. His small group of zealots will join him. Maybe that will be more of a priority than searching for us. Ramzi uses these gatherings to steal the pulpit from Father Yates and make bold promises to those who are loyal to the prince and to him. It is an unprecedented intrusion of the prince's concerns in the Cathedral, the one place where the prince's power does not reach in Valemidas. You can see why Ramzi and Father Yates have growing differences."

Wren smirked and spoke with sarcasm. "Ramzi is such a gracious leader of the faith under Tryst."

"I will make Ramzi suffer for what he has done." My tone must have been harsh, because it wiped the smiles off the brothers' faces. Wary of the malice that Ramzi inspired in me, I shifted my thoughts. "Yes, we can rest here for a few hours. It is safe enough, but we will leave in the middle of the night."

They nodded in agreement, and I leaned back, resting against the wall. "Jon, let's have some of that food your mother packed. Wren, do you remember when we first found this place? You were trying to catch one of the wild stags here in the Glade and you fell straight into the hole. It feels a little like home to be here now."

We talked of old memories for a while longer. The snacks of cheese and flatbreads were as good as I had remembered them. Wren lifted up an aged bag of wine with a smile, and I took it gratefully. The decadent and spicy flavor danced over my tongue. Wren had always had impeccable taste, and now it seemed he had the fortune to indulge it. The small feast and conversation helped relax me enough to ease out some of my painful memories.

I did not tell them about my murders, or my escape. Instead, I shared more about what the Gloaming was, and then about one of my earliest experiences there.

"I tried to organize the men in that dark city, soon after I first arrived." I explained. "The needs of the place were obvious. Men are starving, and they kill each other for food. I tried to gather a few men who might help me establish some order, but everyone seemed to conspire against me. Hunger and fear and darkness made everyone down there distrustful of order. Still, I tried to set up a system for collecting the food and distributing it evenly. More of us would survive that way, I promised them."

"It worked for a short time, precariously, but then the droppings of food became all the more scarce. My followers had grown to ten men, but suddenly there was not enough food to sustain even us working together. Starvation set everyone on edge; a fight broke out between two of my men, and I broke in to pull them apart. There was no kinship, but only terror between us. More men jumped into the fight, and it was all I could do to escape with my life."

"Many men died then, simply because I had called them together. I later tried smaller gatherings, too, but those had the same result. The failures showed me the limits of the Gloaming. No order can last when there are not enough resources to survive. Starving men cannot be controlled, unless you suppress them with the constant threat of immediate death. That kind of forced order is not right for men. Down there, where everyone was struggling to survive, it was impossible to lead men towards the good. Eventually I pushed away the hope of joining with others. Staying alive became my all."

Wren and Jon had leaned in close, with an eager but frightened look in their eyes. I worried about what my face had added to my story. I was not prepared to hide the despair I had faced in the Gloaming, or the pain I felt from the sins that it had led me to commit.

I decided that was enough talk for the night. "It has been a long day, and there will be more time for catching up. We need sleep now."

The talk had exhausted me, especially after the day's efforts. Jon took the assignment of watching the burrow, and I fell into a fitful sleep. I slipped in and out of dreams, none of them pleasant. Each time I awoke to the thought that tomorrow we would march to join a war, except that the war was a mere skirmish delaying my fight with Tryst. I was afraid to think of what I would do if I prevailed and stood over him with my sword at his neck.

Chapter 10

A Woman's Touch

**"Therefore let anyone who thinks
that he stands take heed lest he fall.
No temptation has overtaken you
that is not common to man."**

It was pouring when we awoke, a good omen for leaving no tracks. As I crawled out of the damp burrow, before the sun had reached the horizon, it felt like the downpour would continue for hours. I savored watching the rain soak the ground. It was a natural rhythm that I had missed in the Gloaming.

Jon and Wren walked alongside me with such sluggishness that I felt spritely by comparison. Last night, they had finished off that bag of wine to celebrate the beginning of our adventure. Wren was never an expert at moderation, and Jon tended to follow his lead.

We made slow, wet progress to the bank of the Tyne, where the brothers said they had tied their horses. They were hidden well in a small gulley by the river. I did not see them until we were almost on top of them, but when I did, my eyes saw three where I expected two. I looked at Jon and Wren, their faces beaming with joy and pride.

"Well done, my friends!" The third horse was an impressive black steed. I greeted the horse calmly. He looked built for the battlefield, but there was a shadowed look to him, as if hollowed by some dark experience. "He has good form. Where in the world did you find him between the city and here?"

Wren pointed at Jon. "Ask him. Jon is the one who ripped one of the soldiers off his saddle and grabbed the reins of his horse. While you were wisely charging for the Glade, Jon turned back again and rode into the pursuing soldiers. I watched from outside the archers' reach, but not Jon. He decided he would fight against a host of soldiers in the shade of arrows. I still do not know quite how he did it, but soon after he clashed with the men, he was riding away just ahead of them, with this horse at his side."

"I figured we would need another horse." Jon shrugged and an innocent grin began to spread across his face. "It was tempting, of course, to let this steed go free, just so we could watch Wren try to keep up with us on foot."

"You never cease to impress me, Jon." I grabbed his shoulder in genuine thanks. "I would rather have you and Wren on my side than all of Tryst's knights."

I turned from the brothers and looked upriver. "We ride west and north today towards the town of Albemarle, where the army will make its first stop on the journey from Valemidas. With all of us riding, we should arrive in under two days, maybe before Tryst's scouts."

I mounted the black horse and moved to a trot along the right side of the river. The horse had been well trained, and he followed my lead naturally.

The river bank made for easy riding, flat silt dotted with willows. Beads of rain dripped from my hair to the water's edge below me. I needed to appear as steady as this rolling river if I was to lead again.

The brothers rode behind me in silence for a long while. Eventually Jon sparked casual conversation, about light topics like the forest and the brothers' burgeoning mushroom trade. The ride was a pleasure. The discussion, the horses, the forest, the river, the adventure, the freedom—it was all restorative.

The rain did not relent once during the day. At times, it became so heavy that it isolated each of us in a gray wall. We traveled steadily with a few brief stops to rest and feed the horses. That night we set up camp in a tight copse of trees out of sight from the river. I slept deeply after the long, wet day on horseback.

When the morning broke, we veered north from the river. The rain gave way and the clouds began to break. Around midday we reached the edge of the forest and saw the empty Prince's Road far to the north. While always crowded in Valemidas, where it was called the Path of Princes, the Road was often empty in the countryside. We rode parallel to it, along the edge of the forest, and saw only the occasional farmer in the distance.

The sun was low in the sky when we saw the first hints of Albemarle. It was a simple town that hung like a bead on the Prince's Road, as the first settlement on the long path from Valemidas to the mountains. There was no wall around it, a sign of its dependence on the great city to its east.

As we rode out of the trees, with the day's light fading, I delighted in the view before us. The rolling hills looked like they had been painted with the bright green hues of early spring, glistening after the heavy rain. To the east, there was an ominous chain of clouds that had been the source of all that rain. I hoped that it was drenching Tryst and his army now. We had seen no sign of the Lycurgus approaching from the east, but I suspected the scouts had already reached this far. They would have outpaced us, thanks to the road and our slowed progress in the rain, so I pulled on a wide-brimmed hat and kept my head low.

We rode into Albemarle like three typical merchants. On a normal day, three merchants might have been noticed. The town survived on the business of travelers. This evening, however, we could scarcely command a second glance.

The town was buzzing in preparation for the opportunity that tomorrow would bring. These people would have the honor of hosting the greatest knights in the land. Most importantly for them, they would see their famed new prince. That meant making everything look its best. Men were placing cobblestones on the muddy street. Children were running errands with bundles of goods in their arms. Others were washing windows and scrubbing walls, giving everything a luster of cleanliness that was probably rare to this place.

It was good to see the people's industriousness. The pompous, easy life of Valemidas had not spread this far. Our nation could always count on the rural towns to be a storehouse of lost values. That included respecting the prince, no matter what. It was the prince's duty to return that respect, to enable and inspire the people to achieve their best. Tryst had never been willing to offer them respect. He was too caught up in the scrum of nobles and in his own image.

I thought of his last words as he had betrayed me. Tryst, Ramzi, and six of their men had shown up in my royal chambers in the middle of the night. I had awoken with Tryst, my own knight, holding my own sword Zarathus at my throat. His voice had been a sinister whisper. "You have great gifts, Andor, but not the will to power. Men like us must break the shackles of all these weak people around us. You will learn this where you are going. It is a tragedy to lose you, but the world's progress depends on me. I might come for you after I conquer, and once you are ready to beg to me as your superior. Farewell, Andor." His blue eyes had been ablaze as he slammed the hilt of the sword into my temple and knocked me out of consciousness.

I shuddered at the memory. My desire for revenge was nearly uncontrollable, but I had to control it. Father Yates' guidance upon my return to Valemidas came to me. If I became like Tryst in order to depose him, then he would be the victor. I had to win on my terms, without losing myself in the process.

That was why people like these in Albemarle were so important. They lived full lives antithetical to what my life had been in the Gloaming. They also reminded me of the prince's solemn duty to put the people before himself. I had to find a way to prevail over Tryst within the customs of Valemidas. Otherwise, I would be serving myself and undermining the generations of tradition, just like Tryst.

These thoughts settled into the back of my mind as we passed many others working in the cool night. We rode slowly and deliberately. I tried to keep my head down, to avoid anyone possibly recognizing me. My occasional glances up revealed the opening to the central square a few hundred feet ahead. That would be our destination for the night.

We passed a large blacksmiths' yard on our right. Four men with huge arms and grim faces were hammering away at red-hot swords and horseshoes. The hissing and banging of their blows reminded me of war. This would be their chance to tout their arms to the prince's knights. A giant of a man walked from one blacksmith to the other, checking on their work. His bare chest and shaved head were gleaming in the light of the fires. He was barking orders at man and steel alike, and it seemed that neither disobeyed.

He glanced at us as we plodded by. Before I could look away, his fiery eyes locked with mine. I would never forget those eyes. His name was Granville. He had been the head of the Prince's Yard under my reign. We had almost reached the town square when I dared another look back. It was definitely him and, if he had recognized me, he was not showing any sign of it. No one else had noticed the fleeting exchange, and Granville's commands continued to fill the air.

I had rightly expected that most of my sworn followers would not survive my fall. Father Yates had told me that the knights closest to me had found quick deaths or simply disappeared. Some outside my court had lived, but of those, only a few were certain to remain loyal to me. I could count them on my hands—including Jon and Wren, but not Granville. He had reason to support me, but this was not the time to take any risks, for his sake or mine. The reward from Tryst and Ramzi to anyone who reported on my return would be temptingly immense.

"We need to find an inn *now*," I whispered under my breath.

"Just ahead," Wren pointed to the northeast corner of the main square. "That is the Scarlett's Embrace." His eyes hinted at a smile. He pulled his hood tighter. "I know the tavern well and trust its owner. A few might recognize me there, but they are good people."

We rode the final stretch with each of us pretending to look disinterested. Each side of the square was about two hundred feet long, comprised of a few wealthy homes and dozens of shops and taverns. In the center of the square was a raised stone platform, which had a forty-foot statue rising out of it.

The huge centerpiece loomed over Albemarle and told its history. It was an exquisite sculpture of a man, Prince Jonas. The stone was dark and smooth, almost black, and carved into a god-like body with the prince's harsh visage. He had been prince almost two hundred years ago. He was renowned as a conqueror, both in physical ability and in spirit. History told that he had claimed all the free lands surrounding Valemidas under his domain. Statues never seemed to commemorate peaceful times.

Before Jonas, the continent had many independent city-states, which quarreled amongst themselves over the reach of their farmland and the marrying of their daughters. They were pillaged almost yearly by raiding tribes from the Targhee Mountains to the west. Rulers of Valemidas, itself the strongest city-state, had long been content to leave the other cities to that fate. It had little effect on what happened within the huge walls of Valemidas.

Jonas changed that. Unlike most princes, he was born outside Valemidas, in Albemarle. He traveled to Valemidas at age seventeen and rose by his own strength to prince by age twenty-seven. Men rallied to him because of his prowess and promises of glory, not because they loved him. His background and disposition had showed him two things: first, how much trade and influence Valemidas would gain by conquering towns like Albemarle, and second, how easy it would be for him to conquer them.

His method of attack was the same for every surrounding city-state. He led overwhelming numbers to each one, leaving little doubt that his force would win. Yet some of the independent cities had strong fighters who would not make it easy. So Jonas first offered surrender. He then offered a duel to settle the affair, between the greatest of the city and the greatest of his knights. That happened more than a few times. He always picked himself for the duel, and he always won. He fought with a great spear and the prince's legendary sword Zarathus. He found no equal. To this day, boys in training pretend to be Jonas. I could not recall a single time that Tryst had pretended to be anyone else.

This statue was here in the square because Albemarle, the birthplace of Jonas, had been the first city, and the only city, that had rejected Jonas's offers—both of surrender and of a duel. At that time it was one of the largest independent cities, with strong defenses, and it had elected to fight. The city's council had voted on the decision, and had believed that the fortune of war was more impartial than a fortune depending on a single man. They voted for action, despite their weaker numbers, because they believed that submission would lead to despair, while action preserved for its people a hope that they might stand and achieve greatness. But they did not.

Jonas had obliterated Albemarle, burning it to the ground and sparing only the young women and children. If nothing else, he was a man of his word. He redesigned the city with his statue in the middle.

Before the city's destruction, when the leader of the Albemarle council met with Prince Jonas to reject the offers, he begged to know why the prince would wage war against the city of his birth. Jonas's message was simple, and it was repeated on the huge flag that flew from his spear in the statue: "The strong do what they can and the weak suffer what they must." A cold wind now blew the flag and its message to the east, towards Tryst, Valemidas, and the foreign lands beyond the sea.

I pulled my thoughts away from Jonas and Tryst as stable boys took our horses. The brothers and I dismounted and walked through a broad oak door and into the tavern. The room was clean and subdued, under the spell of an attractive young woman playing the lute in the front left corner. The guests were all so intent on her that they paid little attention to us newcomers. Fires were blazing inside huge stone fireplaces in three corners of the room.

Of the ten round tables spread across the dark wooden floor, seven were being used. About forty people were in the room; mostly soft-looking men, dressed in fine silks. The room reached up two stories, and along the thick beams above there were dozens of hanging flags, probably from travelers who frequented the place. It looked like the most prominent merchants fancied themselves nobility here. They even had their own symbols designed for them. Money and power were always jealous of one another.

I kept my hood up and headed to the back right corner of the room. It was the farthest table from the lute player, the other patrons, the windows, and the doors. Anyone who might have pulled his eyes away from the enchantress plucking the strings would have seen just another merchant looking for a roof and a drink. I sat with my back to the blazing fire and savored the warmth.

The brothers had followed me closely. Their hoods were pulled back and their focus was more on the people than the space. This was their domain, because every inn and town square was a catalyst for trade. Wren, in particular, always tried to bend these institutions to fit his will. I asked him about the flags once they sat at the table.

"You like the flags?" Wren answered casually as he leaned back. "I think they are an excellent addition here. It was my idea to have a pennant designed for our growing empire. You see," he pointed up like a proud father, "it is the one with a sky blue background and a black dragon. We picked the dragon as our emblem long ago, because we attack life with intensity. Jon thought it looked best with black on the light blue. Our mother Selia wove the first pennant."

A quick glance around the room revealed no one paying attention to us, so I pulled my hood back and glanced up. Sure enough, I saw the pennant hanging front and center over the room. The dragon shape on it was a simple, sinuous black, with flecks of silver at its eyes and along its back. It looked more restful and honorable than fearsome, which might have been their mother's intention. Given the prominence of their flag's position, it seemed the brothers were building quite the reputation and treasury.

"The flag has a nice style, but we are in danger here if someone heralds your arrival and draws attention."

The brothers shrugged. "You must understand," Jon explained, "we have been to this fine establishment only twice, and I have not seen a single familiar face yet. We have these flags hanging in dozens of inns around the countryside. It is a small fee for publicity."

Wren looked warily over the table and across the room. "You are right, Andor, there is some risk in this, trying to stay hidden this close to danger. But you are walking straight into it. You could instead escape to a nice estate in the country. Marry Lorien and raise a family. We have a few parcels of land that would serve well. Either declare yourself or do not, but please do not let yourself be caught unaware."

I listened again to the temptation of escapism. This was not the first time Wren had challenged my plan. My mind drifted to Lorien. Her beautiful face had been one of the last hopeful visions that had sustained me in the Gloaming. I had overcome my desperate desire to see her before departing on this journey. My love conquered my duty only in the form of a letter for now. We would be reunited soon enough, if all went according to plan.

My thoughts were cut short by a subtle tightening in Wren's eyes. His stare followed something in the room. Jon began to stand. My hand went instinctively to the dagger concealed in my cloak.

"Dragon brothers!" A woman's voice exclaimed. "Welcome again to Scarlett's Embrace! You were here for too short a time on your last visit, and now you have been away too long. Will I have to send for the Emerald twins again? They said you left without proper goodbyes on your last visit. We can fix that. I will have your usual suite prepared—third floor, front right corner of my inn." Her eyes shifted to me. "And who is your friend here?"

I considered remaining silent, but it would have been too suspicious. "My name is Walt, my lady."

"Why, Walt, you are a fine looking traveler. I will not hold your company against you." She laughed and sat down close beside me. "Perhaps I could show you a proper welcome to Valemidas?"

The woman's unbridled demeanor was matched by her wild red hair. She was stunningly gorgeous, with green eyes and bronze skin, though she looked a couple years older than I. She also looked like a woman who knew what she wanted and how to get it. If I had not been so tense, I might have admitted she was attractive. Any chance for a safe exit from this room now depended on Jon and Wren. The brothers had led me here, and they would have to lead me out.

Wren was the next to speak. "Madame Scarlett, it is good to see you again, very good. Our last stay was a pleasure, and we would not have missed an opportunity to visit your Embrace again." Wren's voice trailed off, as his eyes seemed to be crowding out his other senses.

"All true," Jon intruded. "And you look lovely as always. I am afraid this will be a short visit as well. We leave at first light tomorrow." He nodded towards me. "Walt here is our cousin. He was visiting us in Valemidas, trying to learn the secrets of our success. Now his bride waits for him in their small town at the foot of the Targhee Mountains. They are due to be married in days. We are traveling west with haste."

Jon delivered pieces of the practiced story well, but he left out so many fictitious details that it sounded false. I considered fleeing, but Scarlett acted first, sensing that something was amiss.

"Why no, no, dear Wren and Jon. You have your flag flying here—you must consider my Embrace home, for you and your cousin. I insist that you all stay at least two nights. You must know that our prince will be arriving in Albemarle tomorrow?" She was emphatic, and charismatic.

The brothers nodded but could not say a word before she continued. "But did you know that he will be staying here, at my very own inn? I have added a room that spans the entire top floor—the whole floor is new since you last visited. The prince will be there for at least one night."

She leaned over the table between us, exposing more skin and lowering her voice to a conspiratorial whisper. "A few of the men here tonight are new knights in the prince's court. I am not sure why they would travel in advance of the army's march, and without their arms, but I cannot complain about their spending habits. They welcome pleasure, even if they are a placid lot for alleged warriors. You of course know that there is usually more merriment here at the Embrace."

Scarlett smiled widely at the two brothers. She put her hand on my right shoulder and stared closely, too closely, into my eyes. I returned the stare with my greatest effort at calmness.

"Have we met before?" She asked. "You look very weary, but there is a golden fire in your eyes. Stay two nights here, and you will arrive in time to marry your bride. My embrace is rejuvenating, and these are your last days unyoked." She finished with a whisper, just inches from my ear, and brushed my cheek as she stepped back from the table.

"Now, fine men, what will you be having tonight?" She asked loudly. "We have roasted lamb and fine pork tenderloins. If I remember correctly, you will want some of the Embrace's ale, no?" Before we could respond, she spoke again. "Wonderful, I will have three tankards delivered to you right away. Sionell will be serving you tonight."

She turned and sauntered across the room. Jon and Wren's eyes followed her figure as she walked away, until their attention locked on a new target, another woman who approached our table.

"I am Sionell," she introduced herself like it was an invitation. She might have been Scarlett's younger sister, but with darker hair and open eyes like a doe first spotting a man in the forest. As she took our orders, she held a hand on Wren's shoulder, with only a flippant degree of modesty. The brothers ordered the tenderloin and ale, and I followed their lead.

It was hard to think straight with these women pressing so close. In the Gloaming, I had forgotten what it was like to be around the fairer sex. Everything there was cold, hard, and flat, but this lady was supple and curved, with a siren's smile and a refined voice.

She glided away with our orders and returned with delicious food in short order. Warmth and energy returned to my body as I ate, but with that came a restless sense that the room was closing in on me. Tryst would be here tomorrow, and some of his men were already in this very inn. I surveyed the patrons again. It seemed Tryst had surrounded himself with soft sycophants. None of them would last a day in the Gloaming, and they posed no challenge to the throne.

It was the nobles, not the soldiers, who held the key to unseating Tryst without a complete break in the political order. Even knowing that, I was tempted to challenge him directly when he arrived at the inn. He might accept the challenge. He was always arrogant, and he had always won—except against me. I quieted that line of thought. I had to take power from within the system. There could be no other way.

"We can move to another inn. This is cutting it very close." Jon's tense whisper summoned my attention. "Scarlett is an inquisitive woman, and influential in this town. She has a talent for extracting answers." He looked at me with concern. Wren was staring down at the table, tapping his fingers anxiously.

"This place will be fine tonight," I answered. "I need to get out of this room though. The lute, the comfort, the dresses—it is all too much for my long-deprived senses. Our guard is down and we are in the enemy's den."

Without waiting for an answer, I stood and walked to the stairs. I turned to see that Jon and Wren had risen to follow, but Scarlett cut off their path. Her arms were folded and her posture was stubborn. They would have to answer her questions as well as they could. It would do no good for me to linger, so I retreated up the stairs to seek out the suite that Scarlett had mentioned. On the third floor I found what looked like the right door, and to my relief, it was unlocked.

The suite was well-appointed for a town inn. It had a small antechamber with a fire already crackling in the hearth. I pulled off my filthy tunic and gazed out an open window over the square. The night's air was cold, a remnant of winter, chiseling my focus.

I could almost feel Tryst approaching. I imagined that he was empty and afraid, behind his mask of confidence. He had never led this many men, and had never fought in a battle of this scope. That did not mean he would lose; his gifts and numbers would go a long way to securing victory. But it did mean he would be on edge, without the kind of attention he would need to uncover my plot.

A sound behind me cut off the thought. I turned from the window and froze. Sionell stood in the room. Her posture was innocent, but her open silk robe was not. Auburn hair tumbled down her lightly freckled skin.

"Scarlett asked me to give you this." She reached down to the garter on her right leg. The movement set off alarms in my mind, fearing a dagger or some other threat.

Before she pulled out anything, I dashed to stop her. I grabbed her arms and pinned her down to the couch in the room, with my knee at her chest. She felt frail, and hardly resisted, but I could not take any chances.

"Who do you think I am?" I regretted the question as soon as I asked it. She looked up at me, a blend of fear and curiosity in her eyes. I could not help but notice the smell of jasmine.

"I think you are an honored guest of the Scarlett's Embrace." That was not an answer, so I waited for more. She paused and stared at me before going on. "You must be honored, if Scarlett sent *me* to you, and especially if you are the recipient of the sealed note that you are crushing down there." She smiled and looked down the length of her body.

I moved both of her wrists to my right hand and ran my left hand along her thigh. Her words were true. A crumpled piece of rolled paper was tucked into her garter.

When I looked up again, she plunged her lips onto mine and pressed against me. I recoiled and stood, dizzy from the ale and how her passionate aggression made me feel. I looked down to see that she had hardly moved, except to appear more relaxed, her head resting on her bent arm.

"I did not request your company, but I am thankful for the delivery." I bent down to pick up the note, keeping my eyes on Sionell. "See, the note is safely in my hands, you may go now."

"You have a beautiful way of speaking," she answered, "and I did not ask whether you requested my company. I offered it, and will again."

I had been through so much pain and suffering since anyone had looked at me like that. But the feeling was met by a greater discipline. I had saved myself before, and for Lorien. If I could not hold to that promise now, then what was the point of my prior patience? This was about reason and love triumphing over passion and lust. Otherwise, as Yates had said, I might as well be back in the Gloaming, subjected to a sovereign instinct of the flesh. A stronger force and providence had brought me this far.

"I am promised to another, Sionell. I ask you to go."

She rose slowly, seductively. "Very well, your wish is my desire. Whoever led you to deny me, she must be something special." She pulled open the door, the light of the fire making her slim figure glow. She turned back and spoke in a whisper. "I will leave now, but give me at least one thing before I leave. Please tell me your real name."

"My name is Walt, and there may soon come a time when I can tell you more than that. Goodnight."

Thankfully she did not press further. She bowed gracefully and blew a kiss before leaving and pulling the door closed.

I breathed deeply, my blood still rushing. Only then did I glance at the note. I fell back to the couch upon seeing the seal—a stark, black letter "T", Tryst's seal. Terror clamped me like a vice. How could he know of me already? I pried it open and was surprised to see an unfamiliar, refined script.

A.,

Do not think you can keep this hidden for long. Some suspicions already circulate, but he does not yet know. His helpers will uncover the truth, no matter what you do. Trust me, I am seeing these things from his right hand.

We can find an agreement that gives you time and serves both of us. I believe you can and should succeed, especially with my help and on my conditions. You must swear on your life and your love's life that you will save him if you prevail. He has changed for the worse because of dark guidance. Bring him back and restore him as if he were your brother. If you promise that, I will work for your interests. If not, you and the ones you hold dear will die. You are in no position to bargain.

When you leave the inn tomorrow, paint a black T on your room's windows, and tell Scarlett, "Her word has touched me." I will trust your pledge, as you will trust mine.

My sister cannot know, but her love for you is stronger than ever.

R.

I read the note one more time, flung it into the fire, and sank into the couch. I was shocked, torn by Ravien's request and excited about the prospect of help from so close to Tryst. I would need the help, for tomorrow I would join the Lycurgus.

Chapter 11

Joining the Soldiers

"But each person is tempted when he is
lured and enticed by his own desire.
Then desire when it has conceived gives birth to sin,
and sin when it is fully grown brings forth death."

A sense of dread felt like a knife at my throat when I awoke. I had not slept much, and my dreams had been fitful. The sky was showing its first light, which meant the prince and his army would be approaching today.

That meant thousands of soldiers and hundreds of knights under Tryst's command, just a few miles from me. My blood boiled at the thought of seeing him, of being this close to revenge. Part of me yearned for him to suffer in the Gloaming, as I had, but it could not be that simple.

I stared out an open window and sought calm. The air was heavy and carried with it a chill. Drawing in a deep breath, I used a coal from the dead fire to draw T's in the window, left the brothers sleeping, and walked downstairs.

Several maids were working methodically in the kitchen. There was something established and warm about it—a comfortable routine in the quiet of the morning. The smell of fresh bread filled the room. I pointed at two loaves that had just been taken from the oven, and one of the maids nodded and winked her consent. Grabbing the bread and a jar of fresh milk, I turned back into the hall.

I had taken a few steps when a door popped open in front of me. Scarlett stood inside and beckoned me with her hand. She was hardly awake and hardly clad. It seemed the women had little use for clothing in this inn. I took a reluctant step forward, and she pulled me the rest of the way in and closed the door. She stood close to me, craning her neck to look up at me with amusement.

"My attire is your fault." Scarlett said, perhaps noticing my attempt to drag my eyes elsewhere. "You did not ask my permission for the bread, and you did not give me a chance to dress and bring it to you this morning. So here we are, you holding my bread and trying to avoid looking at me and the bed behind me."

"Here we are, and her word has touched me," I said, turning back to the door and trying to cut the temptation short.

"Is that all you have to say? Will you not stay?" She rose to her toes and whispered into my ear, "*my prince.*"

"If you know that," I responded softly but firmly, "then you know I cannot stay." Based on Ravien's note, I had guessed that Scarlett knew my identity. She could have already betrayed me if she had wanted. So far, she seemed more interested in bearing my children.

She stepped back and bowed. "Then I insist that you come again, once you are in your rightful position."

"I would like to do that. Whether I am able to come again depends on you, and whatever part you may play in this. I will trust the messenger."

"As you wish," she said with a smile and another bow.

I walked out without hesitation. I had delivered the message, and we were now free to leave this place. It would be a relief to be under the open sky again.

Jon and Wren were still asleep when I returned to the room. I woke them and then sat to enjoy the bread—my appetite had hardly diminished. The brothers rose unsteadily, probably because of the prior night's ale.

We ate our breakfast with little conversation, packed our things, and left our payment on the mantle over the hearth. I departed the warmth of the inn with a vision of Tryst in my mind. He sharpened my senses, as if his approach was like another raining of bodies in the Gloaming.

The sun was just above the horizon and people were stirring in the central square of Albemarle. Where there had been excitement in preparations for the prince the night before, there was an air of trepidation this morning. Maybe it was the dampening effect of the weather, or maybe Albemarle sensed that it was about to receive another Prince Jonas. Mounting our horses and riding away from the square, it felt good to be leaving the place. I had trouble finding comfort in anywhere, it seemed.

We kept our eyes on every shadow around us. It was not long before I detected at least one source of my unease. Someone was following us, and doing a good job of it. I had not been able to see the pursuer, but twice he made the mistake of letting his shadow fall onto the street from behind the corner of a building. I signaled this to Jon and Wren with a quick gesture behind us. As accomplished merchants, they would have been the targets of vagabonds before. They would know how to play this game well enough.

My plan was to ride north, through the rougher side of Albemarle, and to approach the prince's army from the flank. Unlike the nicely manicured stretch along the Prince's Road and the central square, the northern section of the town was filled with low, windowless warehouses lining lean alleys. It made for the perfect maze to trap our pursuer.

As I continued my path due north, straight out of town, I whispered to Jon and Wren to break off to either side. They would circle back and follow the tracker until I turned to face him. No one would notice a fight this early on these abandoned streets. It was familiar territory to me, like the Gloaming except for the sky above. I had no doubt we could handle one man, but there might be trouble if he had unexpected company.

The steps of my horse were soft on the hard-packed dirt. There seemed to be no other sound. When I held my breath, though, I could still hear the same muffled steps behind me. I eventually found myself in an alley that would have fit barely three men abreast, with two-story warehouses on both sides. The dark lane stretched forward a few hundred feet before there was another turn.

When I was two-thirds of the way down the alley, I jumped from my horse and turned to face my pursuer. He was a few steps into the alley.

He paused and then feigned casualness as he walked forward with his hood up. He turned his head just as Jon and Wren closed off the alley behind him. He was alone, but strangely calm.

I was at a full sprint in seconds, closing the gap between us. Even without a sword, I knew this would be over soon. I lowered into a crouch, tensed to strike. He yanked back his hood and fell to his knees, holding his empty palms up in surrender. I was not taking any chances, so I slammed my knee into his chest and pinned him down. My dagger was at his neck when I first saw his face.

"Granville?" He must have seen me when I rode into town the day before. Maybe he would be loyal and try to join our cause. "Why were you following us?" The brothers had arrived at my side.

"My Prince." He remained motionless under my weight. "I merely want to serve. I never expected to see you again, alive." His eyes were fierce as always. "It seems like forever since we lost you. Things have gotten very bad, my Prince, in so little time. Tryst has made things harder on everyone, and he rules by fear alone. If you are here, then you must be doing something against him. I want to help."

Rising to my feet, I offered Granville my hand. "It is good to see you, and to know that you are with me." If I could not start to trust him again, then I would hardly be better than Tryst. As he took my hand and stood, I told him that Jon and Wren and I would be joining the Lycurgus today.

He smiled as his gaze shifted to my companions. "It looks like you are building the opposition," he stated proudly. "And with these two, you will have the funds to support it."

"Granville, it is good to see you too." Wren responded levelly. "We are glad to have you with us, but you need to be silent if we are to succeed."

I remembered that Wren had some bad dealings in the past with Granville. They were combustible opposites: a fiery and loud blacksmith, not known for intelligence, versus a sly and savvy merchant. They had clashed over their differences before, but we could not have that now. Disunity among our small numbers would be deadly.

"We will be working together," my words sliced between their locked stares, "but in separate teams."

I began to explain enough to have Granville involved, but to avoid risking too much. He did not need to know all that I had told the brothers. That knowledge was dangerous.

"Jon and Wren will be joining first today. They are too well known to be with me. They will be merchants who want to serve their nation in war. No one doubts Jon's prowess or Wren's strategic mind. The army will welcome them with open arms, and I would be surprised if they do not reach a high rank immediately."

I suspected that Tryst would knight Jon, but perhaps not Wren. The brothers grinned at the game of it but were surely uneasy at selling themselves as supporters of Tryst. There were so many uncertainties about this part of the plan, but I needed to at least try to plant them close to my opponent.

"Granville," I continued, "you will join tomorrow, as a blacksmith. You must know other smiths in the army, and they will welcome your help. You will make a sword and armor for me while the army travels. If anyone asks, explain that you are making them for Jonas Davosman, made at the request of his noble father, Sir Justus Davosman. No one will doubt that you need to spend time making glorious arms for him. You will keep hidden that these arms are actually fit for me." Granville nodded his acceptance with due seriousness.

The mention of Jonas flooded my mind with memories. We shared a father, because Justus had rescued me from the orphanage, raised me like a son, and championed me to become the prince. He was the only noble I had sent a message to since my return. My fate rested in part on his ability to rally support in Valemidas in the coming days. I trusted that he would be one of my champions again when the time came. I could not say the same for my adoptive father's true son.

Watching Jonas grow as a boy, I often chided him for spending more time combing his long hair than polishing his sword. He had become soft, preferring the banter of court to the force of his father, preferring the friendship of Jacodin Talnor to brotherhood with me. When I had learned in Valemidas that Jonas would be joining this march, I decided that it would make sense for a skilled blacksmith to devote great efforts to the armament of the wealthy scion.

"I will be joining the infantrymen later today," I said as I pulled my thoughts back to the moment. "You do not need to know more at this point. If you happen to see me, be sure that you do not recognize me. I will contact you if we need to speak. Otherwise, do your duty and serve for Valemidas. Profess your support of the people and leave it at that. No one questions a professed love for the people, even if no one really means it, or knows quite what it means. Most importantly, remember that I am not alive."

The men nodded earnestly to my words.

We had lingered long enough in the alley, so I mounted my steed and led us out of Albemarle. By the time we reached the hills stretching north from the town, the dawn had given way to a bright mid-morning sun. The hills were beautiful, with a light breeze blowing ripples over the fields of grain. We rode north for a mile and then turned east, parallel to Prince's Road.

I saw the first scout of the army before the others. He was slightly south and east of us, sitting in one of the few trees on the open plains. He saw us just a few seconds later. As he climbed out of the tree and took off at a run, I pointed at him. I had explained that this was when Jon and Wren would split off.

They said their goodbyes and rode at a cantor after the scout. They would reach him at the edge of town and announce their intentions to the army's front line. The scout would surely report that he had seen others, and Jon and Wren would admit as much but claim vaguely they were just riding along together. It might plant a seed of confusion among the scouts. Every hint of discord would help me. I was thankful for the brothers and hopeful that I would see them again soon.

Granville and I rode on, due east, for another few hours. Sweat dripped from Granville's smooth head as the sun passed its peak. The blacksmith looked uncomfortable as a traveler. We had gone far enough.

"It is time, Granville. Your task is simple but absolutely critical. Stay focused on being a blacksmith. It is who you are, and you have special orders from the great patron of House Davosman for his son. Make me the best sword and armor you can with the supplies the army has. The sword will be four feet long, simple and sharp. The armor will be complete but light, leather with thin strands of metal woven through the core spots."

Granville bit his lower lip. He seemed uncertain about speaking anything contrary to me. "But, my Prince, if I may?" I urged him to continue. "Before, I made you a very different set of armor. Do you remember? It was a masterpiece of full plate, nearly indestructible. What you have asked for will leave you vulnerable."

He was a genius with metal, and it was interesting to see his humble point, given his typical commanding style. "Some things changed while I was gone, Granville. It is more important that this armor be very light. I need to have full range of motion more than I need an impenetrable shell. This suit needs to keep glancing arrows and slashes away, but I will avoid anything aimed intentionally at me."

His eyes widened but he said simply, "I will do as you say, my Prince. And the helm?"

I gripped him on the shoulder and grinned, "I will not need one, Granville. Protect my back, my sides, my stomach, my chest, but do not let it weigh me down." He nodded in agreement but still seemed troubled by the instructions. Heavy metal was his forte, but this battle was not going to be won by enduring blows. I had to approach this with more finesse.

Still, Granville's expectations might be shared by others—no Davosman would commission armor without a helm. "On second thought, you are right, Granville. Make me a helm, and make it huge and ostentatious, with a ridge of barbed metal flowing out of the middle. Color the tips of the sharp crest with gold, but the rest should be glimmering steel. Something that demands attention and can resist all but the most serious attacks." The blacksmith seemed more excited with this assignment. "I may not wear it at first, but there will be a time for it."

"It will be done. I am looking forward to this. I ask only one thing in return." He waited a moment before continuing. "I will make you this light set, and it will be strong, as long as you allow me to make you a proper suit of full plate once you are back in your rightful place as prince."

"Deal." I said with a grin. "Once this is over, you can forge a masterpiece for me. I will raise you back to your proper blacksmithing reign in Valemidas." His eyes seemed to reflect the intensity of the sun and a deep gratitude. "For now, though, forget that promise and forget that I am here. Sir Davosman needs some armor and a sword for his son."

He turned towards the marching army to the south. After a couple paces, he looked back with a smile. "You of course will not need a finer sword. Zarathus will be back with its proper owner soon."

"Indeed it will. We will meet again soon. Thank you, Granville."

We parted ways from there. None of them could know that the position of prince, as they knew it, would no longer exist if I succeeded, nor would Zarathus and all the history it carried with it. Those plans were better kept secret. The task at hand posed enough challenge.

I continued riding east, passing more scouts along the way. Some of them arched back towards the camp, probably to report that there was a rider. When the sun was half way through its descent to the west horizon, I turned due south. The tail of the army had advanced past me an hour before. I would approach it from the back, riding hard from a mile to the east—like a straggler from Valemidas. No one important lingered at the back of a marching army. No one important enough to recognize me, at least.

The timing was perfect. Just as I reached the lagging infantrymen, they were reaching Albemarle. The sun was level with our eyes. Many of the men held up hands to shadow the sun. They looked weary, and none of them paid me much attention as I posed questions casually to a few of them. "Where do I sign up?" "Who is in charge of this brigade of infantrymen?" "I finally caught up with you guys; wife held me back. Where are we staying in this little town?"

I got my answers without trouble, and I liked them. This group, the Fourth Marchers, had about two hundred men and could use a lot more. A young knight named Keli Sullivan, who had recently been raised by Tryst for his skill with the pike, was in charge. Everyone called him Pikeli. If I wanted to sign up, I could talk to him or his squire, Laniel. They were both average height, with brown hair, brown eyes. I could find them under the red flag bearing the Fourth Marchers' emblem, a black row of infantrymen with pikes raised.

Armed with that information, I made my way to Pikeli as the sun touched the ridge of mountains far west of Albemarle. When I approached, his men were setting up camp. They would not stay in Albemarle—the town could hold only so many—and instead had stopped beside the Prince's Road just outside the town. An old stone wall, held together by moss and inertia, marked the border of their small encampment.

At the northwest corner of the camp, the corner closest to town, a bright red tent was being raised. It looked like Pikeli's base. Three men were straining to raise it, under the barking orders of an older boy. He was wire thin with a self-important posture, which marked him as the squire. He could not have been more than sixteen, and any of the men working under him could have been his father. All around the central tent, men were putting up small tents for two or three. There was good order to the process.

I caught my first sight of Pikeli from fifty feet east of his tent. I sat on the old stone wall and watched him. As I had suspected, I did not know him, which was a good start. The descriptions of him were correct. Where the infantrymen were ragged, if good-natured, this Pikeli was more of a soldier. His armor had more composed metal in it, as any knight's should. He was maybe twenty-five, with a lively face. His straight dark hair was unkempt, falling unnoticed on his forehead.

He had set up an office a few feet from his tent. Men came with questions, and walked away satisfied. The young knight would look up from the map he was studying and fire off words in quick succession. I could not make the words out, but I could tell they had an air of feisty authority. Between these visits, he would resume his focus on the map spread over the stone wall. It seemed Tryst was at least picking out some talent. I had to be careful, even if this knight did not know me.

With the day's light fading, I walked calmly towards the main tent. Keeping my head low, and slouching, I came to face Laniel. "Good sir, men tell me you are in charge of who joins this fine army."

He swelled with pride at the apparent mistake of his identity. "Well, yes, I am in charge of some things." He glanced over his shoulder towards Pikeli, who was watching us. "Do you want to join? This is going to be a major war, so we could, um, use more soldiers."

"I do want to join. What do I need to do?"

Pikeli practically bounced over to us and offered an answer. "You need to be loyal to Tryst and to Valemidas. A little skill with the pike would not hurt either. Laniel, bring me the scroll. We train twice a day, first thing in the morning and early every evening. In between, we march hard. We stay here in Albemarle one day, and then we are heading north and west. The Icarians are deep in the western ridges of the Targhee Mountains. We are hoping to reach them by the end of the month. But under

Tryst's great command, I am betting we make it in three weeks. He is as strong a leader as the world's ever seen."

He cut off as quickly as he spoke. I smoothed my face, fearing what it might betray upon hearing such adoration of Tryst. Pikeli did not slow a beat. "What is your name, and where are you from?"

I tried to keep my voice bland. "My name is Walt, sir, Walt Francone. I am catching up with your fine brigade from Valemidas. I was—"

"We left Valemidas several days ago," Pikeli cut me off. "Why did you not join us then? Are you loyal to our Prince? Here, sign this scroll if you want to join us." He saved me from answers with his incessant talking. As long as he kept asking questions and giving orders before I could give any answers, this would work out well.

"Yes, my lord, I will sign it now. I just want to serve and to help in the fight, my lord." I scribbled my name, as Pikeli continued spouting words.

"I am no lord, Walt, but I am a knight. Tryst raised me last week. We had a tournament of team melee with the pike. I led five men to victory. True to his word, Tryst knighted me, as the champion, and picked me to lead this here group, the Fourth Marchers. We will be the front line in the great battle. Tryst told me himself that he trusts me. We are going to be the very first part of the victory."

"I am glad to hear that, sir." I was relieved to learn that he was not from a noble house. That would make my rise in the Fourth Marchers easier, as would the position on the front line. Until that battle, I needed to be a simple soldier.

"Walt, it is good to have you with us. Laniel, get Walt here suited up in some armor, and give him a training pike. Then spread the word about tonight's training." Pikeli turned to face the men standing around him and raised his voice. "We start our evening session soon. It will be a free-for-all among small teams. The team left standing wins. And remember, I do not want to see anyone hurt badly. The real battle comes soon enough."

Pikeli scurried away, hastening towards the middle of the camp. I followed Laniel, and a few minutes later, I found myself standing outside a large open circle surrounded by torches. The sun was nearly touching the horizon, and the torches cast a glow on the ground. It felt strangely like the Gloaming. I had a long pike that had its blade removed and replaced by a cushioned tip. My armor was a loose leather smock and an atrocious leather cap.

Pikeli walked to the middle of the circle and yelled out. "Okay men! This is our third night of melee. We train for Tryst, we train to protect Valemidas. What do we do when the horses ride?"

Everyone around me moved into position as they chanted out rhythmically: "Down on a knee, raise the steel pike, forty-five degrees, and roll right at the strike."

"Good, good," Pikeli responded. "And then we fight, stay in tight groups of four. We practice it again tonight. We learn in fading light, because you cannot always trust your eyes in the midst of battle. Now, choose your teams, and remember, it cannot be the same as your team from our last two nights."

With that, a murmur spread around the circle of men. They began to group themselves with their surrounding friends. A group of three beside me was looking for a fourth. All it took was a nod and we were together for the faux fight. Like most of these infantrymen, they looked like simple and wholesome young men. Their weathered faces and hands marked them as farmers or the like—not warriors. On the front line, they would have the honor of being the first deaths in this war.

We had only a minute for introductions before everyone moved into the circle. It was a simple melee, my teammates explained hurriedly. Fifty teams of four would fight until one remained standing. If one man in a team went down, the team was out. None of these men had won in the prior nights, they admitted, but it was rumored that the winning team would be able to join the feast with Tryst in Albemarle later tonight. Just perfect for me, I thought uneasily, the thirst for victory and the threat of premature proximity to my enemy. Before I could fully consider the implications, the fight started.

"Get ready and…go!" I heard the shout and saw another team charging us. In the moments before they reached us, I reacted without thought and yelled orders. We were near the edge of the circle, and I planted myself between my team and the others. "Stand still and watch my back."

Their eyes lifted in surprise. Perhaps they were not used to being commanded. In this position, no one could come from behind us and take out the weak members of my team. "No matter how many charge, stand your ground."

The approaching team was spread in a line, running hard. Only one man had to fall, but more could. I lunged forward with dulled pike aimed at chest level. Just as their two center men spread out, I ducked and swung the pike hard, knocking the legs out from under the man on the left. I began to lose myself in the moment.

The pikes of the two nearest men had plunged into the space where my head had been. I spun the other end of my pike as a staff, landing a second man on his back. My next swing caught the back heel of the fourth man, who was ignoring me and charging my team. He tripped and slid to stop in front of them, their pikes held forward languidly.

I immediately thrust my pike back and felt it slam into something hard. Spinning again, I missed the only one of their team still standing by inches. He turned and ran out of the circle.

Other teams were beginning to close in around us. The threat pressed on me. Looking over my shoulder, I called to my men. "Follow me now. Keep close to each other, behind me, as you are now." Their mouths hung open.

I turned and charged the closest team, which was warily circling another group of men. Their backs were together, facing out at different angles. I leapt up and brought the pike down at the man in the center. He was pinned by his teammates and could do nothing more than crouch and lift his arm over his head.

I heard a bone crack as his wrist blocked the attack. He collapsed and yelled out in pain. His companions fled. Two other teams were closing on me at once. I took a defensive stance, spinning my pike around me in a blur. I lunged forward and the softened tip of the pike hit a flat-footed man in the face. He fell and more men around me ran.

Someone approached from behind me, to the left. It was getting too dark to see clearly. I swung the pike toward him but caught nothing. I came to a balanced crouch an instant before a pike came right at my face. I ducked the blow and seized the attacker's staff under my left arm. I began to swing the butt of my pike at his head.

"Stop! No!" The yells around me came into focus just as Pikeli's face did.

I jerked back, slowing my attack enough that my pike bounced softly off Pikeli's brow. It took only a second then to realize my mistake.

No one around me was fighting, and men were huddling around a few bodies sprawled on the ground. I shuddered at what I had done, as if I had been in the Gloaming instead of a simple melee. The survival instinct cut immediately back towards passivity.

I went to a knee and looked up earnestly at the young knight. "Sir, this was a good fight, good training, and a strong attack by you. My team had able men." I glanced back and saw the three of them staring me with a look of fear.

Pikeli's eyes narrowed, settling into something like a scowl, but he replied calmly—far more calmly than I expected from him. "You fought well, Walt, and your team has won tonight's melee. You are invited to join us for the feast tonight in Albemarle. The great Tryst will be there. I assure you, he will be impressed to learn of your skill with the pike. How did you become so good with it, and not already be in the army? You fought like your life depended on it. You will have to take it a little easier in future melees. Actually, I think you can be on the outside next time, teaching rather than breaking the bones of our

Fourth Marchers." He shut his mouth, perhaps realizing he had talked over his own question again.

I bowed lower and then stood, ignoring Pikeli's question. "Thank you, sir. You are kind to invite me to join you tonight. I have never met a prince before." I could not help letting that sentence sit for a moment.

Pikeli seemed not to notice. He looked past me at my teammates, and at the other infantrymen who had gathered around. "Time to clean up and set camp, men."

He turned to me again. "Meet me at my tent in an hour. We will walk to town together. I look forward to learning more about you." An odd eagerness lit his face.

"Yes, sir." Walking away, I felt the pace of everything rising. This was a major dent in my crude disguise, and it could not fall apart tonight. Not yet. If a game of melee set me back to my crude existence from the Gloaming, the game of politics and the high court could also unleash trouble.

Survival would have to mean silence and humility tonight. Around Tryst, that would be like restraining my very breath. A cold bath would be a good start to the evening.

Chapter 12

The Traveling Court

"But, sure, he is the prince of the world;
let his nobility remain in's court.
I am for the house with the narrow gate,
which I take to be too little for pomp to enter:
some that humble themselves may;
but the many will be too chill and tender,
and they'll be for the flowery way that
leads to the broad gate and the great fire."

"Yes, as you say, my lord." Wren almost retched as the
words left his mouth in response to another absurd line from the
noble's son. It was necessary civility, and Wren was in for an
evening full of it. He could hardly wait for the guests to drink
enough to allow some snide responses to their shallow questions.

This was the beginning of the prince's feast, his traveling
court, in the main square of Albermarle. Jacodin Talnor had
been waxing on to Wren and Jon about how grand the evening
would be. The weather was perfect for a feast, he had said, the
evening air was crisp with a hint of spring's warmth. The lighting
was perfect for grandeur, with hundreds of candles strung above
the square, casting a beautiful soft glow on the guests.

It was all fitting for the resplendent Prince Tryst, Jacodin
explained. He would win over the people of Albemarle and
convince their best young men to join the Lycurgus. Jacodin
admitted that he set his sights lower, at convincing one of the

town's most beautiful young women to join him personally, for he was a man of the world. Wealthy, young, dapper, and unmarried, he would be a prize catch for a merchant's daughter in Albemarle. This was a rare night for those daughters, and for all the people of the town. Those privileged enough to attend— Tryst had told the town's council to select one hundred forty-four of Albemarle, no more and no less—would be seeing the prince himself.

Jacodin lived for these affairs. He had never been much of a fighter, but he thrived in the court. That was why Wren despised him, and why Jon found him an interesting companion. Jon had reminded Wren that a man cannot control who his father is, and that Jacodin had probably inherited habitual political maneuvering, if not physical prowess, from one of the legendary nobles, Ryn Talnor. His legend had only grown after he had rallied the support that Tryst needed to formally gain the throne.

"Look at this, Jon and Wren!" Jacodin was pointing to a round table near the center of the square. "We will be sitting here, quite close to Tryst." He pranced along the table's edge. It had ten seats, and was one of about thirty in the square. "It is the three of us and seven fine citizens of Albemarle. Guess how many are prospects?"

Jon could not help but laugh a little. "What kind of prospects are we talking about, Jacodin? Soldiers or damsels in distress?"

Jacodin responded with a smile, "perhaps both, of course. But here, I will name them and let you figure it out. We will be joined by Lucinda Brink, Katyn Ghent, Dar Silverton, and Mailyn Glen. There are three other local chaps, but I am beside Mailyn and that is good enough for me." He clasped Jon on the shoulder, and added in faux sincerity, "but I cannot get ahead of myself, can I? Look, my fellow high knights are coming now. There are a few political skirmishes to win before I can claim any spoils." With that he spun away, shifting to a different prey for the moment.

Wren was wearing his best look of disgust, and Jon tried to coax him out of his foul mood. "Give him a break, Wren. He is just looking to enjoy the evening."

His brother was having none of it. "He is looking to ruin everything. He is a pathetic excuse for a noble's descendent, earning none of the honor owed to him. I doubt he could win over this Mailyn without his station and guile. Besides, he endangers our task here. He would recognize you know who, a new soldier who thankfully will be nowhere close to the square tonight. Things are risky enough with Tryst knowing we have joined the army. I still cannot believe this sudden pronouncement that we will be knighted tonight. Why would he do that, without even talking to us? You know he never liked me. He must know something, and either way, now we will be under his watchful eye, always close and bound to his immediate command. The position of honor also means we have to put up with Tryst's biggest fans, like Jacodin Talnor."

Jon pulled out a chair and motioned for Wren to sit. He did not understand the risks and politics as well as his brother, but he knew well enough that Wren had to be composed for the night. Too much was at stake to be focused on a non-enemy, particularly with envy involved. Wren had long harbored distaste for those who inherited more influence than he had earned. Jealousy bled easily into hatred, and hatred clouded judgment.

"Whatever you think of Jacodin, we need him on our side," Jon said calmly. "Tryst has questions about us, and the best way to provide answers is through the positive words of Jacodin. While Tryst will not believe us, he may believe Jacodin. Tryst always protected him, and his friend Jonas Davosman, trying to win the favor of their fathers. Remember how Jacodin and Jonas would always come begging Tryst for help in melee training? Jacodin was like a helpless puppy as a boy." Jon was relieved to hear Wren laugh at that.

"Come on, let's find the ale," Wren said, "I need to wash down the stench of those pleasantries I was uttering." The brothers walked toward a bar at the east wall of the square.

The select citizens of Albemarle had begun streaming into the square, giddy with excitement. Some of the older men, perhaps of the town council, seemed more controlled. They had a tense awareness about them. Their unease looked awkward against the merriment of the other townspeople. Just as Jacodin had predicted, many beautiful young women joined the gathering, dressed in their finest. A few young men of the town also entered. They held their heads high, perhaps hoping to earn some station in the army. Or maybe they just wanted to show that they could match the smugness of the prince's court.

The knights and leaders of Valemidas arrived later than the Albemarle folk, gliding in at their own pace. Much like Jacodin, they were by and large an over-important group. They were seated close to the Prince's table, forming a ring of protective praise. Many from noble houses attended, but it seemed no nobles had joined this march. They tended to prefer the protection and comfort of their estates in Valemidas.

The table for Tryst was different from the rest. Shaped like the letter V, the point of the table sat under the square's huge statue and its ends jutted into the crowd. Tryst would be seated at the center. The table was also elevated on a platform above the rest of the square, and anyone entreating the Prince would have to step into the middle of the V, looking up at Tryst as he was surrounded by his highest knights.

"Can you believe this?" Wren said as he took another sip from his tankard. "Tryst is setting the stage to re-chisel the face on Albemarle's statue." The brothers had been watching the crowd grow anxious even as they enjoyed their drinks. Everyone was waiting for Tryst's arrival.

"How many soldiers will the army enlist tonight?" Jon asked.

"No matter how many, it cannot be worth the cost of this feast," Wren responded. "What a pompous parade this army is. We are not marching for war; we are in a beauty pageant."

"I just hope this enemy is as weak as everyone says—" Jon trailed off and nodded toward a young lady seeking a refill of wine. "Look at that blonde, holding her chalice like she owns the place."

She would have stood out anywhere, stunning in a bright yellow dress and red shoes. She was tall, and her hair was cut short above her shoulders, unlike any style they were used to. They were approaching her when the sound of bells interrupted to announce the beginning of the feast, even though Tryst was still nowhere to be seen. The lady took the cue to stride toward her seat. The brothers followed, conveniently, to the same table that held their name cards.

"It is a delight to see that we will dine together tonight. I am Wren." He bowed and kissed her hand before they sat.

She smiled, curtsied, and sat in the seat assigned to Mailyn. Wren did not hesitate in grabbing Jacodin's chair to her right. Jon's spot was to her left. Their table soon filled with the rest of the party. As Jacodin had guessed, four were women of the town, young and unmarried. Both Mailyn and Lucinda were exceptional to the eye, and the two others were fair enough to make good dinner guests. The three local men were young and enthusiastic about joining the army. Jacodin came to the table last, filling the role of knight of the table. He failed to notice that Wren had taken his original seat, the one beside the most attractive woman at the table, or that she was more interested in Jon than in anyone else.

As the feast began, the conversation at the brother's table shifted from the pending battle to life in Valemidas to dreams for the future, and of course, to Tryst. Jacodin had raised a toast to their good fortune just before the royal trumpets first sounded.

Two columns of Tryst's knights lined the path before him. They wore bright red, with white and black bands along their arms. As the only armed guests of the feast, they made a powerful show.

But Tryst stood out above all. He wore his typical suit of luxurious and fitted black cloth, and his gleaming relics—the crown and the sword—left no doubt that he reigned.

The prince took in the crowd with an approving look. Every eye was glued to him and his retinue. Maybe he preferred intoxicated crowds, Wren thought, because it made him seem all the more vivid and sharp. As Tryst strode towards his seat, his knights called out several guests to follow the parade. Two were picked from Jacodin's table—Jon and Wren.

Tryst, without breaking stride, jumped onto the platform elevating his table and loudly called the crowd to attention. Silence fell on the square like a dense blanket.

"Welcome my dear friends of Albemarle! It is an honor to have you join me tonight. Your city has long been loyal to Valemidas. We feast beneath this statue, the symbol of your allegiance, earned the hard way. We celebrate our people's power under my lead, renewing our bond and building our ranks. Between today's and tomorrow's contests, over a hundred of Albemarle's best men will have earned their way into my army. I also have the honor tonight of raising seven new knights. Come forward now."

The men who had been called to stand before Tryst, including Wren and Jon, quickly counted themselves. They were only five. A murmur spread through the crowd. At one table not far from the center, a town elder stood and pointed to a young man at his side. The man stood and approached. He was huge, and wore a dumbfounded look.

"Your city's elders have chosen you." Tryst declared. Wren could tell that the prince was loving the moment, the suspense, almost bouncing from foot to foot. A fanatic look was in his eye.

"There is another, chosen by merit alone," Tryst proceeded grandly. "Each day our infantry units engage in fierce melee. We are training and growing strong for battle. The best are welcomed to my ranks as knights. I am pleased to announce that the randomly-chosen winning unit for tonight is the Fourth Marcher's. Today's melee champion shall come forward."

The guests peered around eagerly. After a long moment, a man stood in the far corner of the square. He was wholly unsuited for the event and the honor—dressed in a simple brown tunic, unshaven, and with disheveled flaxen hair. His first steps seemed oddly sharp for his attire, and he appeared too poised as he walked closer.

It was Andor.

Jon and Wren saw a prince where others saw a rough looking soldier. The brothers' breath froze, as if a cold hand clenched around their throats. They looked to Tryst in terror, but the reigning prince had already looked away from Andor. Tryst had spread his arms wide and gazed up towards the night sky. He seemed not to have paid much attention to the approaching man.

"We have our seven," Tryst declared. "Congratulations to you all. By adding seven knights to our ranks every week, we set a daily standard of conquest. We identify the best and prepare to vanquish all our enemies." He suddenly leapt from the platform and landed in front of the seven men, with Zarathus already gleaming above his head. No one had seen him draw the blade. The crowd erupted in cheers at the show of mastery.

The prince motioned for the men to form a line and began the knighting ceremony. The historic blade dropped onto each shoulder of the first man, as the ancient words of fealty were said. Jon and Wren were second and third in line. Andor was last.

Wren studied the ground at his feet to avoid attention. He questioned why he had left his merchant's life and wondered how long it would be before he would be a trader again, if ever. He feared that he would not get out of the square alive this night. A glimmer of light crossed the dull stone ground and dragged Wren's eyes upward. The first new knight held his sword high, bowed again before Tryst, and moved to the side. Jon was stepping forward.

"Jon!" Tryst exclaimed in a rare break of formality. "It is about time you join our ranks, and it is my honor to raise you as my knight. I would have chosen you among the first, had you been willing. I rejoice that I need not question your loyalty. Your prowess on the battlefield is a thing of legend." He raised his voice. "Let everyone here be a witness that all my knights choose to serve me freely and willingly, not by my command, even if I hate seeing their talents wasted in other pursuits. Kneel, Jon, and say the words."

Wren felt a shadow hit him as Tryst cast a quick, dark glance over Jon's shoulder at Wren. Tryst had always blamed Wren for not letting his brother continue on a military path.

"I swear by my faith and on my life," Jon began steadily, "to serve, protect, and obey the prince until my death, for the sake of Valemidas and our people."

"Before these high knights and witnesses and under my graces, I raise you, Jon Evans Sterling, to be a Knight of the Lycurgus." Tryst dropped the Zarathus blade to tap Jon's two shoulders in effortless precision. "I expect you will be a noble before too long," the prince whispered with an affectionate nod.

Jon rose and turned back toward Wren with a look of joy and relief. Wren walked forward and stood face-to-face with Tryst. He hesitated before kneeling.

The moment froze in the air, before the hundreds in attendance. Where Tryst welcomed Jon with open arms, he held Wren in a scrutinizing stare. This was not the first time they had held each other in disdain, in unspoken challenge. They shared respect, like the respect two roosters have for each other before they begin a fight to the death. The prince surely found it hard to believe that Wren would join him. Jon was one thing, given his warmer spirit and skill at battle. Wren was neither warm nor particularly skilled, and he was known to have spoken against Tryst. Raising suspicions was bad enough, but now it could equal disaster this close to Andor.

Keeping his eyes on Tryst's, Wren slowly went to his knees. He forced the words out of his mouth. "I swear by my faith and on my life to serve, protect, and obey the prince until my death, for the sake of Valemidas and our people." The oath could be said, Wren assured himself, because the only true prince was Andor, standing just behind him.

Tryst spoke smoothly and formally, as if obedience was predetermined. "Brother of Jon, you have always been loyal to Valemidas and you now will be loyal to me. I raise you, Wren Vale Sterling, to be a Knight of the Lycurgus."

Wren felt the famous blade snap down on his left shoulder, then his right, stopping a second too late and pricking his skin. A drop of blood spotted his white tunic. He rushed to his feet and stepped aside, furious. Tryst moved on without pause.

Breathing heavily, Wren watched the next few knightings. He was surprised that Tryst would draw blood, but also slightly relieved that he had not killed him on the spot. He had the feeling of standing in the mouth of a dragon, and the dragon had only gotten a taste before opening its jaws and letting its dinner go. Despite their mutual antagonism, Tryst was calculating enough to know he would gain more from Wren's display of fealty than from his death.

Wren looked to his left at Jon, who returned a satisfied nod. Wren respected his brother's sincerity but could not escape his own feeling of disgust.

His mind flashed back to his first fight with Tryst years ago. Both had been twelve. The boys of that age who had wealth or a noble's support trained regularly under knights on the palace grounds. Twelve was when they began sparring with each other officially. Jon had been only eleven, but his abilities allowed for a rare exception. One of the first days, Jon and Tryst had fought long and hard with light wooden swords. They were the best of the young boys, except for Andor who was a year older and benefitted from the great knight Ulysses' tutelage.

Tryst had won the swordfight that day, as he almost always did. After taking Jon down, he had stood over him laughing and taunting the other boys. Wren had snapped at that point, charging at Tryst with all the force his twelve-year-old body could muster. It did not end well for either of them. Tryst had a black eye; Wren had a broken wrist. Tryst hated Wren for not accepting his primacy; Wren hated Tryst for being better and knowing it. For the years of training that followed, Jon and Tryst always vied to be the best, after Andor. Everyone had a fearful respect for Tryst, except for Wren.

The memories rushed through Wren's mind as he watched the sixth man knighted, the local man from Albemarle. Tryst just went through the motions. His furtive eyes suggested that his mind had already moved on from this segment of the evening.

As Andor stepped before Tryst, he knelt down without ever looking at the prince. It was a proper measure of respect of a common soldier for his liege.

Wren held his breath. He heard Jon breathing nervously beside him and much other noise from the square. The crowd had grown louder by the time of this final knighting, as no one else seemed to care about this last soldier garbed in brown.

Tryst lifted Zarathus overhead and murmured a question about the name of the man before him. Wren could barely hear the words, which were directed at Tryst's feet, but it sounded like "Walt Franken." Wren's heart was pounding. He gave Jon an assuring glance. This would work. It had to.

Tryst dropped his glance to Andor's bowed head as the oath was mumbled in a low voice. With a hint of curiosity in his eyes, Tryst said, "I raise you Walt Francone, to be a Knight of the Lycurgus." The sword dropped and it was done.

Wren thought distraction might now be the best course, so he shouted.

"For Valemidas!"

The Prince's head snapped towards him, as the crowd echoed the chant. The knights standing around began to offer congratulations to the newcomers to their ranks. The guests began to rise and stretch like a pack of hounds awaking from sleep. Amidst the movement, Andor rose and turned from Tryst, keeping his head down. He slid into the pack of welcoming knights.

Wren found himself locking eyes with Tryst. The prince took four swift steps, and in an instant they were face-to-face again. The other knights ducked aside, forming a circle around the prince and his captive.

Before Wren could react, Tryst spun behind him and curved his arm around Wren's throat. Clutching tightly, Tryst whispered into Wren's ear. "I know you, Wren. Do not think that you can prevail over me in anything or keep anything from me." His voice snapped like a whip.

Jon stepped to Wren's side, and spoke calmly and firmly. "My Prince, we are honored to be your knights and look forward to fighting at your side. I vouch for my tricky brother, here," he finished with a laugh, betting on humor to lighten the mood.

Tryst loosened his hold on Wren's throat. "Thank you, Jon, but I was speaking to Wren. What are you hiding?"

"Your excellency overestimates my devices," Wren coughed out.

"Your disloyalty precedes you, hawker. Tell me what you are hiding."

Wren relaxed his body and feigned defeat. "I am hiding that I do not always find you worthy of your position."

"Your lips drip treachery before your first night of service is through." Tryst's threatening tone pushed the onlookers to take a step back. He stepped in front of Wren, clenched his hand around his throat, and lifted him off his feet. Sweat began to bead on Wren's face as he gasped for breath.

Tryst glanced at the surrounding knights. "How do we reward disloyalty?"

"Death," they answered. Each one's voice was timid; combined they were a weak echo of their Prince's passion.

"Death," Tryst responded, "would be a waste with this one. He has strength only to utter disobedience, not to *be* disloyal; his actions have always been wanting in vigor." He threw Wren's body back as if tossing a bad apple. Wren landed with a thud, and Tryst pinned him to the ground with his right foot. In an instant he knelt and held a dagger to Wren's throat.

"Your brother's loyalty might serve for both of you. You will remain my knight, you pitiful son of a merchant's whore. You will valiantly lead our trash squad. Clean up our filth, trail behind the Lycurgus, and leave glory to your betters. Do not forget yourself."

The prince stood, and turned to Jon with a smile. "Now Jon, I raise you to be a Knight of my Council, one of my highest protectors and executors. If your brother oozes any disloyalty, even whispers it in his sleep, I will give you the honor of taking off his head."

Tryst turned from the brothers to walk away. Just as Wren had regained his balance, Tryst spun back and punched Wren straight in the face, knocking him down into a bleeding heap. He gave Jon a quick nod and returned casually to the fawning of his other knights, who were now whipped up into an anxious frenzy.

Wren slowly stood with Jon's help. He offered Jon a dazed smile. Saying a word would have been too dangerous, but he wanted to signal to his brother that this was a success. Unfortunate consequences aside, Andor had passed under Tryst's nose unnoticed. Jon responded with a mixed expression, confused but relieved to see Wren's spirit unbroken. Sometimes he was too forthright to understand fully his brother's intimations.

As the two brothers receded into the crowd, Tryst stepped onto the raised platform, again standing below the immense statue, as if challenging its historic presence. He bowed low before the crowd, like a gracious servant. *So flippantly he terrifies and then beguiles with charm*, thought Wren. He looked blankly at the other guests as he rejoined them at the table.

"My lords, ladies, knights, and good people of Albemarle!" Tryst began. "We have the greatest power in the continent passing through your lovely city and we intend to celebrate it." He grabbed a chalice from the table and lifted it high. "A toast to our new knights and our coming victory!"

The crowd responded in cheers and drank deeply, relieved to feel tension dissipating. Wren marveled at the Prince's charisma. *How could the people love him just because he eases his grip on their throats?*

Wren tried to process what had happened. He found it unbelievable that Tryst's greatest threat could pass that close to him without any action. Andor was just as likely to take that moment to try to kill Tryst as Tryst was to sniff out Andor's presence. The two had a special bond. Growing up, Tryst had always been in Andor's shadow by age, if not by merit. Andor had taken Tryst under his wing and treated him like a brother. This compounded the vileness of Tryst's coup, striking from that position of loyalty. Wren spat at the thought of it, but it was blood that came from his mouth. He rubbed his jaw. He was going to feel the pain of that punch for days.

"Showing off your battle wounds already?" Jon asked lightly. "We have barely engaged the enemy."

"I was just thinking of that last knighting," Wren said in a hushed voice. "We were very lucky the only blood spilled in that encounter was mine. Did you see where he went?"

"No, but I suspect he has duties with his branch of the Lycurgus. He returned to that far corner," Jon pointed, "but I cannot see him in the crowd."

"I hope you are right about him. That was truly a miracle. It was as if he learned to be a shadow of himself."

"Look who's talking to Tryst now," Jon pointed at the prince's dais.

"Jacodin, and the two seem to be having a grand time," Wren said. "Do you think Jacodin is laughing at his own joke, or one of Tryst's? Or are they laughing about me and my glorious new position. Look, they are pointing back at our table."

"Wren, you are a knight, in a position to rise. The more Tryst and his knights laugh about you, the less they will suspect another, more important, man who was raised to knighthood tonight."

"Actually, I think they have more attractive subjects for their enjoyment. Look who our comrade is pursuing now."

Jacodin was beckoning toward the table for the Albemarle ladies to join the prince and him. The women rose eagerly. Mailyn smiled goodbye to the brothers and took the lead in approaching the royal table.

"I bet Tryst chooses the blonde," Wren said. "He always has liked the strong ones. I feel for poor Mailyn, I do. She would have been much better off with me. She has no chance with Tryst."

The brothers watched her stride directly to Tryst, bend low, and plant a light kiss on his right hand. The other three ladies crowded behind, waiting for their shining moment, but the knights standing by readily engaged them.

A moment later, Lucinda was trying to pull away from a huge man in chainmail, Sir Sigmund Crantz. He was a Knight of the Council, like Jon, and he had already become esteemed as the lead executioner for the prince. It was rumored that Tryst tolerated the sinister rake because he never shied from unsavory deeds. Everyone called him Sig.

Now Sig had Lucinda pinned between his arms at the far end of the table. She leaned back as far as possible but could not escape his trap. The brothers saw him murmur something towards her, and she responded with a yell. Shaking her head, she tensed and struck the knight with an uppercut to the chin. It connected firmly yet made little difference to the assailant. He laughed in response, probably to cover his wounded pride.

Again he leaned forward to accost her, when another figure darted from behind, and Sig froze. "There is a blade at his throat," Jon said with urgency. "No one threatens a knight of the Council like that, especially not Sir Sig."

"It is Ravien." Wren whispered, stunned. "What is she doing here?" His throat was tight with emotion. "She hides under that hood, even at this banquet staying shadowed."

Sig turned on Ravien slowly, not daring the sharp edge at his throat. He was twice her size. Suddenly a flurry of motion was followed by the sound of an awful snap. The dagger fell, and Ravien grabbed her wrist in pain. The huge knight pressed closely but paused, probably seeing who she was for the first time.

Most knights would have stopped there, daring nothing that would offend the Prince. But Sig had a history of distaste for the royals and nobles, and he had likely been drinking. He lifted Ravien with ease, and slammed her down onto a table.

Wren jumped to his feet without thought, but Jon stood and grabbed him by the shoulder. He dragged his brother back into his seat as Tryst suddenly slammed into Sig.

The prince pinned him down and began to pound his fists at the knight's face. Several blows connected in a blur before Tryst rose abruptly and walked away. He said not a word.

A pool of blood spread around the head of the fallen Sig. He would probably live, but his scarred face would do the talking for Tryst. Ravien was nowhere to be seen.

"Jon, Wren" a voice said softly from behind, "follow me." They turned and saw Andor crouched beside the table. They nodded and rose. People had scattered enough from their original seats that no one would miss the brothers.

Andor led them to an alley a short way off the square. It was a quiet sanctuary out of eyesight from Tryst's table. Andor sat back against the cool wall and exhaled. "We must remember our purpose here. We risked far too much tonight." The brothers knelt beside him and were relieved to see a wry grin spreading on his face as he went on.

"Wren, I think you saved me with your shout for Valemidas. It looked like Tryst caught my eye for an instant as I knelt before him. He could easily have seen through my crude disguise with more time, but I think he was so flustered by you that he lost focus on me. We put the battle off another day, a day that will come soon enough." Andor's voice trailed off as he looked towards the square.

"I am just glad we made it." Jon broke the silence. "So what now, my prince?"

"Jon, you have won a close position to Tryst, even sooner than I had hoped. You must use that position to find out where his mind is. He may be thinking mostly of the Lycurgus' march or the enemy, although I doubt that. He may be thinking of the nobles or other politics of Valemidas. It could be his thirst for love, which he tries to hide from everyone, including himself. He might seek to satisfy that thirst with one of his mistresses. Stay close to him and be yourself, steadfast in your support. Watch his every move and learn where his troubles lie, his vulnerabilities. Report on what you learn to Wren. I need this information to know when to make my next move."

"Wren, I want you to be a knight, and a good one. Remember, you are suspected from the start. Given your position, you need to provide sound service. Befriend all of the other knights at your level. They will be valuable assets in our campaign. We need to know where they stand on Tryst and this upcoming battle. Learn these things, and seek dissidents in your subtle ways. No one will suspect the two of you talking. Wren, I will find a way to meet you. Do not look for me, but expect me at any moment."

Andor leaned forward and the moon cast his brow and cheekbones in a silver light. The brothers had been listening intently, and seeing Andor's face framed the context of his instructions filled them with hope that this was truly the prince. He was different than before, more serious, more humble, but also more alive, more brilliant. Tryst was going in the opposite direction, perhaps the same direction that Andor had been drifting in before the coup. The power of the prince led them both toward more arrogance, more isolation, and more tyranny.

A look of purpose and understanding showed in Andor's eyes. "Remember our mission, my friends. We must put Valemidas back in its position of greatness, a free city to lead the others by influence, not by force. It cannot be restored as long as a tyrant sits on the throne. I will regain power, and then I will spread it for the good of all. But Tryst stands in my way. So learn more as I rebuild my alliances. My plans are moving fast now."

Andor paused and smiled. "Now you two go enjoy your first night as knights. And Wren, watch out for Ravien. She's a temptress who can unravel even the strongest of men." Their prince laughed lightly as he glided away and melted into the narrow alley's shadows.

Chapter 13

Unbridled Confidence

**"Because the sentence against an evil deed
is not executed speedily,
the heart of the children of man
is fully set to do evil."**

As the Prince of Valemidas, I expected more from my men. "We should have reached the mountains a week ago. Why is this army so slow?"

It was a shame to spoil my morning coffee with reprimands, but I had picked this fight and would win it. These insolent knights were dallying and slowing our pace. My Lycurgus was covering only fifteen miles a day, along the Prince's Road no less. Not a single one of my men, my own Council, would look me in the face. They had plenty of excuses: rain, untrained men, few horses, heavy packs, camp followers. There were always plenty of excuses for failure, but excuses never helped.

"I want to conquer this city within the week. Tell me how we can do it." They were standing around my map table in a half circle. Young faces and grizzled faces, they were nine knights and a priest. I did not miss Sir Sig. The company could have been worse.

"My Prince," Ulysses gazed at me with his old eyes, "the simple answer is yes. We can make it there in five days, marching hard. Our forces should overwhelm theirs, but the mere fact that they have not fled means they have something up their sleeve. We should win, but I fear it will not be a pretty victory."

"A victory is a victory, Ulysses, and we cannot win unless we actually get there. The people need to have confidence in the Lycurgus, and in me. I promised a quick victory, and this march has been less than inspiring. You do not need me to remind you of the numbers."

We had set out with twenty thousand infantrymen and two hundred knights. I had not believed the first reports. Men were deserting. Fine, I had said, bleed out the weak ones. But the numbers had continued to grow. We had lost at least fifty men a day over the past week. Our two stops in villages since Albemarle had brought in fresh recruits, but not enough to replace the losses. Besides, these were scrubs, farmers looking for a chance to fight by my side.

"My Prince," someone interrupted my thoughts. This time Ulysses was looking down. It was the priest talking again. "My Prince?"

"Yes, Father Yates, come out with it." He had been pestering me every possible moment of my short reign about right and wrong, as he had my entire childhood. Debating was no use with the man, but I intended to teach him through actions that power mattered more than his pedantic lessons. Ramzi's doctrine prevailed on that point.

"I have been receiving frightful reports from Valemidas. The people are not doing well. Our harvest will be weak this year, there have been political, ah, changes, and their faith is not what it used to be. My reports say crime is increasing and our churches cannot hold all the homeless. And this spring will soon be turning into a horribly hot summer—"

"Enough." I was on my feet and in his face. "What do you want? Speak it straight, and quit babbling about the unavoidable. The people of Valemidas have always been a mess. What they need is inspiration. They need something to believe in. That is what I am trying to give them. What are you trying to do, priest?"

Father Yates, as ever, remained calm. "My Prince, you are right that the people need inspiration. All I want to suggest is, well, an alternative. It would be more, shall we say, direct if you were there with the people. Let them see you, let them see that you share their concerns, that you are one of them, living, worshipping, and caring for others in Valemidas. That would inspire our people. The community in Valemidas is unbalanced without their accustomed figurehead."

How could the man not understand that this was war? I had to be here for the battle. My face must have shown my thoughts, because Yates quickly changed his tack.

"Or, if you cannot go to the people now, send orders to your administrators in Valemidas. Ramzi is a dark man who has laid too harsh a yoke on the people. They are under twice as many laws as they were a year ago, and they do not understand the reason for many of them. If these laws are born of a man's pride, then they will never sit well, particularly when they reach into the privacy of one's family and home."

I sat back in my chair again and considered the priest's words. He was a strange little fellow, but it was hard not to respect his spirit. He had thought of himself as some sort of father to Andor, and maybe to me before Ramzi came to my side. It was good to keep Yates close. He was creative with his suggestions, like this one. Maybe he was right about Ramzi going too far, especially in my absence. The dark man was savvy, but I had worried about the power going to his head. At least with Yates, I did not have to worry about that. He would still be wearing his tattered brown robes even if he were the one sitting on the throne.

So it was not without regret that I would have to send the priest away. Here, he was weakening my army with his constant teaching about humility. In Valemidas, he would be the perfect foil to Ramzi until my return. His efforts against Ramzi's laws might not change much, but he would help pacify the people and hold my darker advisor back. The people needed to be harnessed if they were ever to achieve their highest purpose.

"Yes, Father Yates, you speak true that the people of Valemidas need me. I will return to them, I assure you, but not yet. You will go in my place, taking a message from me to the people. Something from the heart, something about duty, about pushing through adversity and being strong. Include this: 'only those who obey my law can be free.' Bring me a draft of the speech before the sun falls. Make it good. You leave with tonight's messengers."

Father Yates had been about to speak but closed his mouth and tilted his head to look at me searchingly, obviously trying to read my intentions. Yes, he would be valuable in Valemidas. Let the people grovel in humility, believing in Yates' myths of a greater power and a greater meaning to their pathetic lives. I had subdued enough of the people by force. Now Yates could tame them, distract them—an ideal figurehead for now, just as he suggested.

By the time I came back with the continent under my rule, and with the heads of Valemidas' enemies, the people would be fed up with both Yates and Ramzi. They would be fed up with humility and with obedience. They would be hungry for greatness—the perfect state for turning their praises to me and moving me into the next era of history, unshackled by nobles and empty traditions. I looked up to see Yates still studying me silently.

"You may go now, Father Yates."

He bowed low. "Yes, my Prince. Remember, victory in this battle brings you closer to death if you believe only in your own power."

Another priestly riddle, I thought as he walked out, and a riddle I did not want to try to solve this morning. I stood, returned to the table, and stared down at the map.

"Ulysses," he came to my side and studied the map, "you said we could make it in five days. Make it happen."

"My Prince, I said that we could, but our reports about the Icarians concern me. They are huddled in a defensive fortress. It will not be an open-field battle, so our men and our knights will be at a great disadvantage. With patience, a quarter of our number could lay siege to—"

"No, this will not be a siege. This is war, and we will lose men, but for now we have to get our forces moving. Maybe we lose a hundred soldiers every day. They are probably the worst men of the Lycurgus, which should not host such weakness anyway. My reports, our reports, your reports—they all say the same thing. The Icarians have no more than two thousand men. Thanks to your ingenious bridge, we will storm their stone fortress and defeat them in a single day. But first, we march to the mountains' edge within two days, and then we hike for three. The bridge must arrive safely, along with the supplies for more bridges. You are a leader of men, Ulysses. Make it happen."

I had no more patience for this discussion, not even with Ulysses. He was too cunning, but perfect as the second-commander of my Lycurgus. The men loved him, perhaps even more than me. That was just history and would have to change. My infantry feared me enough to dare nothing, and Ulysses could be trusted far enough. He had served the past two princes well, and he seemed to be capable of nothing short of duty.

After a long moment, Ulysses spoke. "As you wish, my Prince," he said crisply as he bowed. He turned and walked from my tent, the consummate knight. With Yates and Ulysses gone, I was left with sycophants. Well, seven sycophants, and Jon.

"Sir Jon, has a nice ring to it, don't you think?" I posited my question to my cup of steaming coffee. It answered with a sweet fragrance, awakening my mind. One of the knights answered with an echo.

"Why yes, my Prince, very true. Sir Jon is a strong addition." The words flowed out of Jonas Davosman, who looked at Jon nervously, then smiled towards me. What a weakling, a beautiful, formless knight. I hated to keep him so close, but I had promised as much to win his father's support in Valemidas. Too bad for House Davosman that proximity to me was the surest way to find death in this war.

"Jonas, if Jon is a strong addition, what does that make you?" I kept my eyes on the swirling, black liquid in my cup. It would have given better answers than Jonas.

"Um, my Prince, I am not quite sure what you mean. I am your servant as always, and a knight, and—"

"And he has never been a morning person. Forgive him for his sluggish mind." Like a blast of fresh air, Jon's voice spread through the tent. He was neither kissing up nor promoting the old ways. His sincere voice pulled my eyes up.

I looked around at the others in my tent. Jon was looking at me expectantly. Jonas was kicking at the rug at his feet. The other five knights were pushed back against the wall of the tent, close to the opening and ready to flee. My female servants blended against the walls, but the girl from Albemarle stood out, Mailyn. She wore a snug black bodice and studied me almost casually. No one else seemed to look at me like that anymore. I rose to my feet and began to pace.

"Jon, Jon, have you ever been less than brave and true? No matter, Jonas is right. You are a strong addition. My knights have never been stronger." I would have to get rid of Jonas at some point. The other five knights on my Council were not wise companions, but they were loyal men who could handle the sword.

"Thank you good men, for your counsel. Ulysses probably has the men packing camp now. Gather up your squires and prepare for the road." The knights did not waste a second in leaving.

"Jon, please, stay a moment. I have another matter I would like to discuss with you." He paused at the door, looking back at me. It was a hesitance I was not used to seeing from him. But this was his first morning in my tent. There was plenty to put him in awe. "Mailyn, prepare my bath now. We will have a hard ride today."

She strode across the thick carpets and came to my side. Her lips grazed my ear, pressing close as she set a silver tray and coffee pot on the table. Then she was gone as soon as she had come. She had a gift of service, that much was certain.

"We enter the mountains tomorrow, probably in the evening." My finger traced the Prince's Road, the broad line on the map. Jon's eyes followed. "And three more days through the mountains, before we reach the Icarians."

Once off the Prince's Road, the going would be treacherous. As we drew closer to the enemy, there was only one path, and it fit only five men abreast. My finger settled on the little dot of Icaria. They were insignificant, but powerful enough to rouse the Lycurgus for glory.

"Jon, tell me, what do you think of our plan?"

"Why do you ask me, my Prince. You have heard from your more experienced knights. I am a merchant first, and my fighting days are in the past."

"There was a time when you beat me on the field. None of these other knights can say that."

"That was a long time ago, my Prince. We were just boys."

"And now we are the same, grown into larger bodies. I asked for your opinion."

"I think we endanger a lot of men with this plan."

"Yes, and do you think it is worth that potential cost?"

"I do not know the mountains or the Icarians, but I do fear their position. Look, if you strip a talented merchant of everything but a turnip, what will he do?"

"You are the merchant, Jon. You tell me. Eat it?"

Jon laughed lightly. It was good to see a smile. He had always been a pleasure to have around, and everyone's seriousness had been wearing on me.

"My Prince, you are right, you are no merchant if you would eat the turnip. A true merchant would perhaps cut the turnip into pieces, sell it at higher prices. He might even steal another turnip. Then he trades for more turnips, and then he trades turnips for coins. Next thing you know, that desperate merchant has a wagon full of turnips, pulled by two nice looking horses."

"Okay, so some merchant wins some turnips." He sounded too much like Wren. His brother's motives were suspect, and that meant Jon's were too. "Even the best merchant will meet his match, maybe his superior. He will lose out to more powerful forces in the end."

"My Prince, you asked my opinion." Jon's tone was surprisingly assertive. "The Icarians will be fighting with nothing to lose. You have everything to lose, so lead the battle from a safe place, not on the front line."

"What's under your skin, Jon? You are thinking of the boy you knew. Things have changed, and one of them is that I no longer lose, ever."

"As you say, my Prince."

I let silence build, maybe letting him feel some fear. It would help keep him honest, and it might trickle down to his conniving brother. Wren was a pathetic excuse for a knight, with no place in the Lycurgus. The brothers had to be up to something, and my fear was that it had to do with more than just gold. I had Sebastian and his men watching them, but perhaps I could find the truth myself by keeping Jon close.

"As I say, we will win. You are one of my highest knights now, Jon, and that means you join my morning meetings, you dine at my table, and you give me your guidance. Your position requires it, but I choose you because of our past. These other knights do not share what we share."

"Thank you, my Prince, it is an honor. I will serve you well."

"I know you will." I reached out and clasped his arm. Whatever his motives, compared to knights like Jonas, he would be a force at my side in battle. "Observe the knights and the infantry these next days. We will be marching hard, and once we enter the mountains, I need to know what my men are thinking. The discipline of the Lycurgus is wearing on some of them, but they must bear it. Otherwise, the Icarians are going to fill their wagons with our turnips, picking us off in the mountain passes, before I get a chance to break their gate and crush their hidden world."

"Yes, my Prince. You know how I like my turnips." He smiled and turned. Something about his old, jovial self was missing, but it was hard not to like the man.

Mailyn approached as Jon left—just in time to prevent my mind from turning to Wren again. "Mailyn, the water is always a better temperature with you in it."

She blushed and whispered, "I would say the same of you, my Prince."

I thought of the statue in Albemarle as she sauntered towards the back rooms of my tent. That statue was a good precedent, even if it did honor the wrong prince. My victory against the Icarians would be the right start to putting the right prince in the center of every town square of the continent. Pawns we might lose, but the real men of the Lycurgus would be rewarded.

Chapter 14

Discipline and Calling

**"Do you wish to rise?
Begin by descending.
You plan a tower
that will pierce the clouds?
Lay first the foundation of humility."**

Father Yates was troubled. His deepest concern was Ramzi, and the dark forces he summoned from the Gloaming. Yates' God was the light, and he would prevail over the darkness in the end. But no one could say when the end would come. Sometimes Yates felt that his prayers collided into Ramzi's and that the fate of the world depended on the invisible battle between them, but sometimes he just thought that Ramzi was crazy.

As he walked from the prince's lavish tent, he pulled his cloak closer. It was good wool, but old, and the holes allowed a bit too much of a draft this close to the mountains. Striding steadily towards his small tent, he reached out to his God, seeking to channel his frustrated and fearful energy into something good.

He still had hope for Tryst, but the man had proven over and over again his pride. There was no greater impediment to living in the light. For those filled with anger, Yates could show them love and peace. For those with sloth, greed, and promiscuity, Yates could help identify the weakness and seek

God's help in restoration. But for the sin of pride, it often felt hopeless.

His mentor, Father Clive, had spent his life fighting against pride. From the pulpit of the Valemidas Cathedral, Clive had denounced pride as the devil. He had instructed that pride was the complete anti-god state of mind. Pride led to enmity, to separation from the light, and ultimately to eternal death. Yates himself had struggled with the great vice as he had risen to the top of the priesthood, which had its own allure of power. To fight against it, he tried to keep his focus on others, and especially on those whose souls were crumbling, like Tryst's.

Yates had run out of ways to confront Tryst about pride. He had tried for the new prince's entire life. The man had oozed with arrogance since his childhood. He had to beat everyone at everything. As soon as the young Tryst won a competition, he would find another bout in which to assert his superiority. He could not abide others' successes, unless they somehow made him look better. That led early on to his complex rivalry with Andor. As prince, Tryst seemed more focused on himself than ever. Now he had sent Yates away.

There's no use dwelling on this failure, the thought sprang into Yates' mind. Yes, Yates prayed, please show me an opportunity. Valemidas needed plenty of help—anything to counteract Ramzi's idolatry and manipulated order.

But the most important project is still here—Andor.

Yates seized the insight, feeling divinely inspired. He had been avoiding Andor, at the man's own command. Yet it was Andor who needed him most. Tryst remained a puzzle of sin that could not be broken. Andor had long been a similar puzzle with a complicated past, but he had recently been broken. He was now a promising shell, aware of his former self-centeredness and capable of re-orienting his life. If Yates could help refill that shell with light, then there could soon be a righteous prince.

And if Andor could be healed, then who better to confront Tryst?

Yates turned a different direction with a lightness in his step. Packing could wait.

The priest had always loved to walk fast, and this was as good a time as any. Despite his many years, his legs found a warm rhythm as he crested a rolling foothill. Andor was camped on the far south side of camp, which was more than a mile from Tryst's headquarters. *That separation is such a blessing*, Yates praised, as he neared the pace of a jog.

His loose coat was flapping in the wind, and Yates laughed again at what he must look like. *An old priest speeding through camp—on an urgent errand from God!*

As he walked by another group of infantrymen, Yates had to admire the discipline of the Lycurgus. Men were training in all regiments, and every tent was aligned precisely. For all his faults, Tryst ran a tight ship. *If only the man would release his pride, he had talents that could make him a good leader.* A closer look at the soldiers hinted at the negative effects of Tryst's command. They were frightened, even though the battle was days away. Their movements seemed forced and rigid, lacking in the harnessed liberty that made for greatness.

Within a few minutes, Yates had found the Fourth Marchers. A hyper young knight was organizing his pikemen into ranks. He stood before them, barking orders excitedly. The men formed clean lines, practicing their lunges. On the far side, Yates caught his first glimpse of Andor. He was walking along the columns of men, stopping every few steps to show a soldier how to keep his balance when leaning, or where to grip the pike at its pivot point. Joy swelled in Yates at the sight of Andor teaching these men—a good sign of his continuing recovery.

It was clear that the Gloaming had changed the man. He had been born great, and only Yates and Justus Davosman knew the true ancestry and destiny behind that greatness. One year the ritual vessel from the eastern continent had carried Andor on it, when he was only a small boy. That had been the last year the vessel arrived, and the duty of raising the abandoned boy had fallen to Yates.

His suspicion that this was no ordinary boy was confirmed as he witnessed the child grow with a unique force and magnanimity, despite being one of many anonymous children in an orphanage. Yates had convinced Justus to raise him as a son, in part because of the boy's suspected lineage. Justus had sworn to secrecy, but even then, Yates had not trusted him enough to reveal his full beliefs about the role the man might someday play in the world.

Yates had always tried to guide Andor towards the light, and the callings of love and humility. Andor had come closer than Tryst, even though he had grown accustomed to decadence and success in the Davosman noble house. Yates often wondered whether Davosman's care for Andor had fueled Tryst's ambition and envy. Tryst had many of the same gifts as Andor, but he lacked the noble support and the lineage.

Of course, Yates had begun to see the same bad changes in Andor as he now saw in Tryst, once they each rose to prince. The corrupting force of power was inescapable without some greater intervening force. Very few things had greater force than the prince's throne.

That was why Yates was, in a strange way, thankful for the Gloaming. When Andor came to Yates a few weeks ago, he looked like he had climbed out of a grave. He was skinny, pale as the tenant of a tomb, with a maniacal glint in his eyes. His face had lost its fullness, and with it went some of his natural charisma. Worst of all, Andor was haunted by what he had done to stay alive. It changed him to the core, and hung like a shadow over him.

Yates had to admit he had been frightened at first. He had given Andor a change of clothes and a warm meal in a small alcove of the Cathedral. The gift had brought some life back to Andor, and Yates had detected a new and deep yearning in the man. He was broken, but the pieces of greatness were still there. It was like someone had shattered a huge stained glass window that depicted a prince, but the shards of glass could be reassembled into something even better. Yates found no richer joy than identifying the most excellent vessels for shining that light. Unfortunately, those were the same vessels that tended to carry the deepest taint of pride.

Watching him now, Yates could see Andor's progress. It was obvious that he was winning the devotion of these pikemen. Yates had marveled that Andor was knighted within a day of joining the army, and had been shocked when Tryst did not recognize him. The shadow really hid the glory that Andor had worn as a prince. Now the shadow was fading. Perhaps I planted the seeds of healing properly, Yates thought, and now it is time to water them again.

He did not have much time, and it would be too suspicious to call Andor out from the training. Conveniently, a small pile of pikes rested between Yates and the soldiers. Out of two hundred men, Yates thought, no one will pay much attention to an old man with a pike sliding into the back line. Well, Andor would notice, particularly since Yates had no business holding a pike.

The old priest tried to walk like a soldier toward the lines of practicing men, but he stumbled after picking up the pike. The weight of it surprised Yates. He was used to carrying books, not wooden poles taller than he was. He grabbed the pike with both hands and hauled it twenty feet to the line of men. A few of the soldiers eyed him quizzically, and he simply offered a smile in return. Better not to speak, he thought, because no explanation would make much sense, and none of the soldiers were likely to try to stop an old priest.

Stepping into the line, Yates did his best to mimic the men around him. He would take two steps back, holding the pike at his waist. On Pikeli's command, he would join the men in lunging forward in one huge step. Yates found a rich sort of rhythm to the practice. It was too much for him to keep up, but the effort felt good. He had worked up a sweat by the time Andor found him.

"Soldier," Andor playfully mocked the priest, "you are holding that pike like it is a wet fish. Grip it tighter."

A few men nearby laughed at Andor's taunt. He leaned closer to Yates and gave another command, keeping his voice loud enough for the men to hear.

"You have to turn the grip of your right hand thirty degrees to the left."

Yates smiled as he followed the instruction. The men did another lunge.

"That is better, yes, your lead hand should be closer to the top of the pole. You do not want to lose that grip when a horse charges you down."

Another lunge.

"Come now, you have to really plant that front foot. Enough distracting, old man, over here!"

Before Yates could say a word, Andor had grabbed him by the shoulder and lead him away from the line—far enough away to avoid being overheard. He turned his back to his men, with a lecturing posture, and grinned at Yates.

"If this is your idea of disguise, you need some lessons. For a priest, though, you are not half bad with a pike."

"And you are not a half bad instructor. You seem to have earned the love of these men in little time." Andor nodded warmly.

"But remember, you cannot let it drive you to think you are better than they are. Certainly, you are born with great gifts. Those gifts are responsibilities. You have a duty to use your talents as God commands. If you do, he will bless you. If you do not, your fate will be worse than the Gloaming."

A dark look passed over Andor's face at the mention of the Gloaming. Yates worried that he had he said one line too many.

"I do not want to talk about it, Yates." Andor said flatly. "Just let me be."

"Andor, if I let you be, you would know that I did not care about you and your recovery."

The former prince's face brightened. "I never thought I would need that kind of attention. You are not even supposed to come near me and arouse suspicions. Yet here you are."

"Tryst has ordered me to leave for Valemidas tonight. He has become more flippant and angry on this march. I think he senses that the men have no love for him. He has their allegiance only by fear. He claims that is enough, but deep down it hurts him." Andor took the news in calmly.

"What did you do to earn banishment? Does he suspect anything about me?"

"No, no, not that. I, well, I suppose I made him confront his weakness."

"What weakness is that?" Andor did not hide his interest. "Let us walk," he said as he led them further away from the training men.

"I have observed the way Tryst is running this army." Andor's voice was an odd balance of animus and praise. "He is proficient, focused, even if he disregards much tradition and cares only for himself. The authority should be mine, but as I knew when I raised him to my Knight's Council, Tryst is gifted as a battle commander. The weakness must be that he has no right to my throne?"

"Pride." Yates let the word linger. "It is pride, Andor. That is often the great flaw of a leader. It is a flaw in most men, but it festers the worst in a man with power. It eats away at a man until he is nothing but a desire to beat other men and earn their praise. Then he has no morality, no force of his own; he becomes dependent on the opinions of the very men he claims to have bested."

"But men do not become leaders without pride. It fuels ambition." Andor was falling back to arguments he had had before with Yates.

"Greatness is possible without pride. Instead of coming from within, true greatness comes from above, like the very gifts that enable greatness. God can be a purer source of ambition."

"If that were true, the world would have seen some of your godly leaders. Instead, the world has witnessed only leaders who trust in their own capacities. Men can control themselves, so they can control their destiny."

"But where does that capacity come from? It is a blessing, a responsibility, instilled from your very birth. If a man gives up his will to the light, and devotes himself to living for the light, all of that man's capacity and more will be harnessed for the good."

Andor was quiet for a while as they walked. "Yates how can this be?" He eventually asked. "I have never seen such a man."

Yates looked up and saw the sun lighting Andor's face. The paleness had begun to retreat, replaced by the man's prior glowing hue. The priest had little time before he had to return home. He opted for directness and locked his eyes on Andor's.

"My prayer, Andor, is that you will be such a man—that you will be a prince who receives his light from God, and not from other men. You have always had that potential, yet you held your power through confidence in yourself. Tryst is worse, but even he has some potential. Every man does, because the light is offered to all."

"You lost hope in the Gloaming. It broke something about you. You have the same gifts and abilities now, but I think you understand your need to be full of light and goodness from outside yourself. If I am right, then you may be the greatest prince we have ever had, because your greatness will be beyond any man alone. Valemidas will need that greatness in the months to come, because threats loom that are darker than most fear. Only you, Andor, with the fullness of God's blessing, can protect our people."

"You always paint life with a beautiful brush." Andor answered solemnly. "I want to believe you. I want that kind of greatness and light, but I have seen the pit of humanity, in the Gloaming, in Tryst, and—" He paused and gazed at the ground. "And in myself. I doubt that man can be truly rescued from this plight. The whole mess makes me want to retreat."

Andor pointed up at the mountains. "I imagine there is a village hidden in those mountains where men live better. They depend on each other, unconcerned with the greatness that you profess. Perhaps they are sheepherders, carpenters, bakers, and priests, savoring the joy of their individual crafts and shared existence. Sometimes, that is all I want. I am not sure that I want even this greatness that you propose. It is too much, too exhausting, and I have been broken. You said so yourself."

"Andor," Yates nodded, "you are right, there probably is such a village. I appreciate the beauty of such a place. It is rich and good for a man to devote himself to perfecting all that is within his horizon. For some men, that means mastering the art of herding sheep. It can be a joyous existence, as you imagine, but it depends on stability in the surrounding world. A few men have greater demands that allow others to live in peace."

"You cannot run from your gifts, Andor. You cannot flee your desires. They combine to form your calling. Although only you know where the light is guiding you, I must say you have always taken to leadership. The men around you love you, and not because you want them to. Look at these pikemen. They love you because of the man you are, because you were born with the talent of inspiring others. Escapism is a sin when it is thrown in the face of such a calling."

Andor's face looked tired as they returned to the edge of the training ground, but a fire danced in his eyes. After a few moments of silence, Yates clasped his arm.

"Just think on these things, Andor, as you continue on this journey. We will have an opportunity to speak again. I look forward to it."

Andor nodded. "Farewell, Father Yates."

"Farewell, my prince." With that the priest turned and walked away. He held fast to his hope for Andor. God forbid that such a blessed man go to waste.

Chapter 15

The Muck and the Mire

**"The murkier the muck,
the purer the lotus."**

Wren was up to his neck in it. The Lycurgus had been on a brutal march in recent days. Now he faced a wall of looming mountains.

The sun was rising behind him. As it touched the tips of the sharp, snow-capped peaks above, Wren felt a sense of awe at the beauty. He loved these mountains and had not seen them in a long time. Yet, just like every swell of goodness during the past weeks, it was soon dampened. As the sun continued to rise, its rays touched a smaller, gross mountain before him on the Prince's Road.

A month ago, Wren would not have believed that this much waste had ever been gathered in one heaping pile. But so it had, for many straight days. He supposed it was a necessary consequence of thousands of soldiers and camp followers, along with several hundred horses, marching together. What he still could not come to grips with was how this necessary consequence had become his problem.

Tryst. It all went back to him, and Wren's feelings had only intensified with each day of dealing with his army's vile residue. The miserable prince had relegated him to this post, and the true prince had ordered him to do the job well. He had always believed that, if a job had to be done, there was no substitute for striving for perfection. This task strained that belief. Still, he had sworn to Andor that he would do whatever was necessary to overthrow Tryst.

Wren had resigned himself to lead like a true knight. He managed his team of waste managers to prompt, efficient, and sanitary disposition of the Lycurgus's debris. At least, that was his euphemistic spin for the thirty men under his charge. His men, like Wren, were outcasts from other parts of the Lycurgus. Some had picked fights with their own leading knights; a handful were complete slackers, fat and slow; and about half were just weak, whiny fellows with no aptitude for battle. No one left the Lycurgus except by desertion or death, so these men were demoted to this service until they died.

The stench could hardly be stomached, but it forced an odd bond upon his men. Only two had deserted the group since Wren took over. He kept their mood light with crude quips that sold the virtues of the job. Because their work was done by the late morning, he gave the men afternoons off. He also gave them freedom to do whatever they wanted with their nights, which made them a popular center of dicing and other cavorting for infantrymen.

It helped that Wren had been carrying rich spices for trade before he joined the army, so he had fine-smelling scarves fashioned for the men. They were bright yellow, distinguishable. Work is work, Wren would say, and we have the noble task of keeping this fine countryside clean. They had even earned a name for themselves around the Lycurgus—the Yellow Rags.

This morning's work was not too different from the mornings before, except that it was rushed, since it was the last morning before the Lycurgus hiked into the mountains. Wren had his men working the same strict and precise routine. He sent them out before dawn to collect the prior night's waste. They shoveled it onto carts, each dragged by two mules. The pre-dawn collectors would return to the rear of the camp, where the pile building would commence.

Now the heap stood before him, easily twice his height. It rested on a platform of logs that the men were lighting. It would burn through once, and then the men would bury it all in a large hole dug to the side of the road. Wren had insisted that they find an evergreen tree to replant on the spot at each camp. When the Lycurgus marched on, it would leave as little trace as possible, except a few new trees along the road. Wren had grown proud of his work, but tried not to let it show.

When the flames began to engulf the pile this morning, Wren walked to the tent he shared with four other lowly knights who held equally unsavory positions. They were responsible for the cooking, the maids, the mules, and the supplies. Every position required grueling amounts of work in exchange for little to no recognition. The four men were older, quiet, and resolved to their positions. They mostly ignored Wren, and he returned the favor. It was tough to do in their cramped space, so Wren often found himself roaming through camp.

As tight as the quarters had been, Wren knew it was not going to improve in the mountains. The Lycurgus would be leaving the tents behind and marching even harder. This morning Wren saw a different kind of strain among the infantrymen. They were tired from recent days of pushing hard, with meager food and no stops in towns. The weather should have lifted their spirits, but rumors about the Icarians and their strength in the mountains weighed on them.

The mountains built on the fear that emanated from those rumors, Wren thought. Most of these men had come from Valemidas and the villages near it. They had seen hills, but nothing like the Targhees. These were old mountains, sheer masses of rock rising suddenly out of the soft green foothills. Trees had no place in the Targhees, except in rare valley floors. Snow always clung to the peaks. The mountains were frigid and sliced by brisk winds; a rare summer day meant it would be merely cold instead of freezing.

About twenty miles away to the west, the mountains abruptly dropped into the sea. Storms always hammered that coast, and the Targhees absorbed the punishment. They protected everything to the east, huge filters that allowed only nourishing rains to pass.

Somewhere amidst the dense ranges stood the city of Icarius. Wren had been in these mountains before and had heard about this city, but he had never seen it. He had to admit, any people that survived in the Targhees must be strong. Its men would be well-acquainted with harsh realities, which would probably suit them well for battle.

The Lycurgus, by contrast, was full of novices from the mild lowlands. These men were not warriors. Maybe one in two actually knew how to use their weapons. Even a few dozen of the knights were entirely new to war, like Jacodin Talnor and Jonas Davosman, raised by Tryst for some political reason.

Wren decided to seek fresher air with a walk. He stayed far south of Tryst's tent and after a short while came upon a few knights in morning exercises. Four of them had set up a melee, and some infantrymen had gathered around to watch. Wren knew that, being this far from the prince, the knights would be far from the Lycurgus's best, but it would be entertaining enough to join the spectators. He squeezed between a couple infantrymen to lean against a lone oak overhanging the impromptu practice field.

The knights began to dash in at each other, clumsily waving their wooden swords. A particularly plump one tripped over his own feet before he even reached the others. Of the three remaining, one sought valor with a grandiose swing of his sword at the helmed-head of the smallest knight. The little man barely had to duck to avoid the blow, and the assailant was sent spinning by the force of his own swing. The third knight had enough sense to swipe at the out-of-control knight, and a glancing blow landed him on the ground with a thud.

The two remaining knights began to circle each other, with no semblance of footwork. The tiny one looked like a ten-year-old; the other was built well enough, but he held his sword like it was a sheepherder's staff.

This was no way to set an example for the other soldiers, Wren thought. But what he heard himself say aloud was, "it is no melee with only two players."

He stepped towards the mess of men and picked up the wooden sword of the fat fallen knight. As he joined the two circling men, he thought with a broad smile that practice against amateurs might help build confidence.

In mock encouragement, he taunted them, "see men, and everyone listen now, when circling right, your left foot may cross in front of your right, like so." The two knights tripped up as they looked down at their feet. Some onlookers laughed nervously.

"Ah! Now you see, a second lesson, in a merry-go-round of three men, it will not be much of a contest if only one knows the steps." Wren continued circling, amused, as the other two knights picked up the basic footwork. He began to juggle his wooden weapon from hand to hand, bouncing lightly on his feet. A few of the surrounding infantrymen began clapping, enjoying the show.

"Aye, and even three men with training steps makes a weak show." The words came from behind Wren. He did not need to look back to know who was approaching. The laughter and clapping around them silenced instantly.

Ravien held a long, thin wooden pole in her left hand. She stepped into the circling men. "Now, with a woman joining the dance, we'll be sure to entertain everyone."

Wren could see that she was tense and focused. He knew this would not be pretty. The other two men were in a precarious position—either fight against the Prince's sister, lose a fight to a woman, or pull out. They faltered even more in their steps.

"Do not dare consider abandoning our play." Ravien said loudly enough for all the onlookers to hear. "We will be facing real enemies soon. Learn to fight anything that threatens you, that threatens our prince and our nation." Her left foot crossed in front her right, her right crossed behind her left. The circling continued as her words hung in the air.

The tiny man then began to open his mouth, tentatively, as if to sound a retreat.

"My lady, I don't—"

Before another sound left his lips, Ravien pivoted off her right foot and sprang towards the man. She leapt into the air and brought her wooden pole down hard at the man's head. He lifted his stick in time to block the full force and take a glancing blow off the shoulder. But Ravien's momentum knocked him to the ground, and she kicked the wooden blade from his hand.

The other knight's instinct had pulled him in, and he tackled Ravien from behind. The two rolled along the ground, dust and cursing rising from their struggle. The downed man crawled away to the ring of spectators.

Wren approached the grapplers. He told himself that it was only right that he defend the Prince's sister.

The man had managed to end up on top of Ravien, pinning her to the dirt. She roiled beneath him and then slammed her fist into the man's left ear. Just as he dizzily reached up to block the next punch, Wren landed a hard blow to the back of the man's head. He fell over limply.

Ravien was on her feet before Wren could make another move. He ducked instinctively as she swung at his head. She predicted his move and delivered a swift knee to his groin.

As he crumbled down, she slapped him hard across the face and then pushed him to the ground. "Learn well, my friends," she declared to the onlookers. "Soon, we fight Icarians!"

Kneeling down beside Wren, she spoke so that only he could hear. "My bird, I am starting to enjoy your flights. It pleases me to see your wit persist, from wealthy trader to trash knight. Take care to bathe well. I would not take a man who smells. And tell your prince to be more careful to avoid being seen with men like the priest." She sprang up and was gone without another word.

Wren sat still, stunned. He watched as a few soldiers carried off the man he had knocked out. The others dispersed in small groups. There were more men than when the fight had started. Their laughter was not hard to hear.

A familiar chuckle from behind Wren announced his brother's arrival. "That was a fine show, Wren. Ravien seemed to enjoy herself." Jon smiled down and offered him a hand. Wren groaned and reached up to accept the help as he rose slowly to his feet.

"Should you not be with the prince, noble knight? This practice field is awfully close to the rear of our camp, where we do not often see the likes of you. It has been, what, five days since you visited? You should come visit my waste station. The pile should be burning aromatically by now."

"Tempting, but the stench is too much for me. I have come from a meeting in our prince's tent, or movable palace, really. It seems our armed campaign is not going completely to his liking." Jon gestured towards a small copse of trees to the south. The brothers walked towards it, just two aimless knights talking before they broke camp.

Wren shrugged, part in doubt, part post-melee stretching. "Tryst is hard to please. What is not to like? We move into the mountains within the day, and we will be meeting these Icarians soon enough."

"Our march has been too slow," Jon explained, "and we have been losing deserters, lots of them. Tryst is thirsty for battle. I think I accidentally insisted that he be on the front lines, by the mere mention of concern about his safety. But mostly, our recent pace is a consequence of Tryst's anxiety."

"Anxiety about what? Have you heard from Andor lately?"

"No, have you?" Wren shook his head, and Jon continued with a look of concern. "Before, it seemed he found secret moments to visit each of us every few days, even though I feel certain that we are being watched. Andor is too obvious. He has been training the men from his group, the Fourth Marchers, and they are building a reputation of skill where none existed a month ago. At least the leader of his group, a young knight named Pikeli, is keeping the secret if he suspects anything. Tryst will learn soon enough, and I fear he already senses an unknown danger."

Wren sighed. "It was only a matter of time before Andor started to stand out. But if Tryst missed Andor when he passed right under his nose, why would he pay any attention to him now?"

"It is different now, Wren. The pikemen under his command love him. His charisma is returning quickly. Warmth is returning to his face, and you know as well as I do that he cannot stay hidden long once he returns to his old form. Everyone notices him. His men are praising him every chance they get, boiling over in camaraderie and confidence in their leader. Meanwhile, all around us, morale is crumbling. The contrast is clear, and dire. Tryst will not like it when he learns how much adoration is growing for Andor."

"What of it? Andor must declare himself at some point. I believe he has been connecting with other supporters among the knights. We have only a few days until battle, and it will be hard to hide Andor then. Just do your best to keep Tryst distracted until Icaria. There are plenty of challenges in the mountains, so he will not have time to worry about some hedge knight leading a group of pikemen."

Jon nodded. Then he smiled for the first time since he had pulled Wren to his feet. Wren was not used to seeing him so serious, and he relaxed at his brother's lightened countenance. Jon, of course, seized the moment of Wren's relaxation as the perfect time to throw a verbal dagger.

"You are right, and if Tryst has any spare time, I will fill it with stories of young knights wrestling his dear sister to the ground in melee."

"You will not," Wren could not hide the flush in his cheeks.

"Oh, I might. You know how much he loves hearing of your waste-disposing exploits. Wait a moment, to what can I credit this rare blush of Wren?"

"Enough," Wren laughed uneasily and tried to change the subject. "I think we have been away from camp for long enough. We do not want the prince to be missing his most trusted new knight. Remember, distract him, however you can. These next days will be a hard hike."

"Aye. I will find you before the battle, unless Ravien gets to you first. Next time you two are wrestling, it would be helpful if you figured out whose side she is really on."

"I wish I knew," Wren answered. "Her mysterious reputation seems warranted, and I am not sure how much I like being her target. I will find out what I can." Wren turned to walk back. "Take care, Jon."

"You too, Wren."

The brothers departed in different directions. Jon wished that he could believe his brother. While he loved to see the excitement in Wren's eyes, he feared what Tryst would do if he learned about the spark between Wren and Ravien.

Wren thought of how he had grown stronger as the leader of such a messy enterprise, but he was struggling with his weakness to the princess. His usual defenses seemed hopeless. She had caught him off guard and mocked him again, which just left him wanting her more.

Chapter 16

The Path to Battle

**"Order marches with weighty
and measured strides.
Disorder is always in a hurry."**

The Icarian watchman was sweating despite the frigid air. He sat on the crest of a ridge, looking over the other side. The ravine floor was several thousand feet below. Far above, a seemingly endless line of men was inching along the slender path that wrapped around the mountain. The watchman was close enough to make out a few of their faces.

Huge, dark clouds loomed to the west. The marching men might reach Icaria's perched walls before the storm hit, but the timing was going to be close.

Either way, the watchman would do his duty. Not all of the marching men would make it that far. After several hours of scrambling pursuit, he had found the next detonation spot. It would be his third attack of the day.

On cue, the watchman's partner rose from behind a boulder a hundred feet below, half way down the mountain to the soldiers. He lifted his hand to signal that the explosives were ready. The watchman quickly looked at the line of men again to confirm that the attack would have enough impact.

The men were pressed tightly together below the massive boulder, so he crossed his arms above his head to signal approval. In response, his partner knelt, lit a fuse, and began scrambling up the steep rock face.

The army had learned by now to watch the cliffs above them, and they sounded an alarm as soon as they saw the climber. The watchman then stood straight up on the ridge and yelled at the top of his lungs, blasting the men below with the sound.

All eyes below turned to him immediately. That shift in focus caused all the pause that was needed. The explosion erupted ahead of him, sending the massive boulder and a spray of stones hurtling down the mountain. The distraction succeeded: the men below the avalanche turned back just in time to see the rocks crashing down on them.

There was no time to survey the damage. The watchman ducked to the safe side of the ridge and made haste down the slope. He soon came to a tiny opening in the mountainside. If the army sent pursuers, odds were they would never see this place. If they did find it, they would have two trapped and well-trained Icarians to deal with.

The watchman had hardly crawled into the little cave when he heard his partner's voice. "How many do you think we got?" The man had a small torch lit. He was smiling and breathing heavily.

"I think we got at least a dozen, and that boulder may have blocked the path for a while."

"I say we took out fifty. That boulder was in the perfect spot, and those men were frozen in its path. Just the two of us have taken out hundreds these past two days. I believe we will win this fight."

The watchman studied the face of his young partner in the torch light. The face wore the beginnings of a beard, no scars, and unmistakable over-eagerness. The watchman sat back and took a drink of the dark liquid in his flask.

"We will not win this fight, nor will they," he sighed. "Everyone loses."

The watchman offered the flask to his comrade, who drank too deeply and coughed. He tried to hide the cough with a laugh.

"Ha, well, someone must win, and they will be crushed at our gates. We have more of our firepower there. But I must say, their march has been impressive, for lowlanders at least. It will take them only three days to reach Icaria."

"No, not impressive. It has been vain, and reckless. A large force whittled down by several thousand men—the weak flecks chipped off by our mountains and our rangers. This prince wants glory more than victory."

"I say it is impressive if a leader can push his men so. The strong ones remain to fight us, but they have no answer to our fortress and weapons. They have never even seen power like ours."

"Optimism may serve you well, so let's not talk on this further. For now, duty calls and we another hour before dusk. There may be enough time to set up a night attack. They enter the valley below our city soon, and I think this storm will too. Come, let's meet the other rangers at the next hideaway."

The younger man was on his feet in an instant, darting out of the hole and declaring, "for Icaria!"

The watchman followed him out of the cave and summoned the last of his waning energy to follow his spry comrade. The storm would hit soon, as the darkening sky warned. As he ran along the tight path under the lip of the ridge, the man thought again of how his people had gotten into this conflict. It seemed unavoidable that a people with power would fall—sooner if driven by pride, later if lulled into contentment. Icarians always favored the sooner.

Perhaps we are not so different from this prince, the old ranger mused.

*   *   *

"Remind your men, we fight today for Valemidas and its people. Remind them that I will be by their sides in the heat of the battle. Remind them that glory awaits those who prove their honor to me and to our people."

My Council of Knights took my words steadily, with resolve and purpose. "Be strong for your men and for me. If any of your men look weak or afraid, give them a nip of whiskey, a cup of coffee, and a slap in the face. We must be stronger, and we will win this battle today. We attack within the hour. You know the plan, now you will know greatness. For Valemidas!"

"For Valemidas!" They responded forcefully, in unison.

As the knights left my tent, I tried to hold them in a greater measure of esteem. Some merited it—like wise Ulysses and strong Jon. They had all obeyed me and made this march. They had accepted that we would lose men to get to this point. Today they could prove their loyalty and win glory for themselves.

It would be another hour before the sun rose. Most of the Lycurgus was exhausted and asleep. I had not slept a blink the prior night, and instead had spent the hours studying maps and strategy. The days were blurring together, like the continuous assaults that had rained down on my men.

I had expected that we would be in a position of strength once we arrived in the valley under the city of Icaria, but I could not have predicted the storm. It was unlike anything I had ever seen. The blizzard had struck at dusk, when about half of the Lycurgus had entered the valley. Icy, howling winds had whipped through the camp and left two feet of snow in their wake. The storm had lasted that first night and all of the next day.

I could not afford to let the men dwell on the cold and the losses during the march. The snow had at least forced them to rest from the march for a day in their tents. Today, they would have pent up aggression from the day being stuck inside. Today, the sun would shine and we would conquer Icaria.

I stared into the low brazier fire and forced my mind to the next matter. My best knights understood their tasks. I began cycling through the other assignments and meetings to complete before dawn, and then I remembered Ravien. My sister had made a rare request to see me.

"Mailyn, send Ravien in." My admiration of the woman's slim figure was interrupted by my sister's sharp words.

"You left me waiting too long, brother." Ravien glared at me as she strode in, part anger and part amusement.

"It is good to see you, too, sweet sister." I tried to look disinterested. She was always full of surprises. Had she been born a man, I had often thought with amusement and pride, she would be prince and I would not be alive.

Looking at her now, I saw a beautiful, sharp face and unwavering eyes. Her hair fell at various angles, and the dark circles under her eyes showed that she, too, had not been sleeping. She had probably been awake at night plotting, and she was dead serious now. I decided to use a playful, inquisitive tone in response.

"Wouldn't you like to know why I'm here?" She demanded, arms crossed.

"Isn't it obvious?" I smiled as the fib rolled out of my mouth. "You have come to wish your brother the prince well, on the morning of his first great victory as the leader of your nation."

"Why yes, dear little brother, you know me too well." Her return smile was full of dark sarcasm. I loved it. She always kept me entertained because her purposes were the most difficult to detect. "I had a few other thoughts about today's battle as well, if the prince would be so generous as to take suggestions from a woman."

"No, Ravien, I will not take tips on war from a woman. For you, however, my ears are wide open."

"Good," she said, biting her lip. I enjoyed watching her restrain herself. "You have little time, so I will present my points quickly. First, you will not be on the front line. Sir Sigmund and the others on this list will be."

I took the small piece of carefully folder paper that appeared in Ravien's hand. Opening it, I glanced over the twenty names. My sisters both had such marvelous and compact penmanship. I knew half of the men listed and had no particular concern about them surviving the day. I could concede whatever already fit with my plans. I nodded agreement, without any attempt to hide the curiosity in my eyes.

"Second, you will not enter the fight until our men have broken the first gate. When you do enter, you will wear armor. It will not do to have our glorious prince pinched off by a stray arrow from the ramparts."

The timing fit my strategy, but not the attire. "I will wait for the gate to be broken, and I won't be pinched off by an arrow or anything else."

"You don't choose where the arrows fly. Wear armor." She had read my non-answer like a book, and the satisfaction was gleaming from the big sister look she gave me.

"I will have my own protection, and I will dress myself. Haven't I told you, dear sister, that a prince works best in comfort and style?" I turned my head to look behind me, and turned back with a grin. "Just ask Mailyn." Of all that Ravien tolerated, my love life had always gotten under her skin the most.

She paused only a moment before responding, her glare hard. "Fine. Wear your delicate black cloth into the fortress of your enemies. Before you do, please draw up a will naming me as your successor." She did not wait for a retort. "Third, I am leading a dozen men to a hidden entry to the city. We leave within the hour, and we will help prepare the way to the inner keep for you."

"Ravien, you know that you must tell me more if I am to allow this." I stalled to hide my genuine surprise.

I did not mention that my scouts had been circling the city for two days and had not seen any openings, aside from a few grates far up on the wall. Icaria was like an island rising on its isolated peak. Its wall was low, but it grew up from the steep cliffs dropping below it. The only way in was through the front gate. And the only way to the gate was across a ravine. My men had been preparing stronger, fireproof bridges to replace the one that the Icarians had destroyed in an explosion the day before.

Ravien's laughter drew me out of my thoughts.

"Thinking through your strategy, brother? I know you do not believe that a city can survive with only one entrance and exit, no matter how small. The front gate is your army's access point. I am going in another way."

Inquisition rarely went far with Ravien. She was perhaps the only person who harbored not an ounce of fear of me. I had always made my love for her clear, maybe too clear. I was thankful again the people would never accept a woman on the throne.

"This is taking too much time, Ravien." I turned to practicalities. Light was beginning to seep into my tent. The sun would be rising soon. "Tell me how you are getting in. I will not win this battle with my forces divided and outside my control. Besides, it would be a shame to lose you in some foolhardy vainglory."

"Cut the lecture, little brother. Fools hungry for glory walk through the front gate wearing cloth instead of steel." Ravien looked around the tent impatiently. Her eyes narrowed when they glanced over my right shoulder. I guessed that Mailyn was there, wearing something distracting.

"Sometimes secrets are not hidden." My sister continued. "They are standing right in front of you, nearly naked. And it takes the discipline of an army to pretend the secret is unseen. In this case, I will use the Icarians' own secret. Our scouts, as you know, discovered some of this magic substance they have been using to rain boulders down on us. It is immensely destructive. I learned a way to reconstruct their devices. With this power, I am going to blow open the steel grates high up on the wall. I cannot go over the wall, so I am going through it."

"That does not sound like a quiet entrance. Each Icarian will be like a wolverine protecting its cubs in a cave. There are not many of them, but they are an impressive bunch. I admit I have learned from the discipline of their scouts—lessons that will be ingrained in my Lycurgus. My forces will be needed to make them bend the knee."

She stepped closer as if challenging me. "Just say it, Tryst. They are men. I am a woman. That is why, for you dear brother, I promise to skulk rather than fight my way through the city. I'll leave the battle glory to you."

"Dare I ask why you need this adventure?"

"I have my reasons." She took my face in her hands, leaned forward, and kissed my forehead. "You know you can trust me. Let me have some fun."

Then she stood straight with her hand on her hip. Her casual smile was a lackluster attempt at beguilement. She was so devious and hidden about her ways, but she was right. She had always been loyal. This kind of troublemaking was nothing out of the ordinary for Ravien, and it did not threaten my plans.

"Fine. Have your fun. Now, as you seem to be aware, the battle begins soon. A prince has plenty to do at a time like this."

As she turned to go, I remembered that she had mentioned a group joining her.

"Take whomever you like for your group, as long as it is no more than a dozen low-ranking infrantrymen."

She surprised me for the second time this morning by freezing in her steps. So that was her game—something about someone who would be in her little troop. I saw her take a deliberately deep breath, and an instant later she was composed again. Too casually, she turned and said without question, "I had a couple low knights in mind. If I take any of them, you won't notice that they are missing."

She was walking out the tent before she finished the sentence. I sat in silence and wondered about her intentions.

"Sebastian, you heard her."

He slid out from behind a fold in the wall of the tent. As always, he looked like a shadow and acted like a ghost. He drifted towards me lightly and bowed at my feet.

I tolerated Sebastian's strange foreign customs because he spied and managed spies better than anyone. If rumors of his motherland gathering an army had any truth, he would also be a valuable asset in the months ahead.

The whites of his dark eyes shone out from his hooded face. "Low knights, my Prince, yes. Do you have any particular wishes for this task?"

Sebastian never made me say what was necessary, unless I was in the mood. "This time, yes. I want you to follow her yourself. Identify anyone of importance. If this pikeman you have been monitoring is one of her group, send a report to me immediately. And you know Ravien's talents, so take extra care today." He cringed and blinked, probably because of his pride in his skills. Let him take offense; Ravien warranted it.

"Oh," I remembered, "and send your spiders out to make sure these men are in the front line." I handed him the piece of paper from Ravien. "Spare no resources, but you must stick with your battle assignments today. I want a report tonight after the victory."

"Understood and done, my Prince." He rose to his feet. In the few instances when he stood straight, Sebastian grabbed my attention. He was very nearly my size. Eye to eye, apparently pound for pound, he was a bronze-skinned version of myself.

He bowed deeply and the connection was lost. As he slid out of the tent, I thought of his mission and of Ravien's. One was family and the other a foreign brother. They were like alternative versions of me, waging miniature versions of my war. I had no reason to question their love of me, but I shuddered at my increasing dependence on them.

What would become of me without the few I trusted?

Chapter 17

Explosive Strawmen

**"Men think highly of those
who rise rapidly in the world;
whereas nothing rises quicker
than dust, straw, and feathers."**

The Summit stood high above the front gate of his city. An army was gathered below him, larger than any that had ever stood at Icaria's gate. If the reports were accurate, it was almost sixteen thousand men strong. The countless glowing fires of last night seemed to overwhelm the reports.

As the leader of Icaria, the Summit tried to hold his composure and consider what he knew of the enemy. The bright morning and the crisp air helped; the eight-to-one numbers did not help.

The finest of Icaria's rangers, two hundred total, had harassed this massive force at every step of its advance through the mountains. They had used Icaria's explosives, they had rained arrows down on them, and had even engaged them directly in the narrowest mountain passes. One hundred twenty rangers had returned. Their efforts had been more effective than Icaria's most optimistic guesses. Hundreds if not thousands had fallen under the rangers' assault.

But this army marched on. The Summit marveled at their willingness to take staggering losses and continue. He had believed that only people of these mountains could survive the trek while under attack. These opponents had quickly responded to the guerilla tactics by sending out scouts far out-numbering the rangers. The scouts barely knew the mountains and had far less skill, but there were enough of them to slow the pace of slaughter by Icaria's rangers.

Even the mountains' own defenses had not stopped the army's advance. As if beckoned by the Icarians, a brutal winter storm had swept in from the ocean to the west, clouds carrying dense snow driven by gusting winds and blasting thunder. The city's walls had shaken at the force of it. The mountains were left under a serene blanket of snow by the time the storm passed.

The rangers reported that the army had not stopped its march as it was pummeled by the storm. Men with plows were set at the front of the train of men, pushing snow off the thin trail and over the cliff to the chasm below. As men grew tired, relentless groups of reinforcements took up the task. The scouts estimated that over a hundred men had fallen to their deaths during the weather's assault. A ripping push of wind, a loose stone under foot covered by snow, or the cold itself had claimed many soldiers. As if driven by fiery whips, the army barely slowed.

Now they had arrived. Their camp filled to the brim the entire valley that sat below the city. Most of the men were armed and in tight formations stretching out from the edge of the ravine that separated them and the valley from the city's gate. They were a few hundred feet away, but he could see clerics wisping ceremonious smoke among the soldiers, likely saying the final blessing that many of the men would hear.

The Summit understood their courage better when he saw the famed prince. The man emerged from the center of the army's long front line. Even from the distance, the Summit could see that he stood apart, leaner and straighter, than those around him. His blade and crown gleamed brightly, reflecting the snow.

He turned his back to the city and roared words to his men. It looked as if he was wearing no armor. Just mere cloth, and it was all black.

If he would not suit up for battle, the Summit thought, the Icarians would bring it to him. He made an instant change to his plans. Arrows could be wasted. This recklessly bold man had to be taken out. He whispered a few commands to the strongest archers around him on the wall. He had hoped to save their few arrows until the army attempted to cross the ravine and was an easier shot, but this opportunity could not be missed.

He raised his hand, and the bows went up with it. The snap of the bowstrings left a heavy moment of silence. The prince below had stopped his speech and turned to face the city. The Summit's heart raced as he followed the arrows' path. There were at least twelve arching toward the man.

The next movements happened so quickly that the Summit could hardly tell what happened. A few glimmers of steel and black blurs, and then all was still again. The prince was standing, as if he was the only one who had moved. A handful of arrows were pinned into the ground around his feet. The prince seemed to have dodged or deflected the ones that were on target.

He held his sword raised overhead and roared at the city, echoed by the men behind him. Where no one had been before, two knights crouched at the prince's side, huge shields now at the ready for any new attacks.

The Summit had figured the arrows would miss, but not that they would be dodged. Perhaps some of this prince's brashness was deserved. The Summit would keep that in mind through the day, but now he shifted his focus to the army bringing forward its first bridge. The Icarians still had the high ground and impregnable walls. He looked to his sides, along the line of men. Several of the remaining rangers stood near him. Their faces were grim, almost resigned. The younger common Icarians around him looked terrified.

"Icarians!" The Summit shouted it, and the surrounding heads snapped towards him. "We have a thousand more arrows, let him shrug off the first few. Let's see how his army stands against our bombs. They come in through our front gate or not at all. There, we face them one on one. These lowlanders will be the overwhelmed ones."

The words had some effect. He saw several of his men glance at their feet, where piles of explosives were gathered. It was those weapons that had gotten the Icarians into this fight, and they were the only hope of getting them out of the day alive.

He reached down and grabbed a round bomb the size of an apple. He lit the fuse and looked at his men again. With a yell he hurled the ball over the wall. It was near the middle of the ravine when it went off. The sound, like a thunderclap, grabbed the attention of soldiers on both sides. His men shouted with fervor.

The army below stirred in its place, seemingly shaken. But the prince stood motionless, staring at the city. Lifting his arms, the prince seemed to be calling forth a bridge. The Icarian rangers had taken out one, but also had seen pieces of others towed along with the army through the mountains. They could not tell how long it would be, or how many there were. Some estimated five bridges, while others said there were only two.

The Summit had explained the simple plan to his men yesterday. Litter any bridges with bombs and watch them fall to the bottom of the deep ravine. No army could take Icaria without some way to cross that ravine and surmount the walls.

A long plank began to rise up from the ranks of men below. It was drawn up with ropes anchored to pulleys. It rotated up slowly and steadily. The Summit was taken aback by its size. When it was perpendicular to the ground, the bridge looked like a thin tower far overhead. It was several times the height of the wall that the Icarians stood upon. Set against the low morning sun, the impromptu bridge cast a slender shadow over the full length of the valley.

The shadow rotated as the massive structure began its fall. It seemed frozen at first, let out of control of the ropes. As the men far below dropped the ropes, the bridge dropped too, racing down towards the city. At the last moment, the Summit saw that the bridge was not aimed at the city's gate. It was falling several feet to his right. As he dove and rolled along the wall, he was already cursing himself for not guessing this. This was not a bridge *to* the gate; it crashed hard *over* the wall.

Two men had misjudged the bridge's landing and were crushed beneath it. The day had its first deaths, and now the long plank extended over the wall by maybe twenty feet, hanging above the city below.

"Bombs! Now!" The Summit shouted. The lowlanders had already scrambled onto the bridge and were sprinting to the city. The bridge was wide enough for two or three men to run along it abreast.

As the first men reached the half-way point, the Icarian bombs began landing in their midst. A few were slapped away and exploded innocently in midair. Others did better service for Icaria. Each small device that went off near the bridge sent men plummeting to their deaths. The force of the explosion was enough to knock off a handful, splitting limbs and bodies. The noise and disruption would then take out another few soldiers. Already the Summit had counted ten good detonations. And almost every one of the Icarians' arrows found its mark at this range. Dozens of lowlanders were dead in less than a minute.

As soon as men fell, others racing behind them took their places. The bombs and arrows were wreaking havoc, but they would run out too soon at that pace. Even worse, the bridge held fast. In moments the men would reach the wall.

The Summit studied the composition of the bridge, which seemed to be dark wood covered with a hard gray substance. The lowlanders had brought their own competing science. Each bomb could weaken the bridge's joints, but it seemed too weak to break it entirely.

The Summit made his way to the crux of the fight, where bridge met wall. His Icarians were fending off the attackers, who came two or three at a time. They came at intervals that left his men enough time to brace for the next small wave.

He ran the numbers in his head. Maybe they had powder for five hundred small bombs. His thousand men could hold off two thousand at this pace. Icaria might survive another two hours, but it would not make it many more. But so his people had chosen. We stay and fight. We go down with our home.

That set off the spark in his mind. We go down with our home, or we live and move on. He surveyed the men surrounding him. It would have to work.

"Nalin and Therron, fall back and bring a powder keg to this exact spot. Now!" His words took them aback. The battle frenzy was in the two rangers' eyes, but they obeyed without hesitating. As they sheathed their swords and sprinted away along the wall, two other Icarians took their spot on the thin front line.

More lowlanders ran onto the wall, only to find an Icarian spear sticking through their bellies and out their backs. The sound of bombs exploding drowned out screams and punctuated the devastation. It seemed like a thousand soldiers had died on the dangerous run along the slender plank hanging above the deep ravine. Most were taken by arrows or bombs, but some fell to their deaths amidst the smoke and confusion. Only a few hundred men had actually engaged in face-to-face fighting by the time the two rangers showed up again at the Summit's side.

They had a powder keg. It was one of the last two the Icarians had in storage. The Summit knew that Icarian women were working furiously to assemble more bombs with the last of their black powder. They had more forged metal shells than powder to fill them. Time was running short, and the small bombs were not going to save them.

The Summit pointed to the spot where the bridge had landed on the wall. The fight was intense there, but this had to be tried. He charged to the spot with the two men following. Swinging his spear wildly, he took out one man and turned back. He grabbed the keg and helped Nalin roll it to the crux of the bridge's hold. Without hesitation, he pulled a fuse from his waste, connected it to the keg, lit it with a small match, and ran.

As he fled, the Summit yelled, "Run now! Turn and run!" The rangers and the rest of the nearby Icarians followed on the Summit's heels.

The lowlanders flooded into the spot like a river breaking free of a dam. They had expected confrontation but were met with the fleeing backs of their foes. It caused a short-lived pause and moment of strange silence, as if the sound and all of Icaria's hope was sucked into that one burning fuse.

The blast shattered the precious moment of quiet. The Summit had never seen such an explosion. Stone and shards shot out and showered down. He could hear nothing but a ringing, and found himself flat on his back, nearly blown off the wall. Where the keg had blown, the wall was gone. It left a hole thick enough for five horses to stride through abreast. Most importantly, the bridge was gone too. Staggering to his feet, the Summit peered down the ravine and saw its remnants far below.

Another roaring sound rose around him. Combined with the ringing, it was an exhilarating rush of noise. His men rallied into small groups behind his captains, his best rangers. They were down a hundred men and had one keg of powder left, but the lowlanders were down two thousand. The crashing bridge must have taken two hundred more, he guessed.

The optimism died fast, as two more towering bridges began to rise from the army below. The Summit had guessed that there would be more, but he did not have enough powder left to destroy them. He issued orders to his leaders to form lines where the two next bridges would fall. One was aimed at the hole in the wall. It would be a straight road into the city. They would hold the line as long as they could, but then would have to fall back.

After his men split and charged to their positions, he felt alone. They had no more surprises. As the ringing continued to pound in his ears, he accepted that he might die without another pure sound. It was time to lead this battle from within the city.

As he turned towards Icaria's grand hall, he saw the black blur of the prince and his retinue racing across the bridge. If this was his people's final stand, he would do all in his power to make the price of Icaria be the life of this prince.

Chapter 18

Glory Cannot Hide

**"It is not enough to conquer;
one must learn to seduce."**

Wren had slept soundly until he awoke with a face one inch from his. Just as his eyes jerked open, a hand covered his mouth and he felt lips against his ear. Ravien's voice commanded him to wake and gave him to the count of fifty to follow her, ready for war.

From that moment the day raced out of his control. He hurried after Ravien while she skirted from camp to camp, gathering men who also seemed to have no clue what the prince's sister was doing. She left a sealed note where each man had slept, presumably authorizing whatever excuse she had for taking them. Ravien stonewalled every one of his questions with commands of silence. Because she knew about Andor, and remembering her words on the rooftop in Valemidas, he resigned himself to do as she said.

The fourth man Ravien recruited was Granville. That gave Wren some concern that she was picking off Andor's supporters, but other reasons could explain it. Ravien was gathering a battle-proven and tough group, with diverse skills. Granville was the only blacksmith. The second man, like Wren, was a merchant-turned-soldier, except that his trade had been limited to fine spices. Ravien had demanded that he bring two of his finest spice boxes, into which she placed ten odd spheres as if they were as delicate as black dragon eggs. Since the spheres were metallic, Wren figured that having a blacksmith around could prove useful. The third man was renowned as a healer, with a specialty in ointments to soothe severe burns. Wren did not know the next two men, but they had stern faces and scars suggesting they were no foreigners to war.

Nothing about any of those men lessened Wren's shock at the last recruit—Andor.

Out of an army of thousands, Ravien had pulled out a group of seven that included Wren, Granville, and Andor. Wren had long suspected that she would act on her knowledge, but not this boldly.

When Andor stepped out of his tent, he nodded calmly at the other men. He did not spare attention for Wren. He did not question Ravien. It was closer to the opposite—he clasped her shoulder, then bowed low in respect. That gave Wren some comfort, as he pieced together Andor's hints of allies close to power with Ravien's veiled messages. But he still did not like it.

After Ravien gathered up her little band, they fled the awakening camp. A few scouts eyed them but none tried to stop them. They made their way, by her direction, to the northeastern edge of the ravine encircling Icaria, so that the city stood between them and the army. They arrived at a spot where the ravine was narrower than on the other side of the city. Where the other side opened into a valley, this side had a steep mountain face rising high behind it.

Ravien spoke quietly to one of the men who Wren did not know. The man did not respond in words, but loaded the large crossbow that he had been wearing on his back. The bolt had a strange point, like an inverted claw, and a thick rope tied to it.

The man steadied himself and shot the bolt across the ravine. It fired through a small metal grate on the other side, and it seemed to catch. The man then wedged the crossbow behind a huge boulder and drove a stake through a loop in the rope that was tied to the crossbow. He tugged the rope firmly and nodded at Ravien.

She waved the group to follow as she grabbed the rope with both hands, swung one hand past the other, and slid off the edge of the cliff.

Wren watched as Ravien and the other men made their way across the gap, hanging onto the rope as their feet dangled above the chasm. No one had asked him whether he was willing to do this, and he did not like the idea. They had left him with little choice. He noted wryly that he was finally receiving the action he had sought.

He took a deep breath and clenched the rope. It held strong as he swung his hand forward and proceeded over the ravine. He tried to keep his eyes on the rope, and he dared not look down.

Upon reaching the other side, he saw Andor offering his hand with a smile. Wren took it and gave thanks when he felt the solid ground beneath his feet. He caught his breath as he studied the surroundings. The peak of Icaria loomed high over them. What had looked like man-made wall was actually a rocky cliff for nearly a hundred feet up. From there, the cliff turned into a stone wall for another fifty feet. It seemed to reach to the highest point in Icaria. Only the surrounding mountains stood higher.

"Up," Ravien whispered and pointed above. Without another word, she began climbing up the cliff face. Andor was the first man to tackle the wall after her. His hands seemed to have glue on them, as every grip locked onto tiny ledges and crevices in the stone. He quickly came to an even spot with Ravien. The other men followed more slowly.

Ravien and Andor were already fifty feet up, and the other men were well on their way, when Wren began his climb. He grabbed a small hold of stone jutting out from the wall and pulled himself up. He tried to wedge his shoes into any crevice that he could find. Where Andor was a spider, Wren felt like he was a goat bouncing upwards without any flow. When he was about half way up, he risked a look down. His head dizzied at the distance between him and the ground. He would die if he fell. He resolved not to be last for whatever they did next.

Wren looked up and resumed his climb, sweat dripping down his brow and falling to the ground far below. Just as he pulled up to another small ledge, nearing the top of the cliff, his focus was shattered by an explosion above him. Stones crashed down to his side, and a cloud of dust enveloped him.

Wren shuddered at the temporary blindness, clenching even harder with his exhausted hands. He was having a hard enough time climbing when he could see, and he could hold on to this thin ledge for only so long before his grip would give. He wondered if Jon was faring any better than he was, fighting at Tryst's side.

He thought he heard shouting somewhere above when a hand reached down through the dust and clasped his forearm like a vice. It pulled him up and then grabbed him around the waist.

"Hold tight to me. They will pull us up." Andor then added in a whisper, "And you can trust her, for the most part."

"Trust her with what? Where is she leading us?"

"What makes you think she is leading?" Andor winked and yanked the rope tied around him. "We are going to win the battle for Valemidas while saving the Icarian people. I will also ensure that Tryst returns home in defeat. Nothing complicated."

Wren wanted to ask more, but suddenly they were hoisted up. The rough wall ended in a ledge after they had been lifted a few more feet, and Andor nudged him into the emptiness. Torch light flooded the small space. Ravien and the other men were in the tiny room. There was a bed of straw tucked into one corner. The wall to his back was gone, open to the chasm below.

"You sure were taking your time, Wren." Ravien's voice taunted him, as usual.

Granville's voice followed. "She is right about that. You let a hefty blacksmith like me beat you up here." Some of the other men chuckled.

Wren was out of breath and out of patience. "Someone had to be ready to catch all of you if you fell," he said. "Let's not waste any more time. That explosion is sure to bring their attention to this place." Wren hated not knowing more of the plan.

"He is right." Andor said, taking on an air of command. "We are in the Icarian prison, which is small for a city this size. Their grand hall is not far from here."

"Antony," Ravien cut in, "stand guard in this room. The rest of you follow me." Wren caught a rigid glance between Ravien and Andor. He could not be sure, but it looked as if Andor had interjected leadership before either of them expected it.

Ravien ran out of the room. This time Wren made sure he was close after her. She led them upwards through a winding series of tunnels and tight stone stairwells. In three places, when Wren heard Icarians near, Ravien halted the group and commanded silence. She lit a fuse and set off a small explosion nearby. The first time, it seemed the blast was nothing but a distraction. The next two times, Ravien blew off locked metal-grate doors and led the group through. They did not pause for an instant to catch their breath, and they saw not a soul as they left the prison.

It was not long before they escaped the cave-like inner passages of the city and entered an alley that opened to the clear, midday sky above. Ravien led them to the end and peered around the corner. She waved Andor and Wren forward.

Wren peeked his head out and saw that they had made it to the plaza before Icaria's main hall. The hall was a huge, smooth stone building, rising from the peak of the city. The plaza had been carved into the stone itself. It had two ancient, twisted pines framing the entrance to the hall. Wren counted six guards surrounding the square, with two of them by the sides of the door. He heard the battle raging somewhere within the city, but it had not reached this far.

Ravien pulled Wren back from the corner. She issued orders to the six men. "Two of the guards are rangers, which means the Summit has left the walls and is inside. It sounds like most of the Icarian soldiers are still near the wall, plugging the holes of the dam that will soon break forth with our army. We must make this quick and quiet." She beckoned the man who had fired the bolt across the ravine. He pulled out six small crossbows from his bag.

"We each get one shot," Ravien continued, "on my count of three, step out and fire. Wren, take the far left guard. Granville, the one to his right. Hal, the next to the right, and Andor, the one after that. Aim for the neck, and immediately charge your target. Put on his helmet and take his spear." Without more, she said "one." Each of them went into a focused, tense crouch. "Two." Wren swallowed and tried to steady himself. "Three."

Wren followed the order exactly. He shifted to a stable firing position and released the bolt at the guard to his left. He hit the target. He dashed forward to seize the fallen man's helm and spear. The Icarian's face was framed by a long beard peppered with gray. The helm was a bit too large but comfortable. It had thick wool puffing out of the base, an open face and a soft leather shell. Wren guessed that it protected more from the cold than from battle. The spear was sturdy wood with a small blade at the end.

Wren rejoined the others by the door, as he tried to push down the sense of wrongness that accompanied his new arms. The other guards had all been downed as well, it seemed. Icarian helmets put them all in crude disguise, but they could not so quickly replicate those beards.

Ravien again commanded silence and gestured to Granville, who pulled out another of the explosive spheres from his pack. Wren noticed that it was a heavier sphere with a longer fuse. Ravien hurried away with the sphere, around the corner of the main hall and out of sight. She returned a moment later and motioned for them all to stay quiet and keep watch.

As Wren knelt in silence alongside the others, he fought the urge to both laugh and cry. Ravien filled him with emotions he still could not comprehend. He wanted to escape with her to somewhere safe, but she seemed drawn to danger. And that made him all the more drawn to her. This morning he had expected nothing of the day but the worst kind of cleanup, mired in the grotesque decay of an exhausted battlefield. Instead, Ravien had come, and now he had killed a man under her command. So, here he was, maintaining a façade of composure, because showing fear was no way to tempt a temptress.

Love led to funny things in the middle of battle, Wren admitted. Ravien was staring out over the Icarian plaza. Aside from the few drops of sweat that beaded at her temple, she looked composed enough for the royal court. And yet, while her brother's full army tried to ram its way to this exact spot, Ravien had beaten them to it. It seemed her force of will could have taken down the city on its own.

She turned to Wren and caught him watching her. A smile crossed her face. "You have done well today, Wren. We are together in this."

Something about her words set him reeling even more. He was trying to find the right response when the explosion ripped through the air.

This one was the most intense yet. Ravien led the men the way she had gone before, around the corner of the hall. When he rounded the corner, Wren looked through a cloud of dust and debris at a small grate blown open in the side wall of the great hall.

Ravien had ripped open the city's heart, and now she nodded to Andor, with her hand held out as if she were merely an escort.

Andor led the way in. Wren and the others followed him closely, still in their crude Icarian disguises. They stepped into the cavernous inner hall and were met with a flurry of activity. Maybe three dozen men stood with spears at the ready, and hundreds of women and children hunkered behind them.

There was terror and tenacity in the air. It was the first time today Wren had felt within death's grasp. Wren remembered enough of Icarian politics to know that taking out the Summit would leave the city paralyzed, and that they would do anything to defend him.

"I demand the Summit!" Andor yelled as he stepped forward and kneeled. He rested his sword on his palms, parallel to the ground.

The Icarians seemed shocked for an instant before they all lurched forward and surrounded Andor and his small band. So much for the disguises, Wren thought. They were at the Icarians' mercy now.

Andor lifted his head and shouted again. "I demand the Summit!"

Wren followed Andor's gaze to a small cliff ledge far above them. Ancient runes were carved into the surrounding stone. The hall was eerily quiet, as if weighing its answer to Andor's demand.

"You have the Summit," Wren heard from one of the men surrounding Andor. A man lifted his spear and stepped forward. The other Icarians seemed to relax an inch. He was elegant and as tall as Andor, and he pulled off his helm to reveal gray-silver hair that fell to his shoulders. Unlike the Icarian soldiers around him, he had no beard and seemed to exude calm, rather than fury.

"You call upon an old Icarian law." He reached out a hand to Andor. "He who demands the Summit must know the Summit's calling."

Andor clasped his hand and stood. His sword hung ready in his left hand. The two men met each other on an equal plane, and the room seemed to wait on every breath from them.

"The Summit commands the mountains, for he leads the Icarians. But you, Summit, have led Icaria to destruction. Give up your life now to me, and I will save Icaria's ways." Andor said loudly. Wren did not quite know what the words meant, but it was obvious they carried great significance to the people because they had paused this battle.

"You have the Summit," the Icarian said again. He turned to face the Icarians behind him. "You have heard the call and the answer, Icarians. Now I put the full vote to you. Do you give the summit to the man who demands it? Kneel to him now to answer aye." No one moved.

The Summit turned again to look at Andor. He stood still and silent, and Wren could see a mix of sadness and satisfaction in his face.

Behind him, the women began to kneel. The Icarian soldiers looked back over the hall, all of them still standing. One of the older men—with a grizzled veteran look about him—approached the Summit, clasped his shoulder, and nodded before going to a knee. The other soldiers followed, dropping their weapons as they knelt. Each of them seemed to be saying goodbye to their leader.

Once all around him were kneeling, the leader graciously handed his long blade to Andor. It seemed as if this was all part of a ceremony.

"You have the Summit, and you are the Summit, my life to give," the leader declared.

With those words he fell prostrate, his head held out before Andor. It had been mere minutes since they walked into the hall. Somehow they had gone from surrounded in a death trap to standing over a huge number of kneeling men and women. Wren could not believe it. Andor had always been great, but now he seemed to have a touch of the divine about him.

The leader pulled his long hair away to reveal the bare back of his neck. Wren heard a woman begin to cry within the hall.

Andor lifted the leader's sword high and brought it down swiftly, stopping just above the older man's neck. He raised it again, the blade reflecting the candlelight that filled the hall. He looked poised to take the leader's head off.

"I call for a vote." Andor commanded to the hall. Men and women alike gasped at his words. Murmuring spread through the crowd like wildfire. Wren heard "this is not the custom" and "he cannot be Summit until he takes his life."

"Silence, Icarians," Andor demanded. He dropped the blade and placed his hand on the back of the older man. "Your Summit rules until he gives his life, which he has done because his life is now mine to take. An army stands ready to put you all to the sword. I believe it is too great a sacrifice to lose the nobility and goodness that pulse inside these walls. As your Summit, I may call a vote, and I trust that you will elect the right destiny."

Andor knelt and whispered something into the leader's ear. The Summit stood and spoke to the hall. "Icarians, it is unbearable to see the fighting men of Icaria disarmed. It is equally unbearable that others who have rendered me devoted service should now die. The time has come to bear the unbearable. Swallow your tears and keep your lives. You must vote now as your Summit demands." He looked to Andor.

"I call for a vote: kneel again if you wish to live, to keep me as your Summit, to keep the old laws within these mountains, to give up all your weapons, and to give up sovereignty to the Prince of Valemidas. Or, stand if you refuse surrender and want to die at the hand of the Prince of Valemidas; if so, we will begin by taking this man's life." Andor pointed at the former Summit at this side.

This time the soldiers knelt first, followed soon by the women and children behind them. Again, Wren marveled at the unity of these people. The former Summit clasped Andor's hand and lifted it high.

"For the Prince of Valemidas and Icaria," he yelled.

"For the Prince of Valemidas and Icaria," the crowd chanted back.

"For the Prince of—" Andor began again, but was interrupted by a loud bash against the main door of the hall.

Another bash followed, and the door crashed open. The few Icarians between Andor's group and the door retreated further back into the hall.

Tryst strode in with his blood-drenched sword, Zarathus, at the ready. A company of knights followed him, and Wren was relieved to see Jon among them. Shock swept over Tryst's face as he locked eyes with Andor.

"This is my fight!" Tryst screamed in fury and charged the short distance between them.

"Stand back," Andor commanded as he stepped forward with the Summit's long blade pointed towards the charging prince. The two men's orders, and the speed of their collision, momentarily froze the surrounding fighters of Icaria and Valemidas.

The princes sprang into a lethal dance. Tryst attacked with relentless fury, slamming Zarathus down at Andor. Andor managed to deflect the blows and maintain his position. He ducked under one of Tryst's violent swings at his head, and then lunged at Tryst. The two men tumbled onto the ground, both with blades still in hand.

Andor landed a knee into Tryst's head and managed to pin down his sword arm. Tryst writhed under Andor and pulled a dagger from his waist. He sliced Andor's side just as Andor pointed his blade at Tryst's neck.

An instant passed when Andor could have plunged the sword into his nemesis. From his back, Tryst swung his dagger wildly again and forced Andor to release Tryst's sword arm to dodge the attack. Andor kept his sword at Tryst's neck.

Before either man could strike again, a dark figure dashed at them—Ravien. She spun behind Andor and pressed a dagger to his throat. Neither prince dared another move, but Andor spoke suddenly, steadily.

"Icarians, your prince lies before you. He is your conqueror and, following your vote, I as Summit submit our city to him." Something about Andor's voice sounded both triumphant and humble to Wren. Andor had so thirsted for revenge. His restraint from killing his betrayer must have been a victory.

Andor slowly moved the point of the sword away from Tryst. As soon as it was an inch away, Tryst surged up and slashed Zarathus at Andor. Panic struck Wren as the sword sparked against Ravien's dagger. The force of the blow knocked both her and Andor back to the ground, but Tryst had not spilled their blood.

Tryst's attack jolted others into action. Icarians and Valemidans charged against each other in apparent confusion.

"No one move!" The former Summit shouted as Icarian men surrounded Tryst, Andor, and Ravien with spears facing out. "Foreigners' blood may not be spilled in the Icarian hall. The city is yours my Prince and my Summit." The man dropped his spear and knelt before Tryst. "Tell me how the Icarians can serve you." Tryst glared at him, furious and robbed of glory.

"Very well, Icaria is mine." Tryst announced to the room. "Knights, disarm these men and"—the Prince turned back just as a series of small explosions began along the floor. A cloud of smoke billowed up through the hall.

It cleared moments later, but Andor and Ravien were nowhere to be seen.

Tryst let out a shout. "Close off the city, now! No one leaves!" He sprinted out of the hall's door, yelling orders to seize Andor.

Wren was close to the hole that had been blown open in the wall and was the first to slip outside that way. He glimpsed Andor and Ravien darting out of the plaza, out of sight from the main hall's door. Tryst ran out into the middle of the plaza a second later but they had vanished.

"What happened back there? You alright?" It was good to hear Jon's voice. He had shown up at Wren's side.

"Yeah, I am not sure. You alright?" Wren turned to his brother.

"I think I am doing better than you," Jon answered with his typical smile.

"Why is that?"

"For starters, the love of my life did not just steal the prince who returned for the throne."

Wren let himself laugh for the first time today. "I think she can take care of herself, and Andor, and the rest of us."

Chapter 19

A Fine Grapevine

**"Wine can of their wits
the wise beguile,
Make the sage frolic,
and the serious smile."**

Lorien's desire for information was deeper than hunger. Since Andor's letter, she had been fighting for Andor's cause in every way she could, coordinating pieces of his network under many guises. It made her feel closer to him, and it became the consuming passion that awakened her from sleep each morning.

Living in the palace made her work easier. Any other betrothed of a former, deposed prince would be gone and probably dead by now, but Lorien was the half-sister of Tryst. He had demanded that she stay in her quarters while he was gone, for her safety, of course. Even locked away there, she had royal privileges and needs that required a wide variety of visitors. No one suspected anything amiss when a noble lady, a priest, or a physician came to wait upon the princess.

Still, the trickle of meaningful information had slowed recently. Her last news of Andor, delivered by Father Yates in the ruse of a private prayer, had been too short—just an assurance that Andor lived and recovered, and that he planned to move against Tryst soon. She would not be much help until she learned more, so she focused on arming herself with knowledge. Today of all days that would be essential.

This morning her maids had told her that Tryst had returned victorious, and that he wanted to see her soon. She shivered at the thought, despite the summer air. It was hard to see how he could return in victory, unless Andor had been caught or had abandoned his plans. To avoid complete betrayal of her emotions when Tryst visited, she had to know if, and how, Andor had returned from the journey.

And so she had called on the best storehouse of knowledge, Selia. The mother of Wren and Jon knew everything about the city and could be trusted. Lorien had called on her only twice since Tryst had left, to avoid rousing too much suspicion. They had met under the cover of fashion, because Selia was a prominent figure in the city's garment trade. Her expertise in dresses was popular among many noble ladies, so her presence in the palace would surprise no one—as long as it did not become too frequent.

Lorien had called for the Prince's finest summer wine to be brought from the cellars. It was a dry, crisp white wine, from the foothills of the Targhees. The grapes had enjoyed a fabulous harvest last year, and this was from the Prince's private vineyard. Sipping slowly, Lorien took in the view. Her quarters had three rooms—an anteroom, a washroom, and a bedroom—and one of the palace's rare balconies. At least seventy feet up in the slender tower, the balcony afforded a view of almost the entire city and the river stretching below its southern wall to the sea.

Lorien was thinking of where Andor might hide in the city when her serving maid knocked on the door of the anteroom. Five knocks meant that Selia was here and her arrival had gone smoothly. Lorien took another sip of wine and braced herself for any news.

"Send her in," she said to her maid as she rose to her feet.

Selia swept in with a flurry. Her dark hair had gray streaks and spunk. Her eyes wore light wrinkles and cheerfulness. As much as Lorien may have doubted her subtlety, she always found herself warmed by the woman's presence. She wore her passion like she wore her bright red flowing dress.

"Lorien my dear! It is an honor and a pleasure to see you, as always. And my, what a view! This must be one of the prettiest spots in the whole city. Fitting for a princess, of course. Did you set this wine out for me? That was very thoughtful of you. My lady, you know me too well."

Lorien could not help but smile. "Selia, thank you for joining me. Please, have a seat." She gestured toward the chairs and made eye contact with the maid, who poured Selia a glass of the wine. Lorien reminded herself of her mission: she must learn as much as possible, while revealing as little as possible to her eavesdropping maids. She had seen enough signs to know that everything spoken above a whisper in her quarters made its way to Ramzi.

"That is a beautiful dress, Selia. Which designer have you been turning to?" Lorien looked attentive as she eased open the flow of information.

"Thank you! This is by a Valemidas local known as Guillermo. You really must meet him. Lady Talnor has given him a full time position in her House. She snaps up all the best young designers. In fact, I think he is having a show there just this week. Won't you consider joining me? The Talnor House always throws the grandest parties. Or maybe I could convince him to hold a special show for you?"

Lorien hid her frustration—it was not Selia's fault that she could not leave this tower. No, that blame rested with her brother. Of course, if she could leave, she would not be spending any time in the Talnor House. They had been among Tryst's strongest supporters.

"That is quite thoughtful, Selia. I will think on it. Tell me, what makes you like his style so much?"

Selia continued in cheerful monologue, discussing the ins and outs of Guillermo's styles and those of other prominent designers. Lorien prodded the discussion along, dropping in exploratory questions whenever Selia paused for a breath or a drink of wine.

She had finished her first glass by the time Lorien shifted the focus to her second innocent, yet transitioning topic. The maid poured another full glass for both of them, nearly emptying the bottle. Lorien hoped the talk of dresses would lull the maids into inattention.

"I think you are right that Guillermo is the most promising. With winter coming, though, I may need something heavier. Perhaps next time we meet, you could bring me a few samples from designers outside Valemidas. I would love to see dresses done by one of the designers from the mountain region. Speaking of the mountains, how do you like the wine?"

"The wine is delicious." Selia chattered on, "Is this one from the mountains? I do love the mountains. Any view of the mountains will make my day. You said you would like some dresses from that region. Why, I would be delighted to gather some for you. I even know one designer from Icaria." Perfect, thought Lorien, relieved to detect Selia's transition to what she really wanted to know.

"She is a good designer, nothing fancy mind you, but delightfully solid and comfortable woolen wear for the winter. Just a week ago, I might have doubted whether she would be designing anything this year. Now I'm confident that she will be, since Icaria has surrendered to Valemidas. An Icarian designer would be honored to fashion a dress for the prince's sister. What color did you have in mind? A lot of the mountain styles are in gray and other neutrals."

Lorien calmly sipped her wine. "I was hoping for something more celebratory, maybe white or red? Anything dark would be out of place, wouldn't it?"

"Why yes, something celebratory might well be suitable. Certainly no black dresses will be called for." Selia winked.

The words washed over Lorien. So Andor lived, and he still had a chance of success. "You mentioned something about the Icarian designer perhaps not making anything this year. What do you think could stop the march of fashion?"

"Lorien, my dear," Selia answered, "you are right that the march of fashion cannot be stopped. I just meant that this particular designer might have gone out of business because of the war against Icaria. I had started to grow worried since your brother and his Lycurgus had been gone for so long. I figured they would have had little trouble with a mountain village like Icaria. Even if we did win, we lost many good men, I hear. I hate war, I really do. It leaves mothers like me helpless at home, in constant fear for our boys. Can you imagine my relief when I learned that Jon and Wren were alive and on their way home? Those boys are always up to trouble. I mean, I wasn't worried. There's no use in worrying, you know. I was concerned, that's all. I had faith that they would come back safe."

"It is encouraging to hear of your faith. Have your sons made it back home yet?"

"Thanks to God, yes. They returned with the prince last night, and Wren spoke with me briefly before tending to his many duties. As I told you before, they were both knighted. Well, it seems Jon was even invited to join the prince's Council of Knights. His new position kept him from coming to see me."

Selia sat back in her chair and took the last sip of her second glass of wine. She tapped the glass, and the maid began to open another bottle. "Do you plan to see your brother soon?" Selia asked.

"Yes, he plans to visit me." Lorien leaned forward, hoping that Selia would detect her urgency. "That is a great honor for Jon. Does that mean he was in the thick of the battle for Icaria?"

"It sure does. In fact, the craziest part of Wren's story was how they took the city. It seems that Jon was with the prince the whole time. Once they got over the walls, the prince and his men marched right in. By all accounts, Wren said, your brother was a force during the battle. He killed dozens of men as they took over the gate to the city. Can you imagine that? A prince in the thick of the fight? Anyway, it sounds like they waltzed through the city untouched after taking the gate. The prince went straight to the main hall of the city, ready to declare victory. Only, when they arrived and battered down the door, the Icarians were kneeling throughout the hall, with their weapons down."

"You won't believe what Wren told me next. The prince charged at a man who was a master swordsman much like himself. The other man was taller, with golden eyes, light hair and a beard."

Lorien nodded eagerly and looked down at her hands to avoid betraying that she knew it was Andor. Selia seemed to understand as she continued. "The two men fought fast and hard, and next thing you know the other man ends up on top of the prince with a sword pointed at him. Then, of all things, your sister appeared and somehow stopped this other man and saved your brother. I don't know the details, but it seems an Icarian leader started talking to the prince at that point. He said that the city had been handed over, that an official vote had passed the rule to Valemidas. The prince declared victory on the spot but seemed upset to have the city handed to him like that. By that time, your sister and the other man had disappeared, which made the prince furious. You have to spare any exaggerations of course. I'm just relaying what my boys told me. They are quite the storytellers."

Selia finished and silence hung in the air. Where Selia's meandering words had filled the small anteroom with a comfortable feeling; it now felt empty.

Lorien stood, eyes open wide, failing to contain her emotion. Where she had been surviving on morsels of information, she was now overflowing at this feast. She began to pace.

"Is he well now?" Lorien said quietly, emphasizing the "he" in a way that meant Andor but sounded like her brother.

"I think so," Selia answered. "The rumors have been all over the place. You can't trust half of them."

"You certainly can't trust the rumors." Lorien tried to recover some of her composure. "What happened next?"

"Wren heard from Jon that later that night Prince Tryst got heavy into some wine. As you know, he's not one to indulge in drink, so it had quite the effect. Apparently he kept saying the name of that other man and demanding that anyone in Valemidas or anywhere else who supported him be rooted out. He put Jon in charge of the search. The next morning, Tryst set the Lycurgus off on a brutal march, even faster than their trek into the mountains. Would you believe it if I told you they left the mountains just a couple weeks ago?"

"What happened with Jon's search?"

"Jon and his men have not found anything yet. It is said that many soldiers and knights have begun declaring their loyalty to this challenger, but do not worry about your brother. There has been no attempt at a coup." As Lorien sat back into her seat, Selia continued in a quiet and serious voice.

"Even here in Valemidas, people are whispering that the other man could be our last prince returned, and that he should have the throne. Now that is treason in my book, but it sounds like maybe the nobles have forgotten that. They are supposed to be the stable force in this city, but lately they seem as fickle as everyone else. The streets are bustling with some sort of hope I haven't seen in a long time. Surely that is because your brother has returned, right?"

"Surely it is," Lorien answered. "But I am concerned about this threat to my brother. How can we help Jon's search?" She posed her question loudly, to make sure the maids heard her spoken loyalty to her brother.

"Well, I think Jon has enlisted good helpers, like Ulysses and Father Yates. They will find him, do not fear. But maybe you can help by talking to the prince about it. You know he can trust Jon, so encourage him to give Jon as much authority as he can."

"Yes, I will take that under advisement." Lorien breathed in deliberately. Andor was alive and well enough to take back what was rightfully his, including Lorien. She exhaled. Selia had an amused grin that Lorien met for an instant of shared understanding. She then put every air of rigid royalty into her words.

"Thank you, Selia. You have been helpful as always. I do look forward to seeing the Icarian dresses when we next meet." Lorien rose to her feet, and Selia stood and bowed low.

"If I may be so bold," Selia whispered, "there is one more thing I should mention."

Lorien motioned for her to continue, exuding calm.

202

"It's a message that Wren wanted me to pass along. He said you'd know it, something an old bard once said about young love. 'My bounty'—wait, let me make sure I get the cadence right." Selia continued in a measured voice, "The message is,

"My bounty is as boundless as the sea,
My love as deep; the more I give to thee,
The more I have, for both are infinite."

Fighting the wave of emotion, Lorien replied with a simple farewell. "Thank you again, Selia. I look forward to our next meeting."

"Farewell, my dear lady." Selia turned and walked out the door.

When she could no longer hear Selia's steps, Lorien realized that she was holding her breath. Releasing a huge gasp, Lorien fled to her bedroom and slammed the door behind her, shutting out the maids. She let go of all the trembling and joyous tears that she had held back. He was alive, and his message meant that they would meet and they would marry as he had promised in his letter.

She could not even begin to imagine how he would make it happen, but he would. She laughed at the thought that her Icarian dress would not be ready in time.

Chapter 20

Fear Mongering

**"The essential vice,
the utmost evil, is pride.
It is the complete
anti-God state of mind."**

Ramzi was not looking forward to Tryst's visit. He would be in a foul mood, returning to Valemidas without the head of the Icarian leader. He would not have set off to conquer the insignificant city if conquering meant only another subservient outpost. And, if Ramzi's reports were right, a leader had sprung up against Tryst's will. It certainly did not help that the leader was rumored to look like Andor.

Ramzi still could not believe that it was possible to escape the Gloaming. But what if the deposed prince had? We can recover that ground, Ramzi thought. He and his followers would find Andor and assassinate him. His god had answered his prayers before, and he would do so again. More sacrifices to the Gloaming would be needed. No more leaving anything to chance.

Tryst's journey had also brought successes. He had won his victory over Icaria, and there was no question that the city served him. The only question now was how obedient it would be. Those were the perfect ingredients for exporting a noble house to deal with the frozen place. And Tryst had subtly grabbed power in Albemarle. That town was a plump treasure—much finer than Icaria—and Tryst could perhaps even satisfy Sir Talnor by giving him control there. Tryst could quickly steamroll a few closer villages to clear out other nobles.

Yes, Ramzi assured himself, we will dismantle the nobles and eliminate the limits they impose on the prince. That was the only sure way to his victory. When Tryst gained complete control, then Ramzi believed his god would give him control over Tryst. Control must reside in the ultimate source of power. Ramzi would convince Tryst to swear fealty to his Sunan people if they invaded. If they did not invade, Ramzi and his god would be the master of this city. Valemidas would be a city of power, control, and obedience.

So it was not the nobles, the Sunans, or even Andor that troubled Ramzi most. Instead it was the weak loyalty and faith of the Valemidans. They had bristled at Ramzi's guidance, shunning the regulations designed to make their lives better. These were little things. If they signed up for identification numbers as demanded, then the city would have a full registry of inhabitants. If he had a full registry, then Ramzi could ensure that everyone cooperated with giving first sons to the Lycurgus. The Lycurgus would be faithful to Tryst and to him, which would ensure unity and discipline and peace. Ramzi could not understand why the people rebelled—his rules were for their own good.

Whatever their reasons, Ramzi would need to report a few failures to Tryst. It did not bode well, as the prince had already seemed less appreciative of Ramzi's guidance in recent messages.

He considered again the ways he might phrase his report. The word "failure" surely would not be said, nor would "rebelled." He would explain to Tryst that the people were just taking time to come around. All of his new laws made sense, and the people would come to understand that. Indeed, yesterday Ramzi had ordered that all the older children of Valemidas be schooled in the virtues of the new system. They would be taught a more orderly life, because it would be a safer life. Maybe change could not be finished in the short time while Tryst was gone, but at least the right changes had started. If the people could not be faithful by their own willpower, his laws would make them.

Ramzi heard a knock on the door behind him. He had instructed his clerks to inform him as soon as the prince had gone to his chambers. "You may enter," he said as he turned. The man who sauntered through the door was the last man Ramzi would have expected.

"Ramzi, good evening!" Jacodin Talnor smelled of ale but had clear eyes. "You sure don't look happy to see me. Were you expecting your dear prince?" Ramzi stared down the pompous young lord, who took a seat in the lone chair of the chamber, without asking. It seemed the night was not too young for a loose tongue and intentional mocking.

Noticing the sword at Jacodin's side, Ramzi first deflated his own tension. As much as he would like to belittle the noble's son, he could not risk a fight. He leaned against the window, facing the young man. "Jacodin Talnor, I always liked you half as much as a noble's son, and now it seems you are a knight. Did you kill any Icarians?"

The question had its effect. "Well, no," Jacodin stammered, "or not directly anyway, I mean, I was there for the battle. You should have seen the men of Valemidas storm the walls. We crushed them!"

"No doubt," Ramzi said dismissively. "But now you interrupt your celebrations to visit me. Why do I deserve such an honor?"

"Ramzi, you're a dark one. Never up for fun, are you? Anyway, yes, this is my first night back in Valemidas and the Prince is throwing the first feast for the nobles in honor of the victory. I was just warming up for the party when my father gave me a message. He insisted that I deliver it to you in person. It's not about the Icarians. Whatever the point, here are the words of Sir Ryn Talnor. He said to tell you that—it was something about—" The boy belched before he could finish his sentence.

"Out with it!" Ramzi did not have time for this imbecile.

"My father said: 'The gathering will be called tomorrow. House Talnor stays with you, but others are drifting. Beware of

House Davosman. Much is at risk.' That's the message. I guess it's up to you to figure out exactly what that means. He didn't tell me anything else. If that's all, then—" Jacodin stood and stretched into an arrogant pose, like a rooster about to die in a cock fight.

"If that's all you have for me, Jacodin, then you may leave." Ramzi's mind was dicing through the concerning implications of the message, and why the noble would possibly have used his son as his messenger.

"I know I can leave, Ramzi. For a dark puppet of the Prince, you sure do pretend to have power. Don't forget who the nobles are, Minister. I hope you'll join the festivities tonight. You look like you could use a drink."

"That's enough, Jacodin." The boy has no discretion, Ramzi thought. He was just the kind of man who needed stronger shackles of law. "Enjoy your evening while you can," Ramzi said as he prodded Jacodin out the door.

Ramzi forced his mind away from the incompetent knight. The message was more important. "Others are drifting"—he pieced the words together again. They could only mean that Tryst was losing the support of the nobles.

That could not be happening already. Ramzi's efforts had been nothing short of groveling for the nobles. Surely they had seen his increased taxes on the people. Ramzi had not applied his laws to the nobles' traditions, taxes, or politics. They had served their purpose in putting Tryst in power. It was not yet time to end their purposes once and for all. No, Ramzi thought, the people must fear the prince more before he can pull his sleight of hand. Only when that fear has gripped them will the nobles be ripe for destruction. Then Tryst would truly rule this continent.

As he began to pace, Ramzi again considered how he would present this to Tryst. It was bad enough to start with the prince's foul mood. On top of that, Ramzi had to report on the setbacks in Valemidas. That was a simple report—the people were still learning obedience. Ramzi resolved not to mention the Talnor message to Tryst, not tonight anyway. He breathed more easily having made that decision.

He sat in the chair that Jacodin had occupied and stared into the fire. It was burning low and needed wood. He rubbed his hands together to keep away a growing chill. Where were his clerks, anyway? Tryst must have returned to his chambers by now. He decided he would put on another log himself.

As he rose to his feet, he felt cold hands clamp down on his shoulders and push him back to the seat.

"I'd suggest you not try to move from that chair. I don't want any loud noises, either. I hope you can keep your patience better than you did with that young knight. You need to tell me a few things."

Ramzi's stomach roiled at the voice of Sebastian. This was not the first time he had appeared unannounced in his room. Why did the man always have to show up at his back, catching him off guard? Being around him was like sitting in a tub of cold water, under Tryst's shadow.

The tall man walked around Ramzi's chair. He was wearing all black as usual. He casually picked up a round log resting by the fireplace and poked at the dwindling flames. Fear swelled inside Ramzi as each second passed in silence.

"You see, Ramzi, if you leave a fire alone, it goes out peacefully. The coals slowly burn away, leaving only a pile of ash. You can then toss out the ash and make ready for your next fire." He tossed the log into the fire and crouched to watch it burn. The flames licked the edges of the dry wood and ignited it, refueling the blaze.

Ramzi felt powerless in Sebastian's presence. There was no doubt who would win a physical struggle between them.

Sebastian stood, took two steps closer to Ramzi, and crouched to one knee. "If you add more logs to the fire, Ramzi, it just keeps burning. The fire gets bigger, and then it's not so easy to put out. There's nothing peaceful about it."

Ramzi could not keep his patience any longer. "You are wasting my time, Sebastian. Quit hiding behind riddles. If you have no official business here, then I will be going. The Prince will want to see me tonight."

"You are such a fanatic that you can't see your excesses. The Prince certainly does not *want* to see you tonight. You have failed miserably as his Minister. This city is boiling with discontent. The people will not abide your yoke."

"I did only as the Prince and I had agreed. The changes I made are minor, designed to improve the lives of the people. The Prince will understand, even if you can't. You lurk in the darkness. I am bringing justice—law and order as revealed by my faith, which I am giving to the people. They are the ones with excesses that must be restrained. Fighting, drinking, the public show of women's skin, disorderly streets, loud voices, unfaithful children—these vices are a plague on the people. You must know this, we share it as Sunans." Ramzi touched the tattooed stars by his eye, hoping to remind Sebastian of his own symbol and what it meant.

"We share nothing but the city of our birth. You are a plague on freedom, and you have left a stain on the Prince's reputation. For that, you will be punished. I did not come here to listen to you babble about your politics. I want answers. First, what did that message from Talnor mean? Why beware of Davosman?"

Ramzi hesitated. "That message was for me and the prince. Before I say a word, you have to show me some authority for your questions. You have no privileged position with him, compared to me."

"You know my authority is from the Prince," Sebastian responded as he leaned into Ramzi's face. He then whispered, "But tonight you will answer my questions because I will kill you if you do not."

Sebastian raised a curved blade, which glinted in the fire light before his eyes. "And if you do not answer my questions well enough, I will pull the answers out of you." He leaned back against the mantle and began whittling a piece of firewood. "I will ask one more time. What was that message from Jacodin Talnor about?"

Ramzi stammered out the rough outline of his thoughts. He was relieved that he could say without lying that he did not know exactly what the message meant. He was more relieved that Sebastian accepted the explanation.

Sebastian sat quietly for a while before speaking again. "My second question is about Ravien. What do you know about her relationships?"

Ramzi could not suppress a laugh. "Come on, Sebastian, what kind of question is that? You are the spy here. I know hardly a thing about the prince's sister. She is more secretive than you are."

"What do you know about her relationships?"

"I know next to nothing. I know that she wants me to know next to nothing. I will admit this, because I think many have the same story. Long ago she rejected without compromise my attempts to entreat her. No man in this city can ignore the stunning woman, but she operates as if men don't exist, except for her brother, of course. I would love to know about her relationships. Once upon a time, I would have loved to be a part of them. But all I know about Ravien is that she holds her cards closer to her chest than anyone."

"What do you know about a merchant named Wren?"

"Less than I would like. I know that he was part of the opposition to Tryst, before he became prince. I haven't heard a thing about him in a long time. Again, you are the spy here. Why are you asking me these questions?"

Ramzi's question lingered unanswered. He wondered whether there was some connection between Ravien and Wren. He doubted it. She would never stoop for a merchant, particularly a greedy one opposed to her brother. Ramzi was more intrigued by Sebastian's questions—signs of weakness. Maybe this was all bluffing by the spy. He should know better than to seek answers from the Prince's advisor. The advisor analyzed information and guided the prince. It was Sebastian's job to provide the information in the first place.

Sebastian interrupted his thoughts. "One last question, Ramzi. What do you make of these rumors that Andor showed up in Icaria?"

Ramzi jumped to his feet. "Andor is gone!" He shouted. "He is in the Gloaming, and Tryst is our prince. Even if Andor came back, he would have no power, because my god, our Sunan god, would personally see to it that he dies. His Excellency in Sunan commanded it!"

Sebastian's eyes burned with excitement. "Thank you, Ramzi. We are finished here. Tryst is not going to be pleased."

Ramzi lunged forward in anger, which was a mistake. He saw the punch coming too late. Sebastian slammed the hilt of his blade into Ramzi's head, knocking him unconscious.

*   *   *

Sebastian was pleased that Ramzi knew less than he had feared, but it was better to leave him incapacitated on the floor than free to maneuver this night. The traitor moved on to his next mission—kidnapping the prince's sister.

Chapter 21

Becoming One

**"Let me not to the marriage
of true minds admit impediments.
Love is not love which alters
when it alteration finds."**

Lorien had thought she would never see this day. She laughed inside, because she also never thought it would happen like this. Sebastian had appeared in her room after dusk, drugged her maids to sleep, and rappelled out of the tower with her in his arms. She had left the city hooded on the back of his horse, with a few treasured belongings.

She had envisioned months to prepare for a wedding with hundreds if not thousands crammed into the Valemidas Cathedral. The people and the nobles alike would have craned their necks to see her in this dress. It was structured at the top and freeform at the bottom, with infinite layers of silk spilling to the ground from the bodice. A diamond pendant plunged down from her bare neck, and a silver diadem framed her hair.

Running her hands along the white fabric, she thought of her mother who had given the dress to her. It was a pleasant memory for a blink, before her thoughts bounced from her mother to her father to her half-brother. *I will not let Tryst spoil this,* she insisted to herself. *This is our night.*

"What ill thought just swept over your face?"

Lorien had almost forgotten that she was not alone. The small stone cottage in the countryside outside Valemidas seemed like a solitary haven. It had a single room, with a mirror and a fireplace. That was all Lorien really needed to prepare, even if her royal quarters would have been more comfortable. As her mother would have said, a princess wears her royalty inside, and she brings it to every place she goes.

Looking into the mirror, she thought that her mother would have looked a lot like this on her wedding night, with the same long curls framing her face. Lorien turned her glance to a deeper place in the mirror, at the other face. It was sharper, darker, but with the same mouth and the same eyes.

"The thought was of our brother, Ravien. It came, and it is gone. I will not be thinking of him again tonight."

"Tryst will recover," Ravien whispered as she stepped closer and began to tie the delicate ribbons that stretched from Lorien's mid-back to low waist. "He shares more of my blood than yours, and I believe that he holds to truth in his core. But you are right, no more thoughts of him. Tonight is about you and Andor. I still do not understand how you managed to entangle that man."

Lorien laughed softly. "I wish I could claim some superior knowledge or tactic. I also wish I knew more about his past months. Surely he has changed, but it has been too dangerous for us to communicate beyond a few sentences here and there. Whatever it was that happened, Yates and Selia hinted to me that it has drained some confidence from him, leaving more resolve and humility in its place. His written words have seemed more prone to melancholy. Even so, I believe he has enough spirit and goodness within him to unseat Tryst and rule again."

Ravien lifted her brow at the mention of her brother. Lorien grinned innocently. "I said I would not think of him, didn't I? Well, I suppose it is okay if I am comparing him to Andor."

"Let's not compare. Tryst will recover, and I believe he will help Andor in the end. We need both of them. More than that, we need them working together." Ravien raised her eyes from Lorien's back and looked intently at her sister through the mirror. "Remember what our father said on his death bed?"

Lorien nodded. Her father had looked so weak. Covered in a light sheet, his body was half its normal size, pale and fragile. Where a huge, powerful man had once laid, a shriveled body had rasped out its last breaths, under the weight of poison from an unknown source. He had called his two daughters forward before he said his last words to his teenage son, Tryst. The words to his daughters had shaken Lorien then, and they still did.

I leave Tryst in your keeping. He needs your protection, not from those outside, but from what's inside. Love him, and make sure Andor stays close to him. Andor would be the better prince. My son should never have the throne.

"Is that what's been driving you all these years?" Lorien asked.

"Among other things, yes. I think father was right all along. He always did have a talent for prediction."

"He predicted this night." Lorien took one last look at herself in the mirror and turned to face Ravien. A rare look of surprise graced her sister's face.

"Truly? He predicted that you would marry Andor? We were young—you had just become a woman. Andor was barely older than I, but five years older than you. What did father say?"

Lorien smiled at the memory. "Father told me, a few years before Andor became prince, that I must be kind to Andor. I was fourteen at the time. It was a strange statement, so I asked him why. He was wearing that wry old smile that stretched over his entire face. He knelt down to me and whispered, 'Lorien, you will marry Andor. I have seen it in both of your eyes. Trust me.' I told him that he was silly, that a potential prince would never marry me when he could have anyone he wanted. Father laughed at that and scooped me up into a great bear hug. Despite what I said then, I took his words to heart. I think my feelings for Andor gained the hope they needed to thrive that very day."

Ravien wiped a tear from Lorien's eye, and embraced her tightly. "I wish father were here to see you tonight, Lorien. He would be so proud of his beautiful daughter."

"Of both his beautiful daughters." Lorien smiled at her sister. She had always admired Ravien's way of beauty. Tonight she wore a long black gown, open at the back except for thin strands that crossed like loose laces. Her hair was up, revealing lean porcelain shoulders sculpted by years of play at battle. As striking as it was, Lorien thought white would have been better this night. "I think father would be confused to see you wearing black, Ravien. Even tonight?"

"Tonight of all nights. You know I wear black to reflect my sadness, but also to dim my joy. At least it is a gown of luxury, rather than leather. The man I chose has that refined taste. Besides, if someone were to spot me after the wedding, it would be a shame for me to give away that the happiest occasion in a long time is happening this very night."

"True enough. And you might look odd in white. The contrast with your sinister smile would be too much for mortal men."

"That is why I would never settle for a mortal man, with perhaps one exception."

"A mercantile exception?"

"A sharp and driven and cunning exception. No one makes me laugh like he does."

"His humor will do you good, my dear sister."

A knock on the door interrupted Lorien.

"Wren! Please come in!" Lorien announced as she flashed a grin at her sister.

"Thank you, my lady," Wren said and bowed low. "You look stunning and," his gaze shifted to Ravien, "ravishing." He stepped closer and took the darker sister's hand. "All is ready. Are you?"

"Yes," the sisters said.

"Then it is time." Wren led the sisters out, one on each arm.

Lorien soaked up the energy of the warm summer night. She could hear the chorus of insects and frogs all around. It may not have been the grand wedding she had expected, but nothing had gone quite as planned. Her expectations and wounds from the past evaporated in the moonlight as she was caught up in the excitement.

It was a short walk to the small structure on the bank of the River Tine. The barn was built of river stones, covered in ivy, and hardly big enough to hold a dozen horses.

Father Yates was standing at the entrance. He leaned against the worn wooden doorway. As usual, he wore a plain brown robe and a smile.

"The wedding party has arrived!" Yates announced cheerfully. "And the bride, my how she shines like the divine light."

He bowed and made way for Ravien and Wren to enter. They slid through the cracked door, and Yates pulled Lorien gently to the side.

"Thank you, Father. How is he?" Lorien tried to sound calm. Earlier that evening, Sebastian had passed a short, sealed note to her from Andor. He had written again of his love for her, and had explained that they would have more time to talk tonight, but that the wedding would have to be hidden, official, and brief. Things were still too perilous with Tryst's anger high, he had written, and the real celebration could come later. She accepted the wisdom of it, even though she yearned for more.

"My dear, he is doing as well as we could hope." The priest's eyes looked deep into Lorien's. "He will have great need for your tender touch in these days to come. I believe no other man could have survived what he did. You will be the one he needs most. The path ahead is fraught with risk."

Lorien nodded. She would not cower at the uncertainty. She would trust Andor.

"Come," Yates said, holding out his arm. "I will escort you in."

As they walked through the door, the brightness and the faces overwhelmed Lorien. Ravien was waiting to take her other arm. Lorien reached for it and found strength.

The tiny building was packed. It was lit by candles glimmering along the walls and the ancient wooden rafters above. The soft light shone on the faces of maybe fifty people crammed into every inch of space. Lorien knew some guests would be there, but she had not dared hoped for this. Many were friends she had not seen in months, all of them loyal to Andor. Their smiles blended into an overwhelming warmth.

Andor stood on the raised platform at the far end of the room. Wren was at his side. Once Lorien's eyes met his, everything else melted away. He was more stunning than she had remembered. Standing before the room, his presence was commanding, like that of a god among men. His eyes reflected the golden light of the room, and his smile reached from one end of his face to the other.

She was walking down the aisle before she could catch her breath. He reached out his hands as she stepped up to his side. He looked at her with the same intensity she remembered. He swept her into his arms and held tight, as if he would never let go. She buried her face into his chest and wept in joy. She prayed that the moment would last forever, but he gently kneeled down and looked up into her eyes.

"Lorien, my love, you are more beautiful than ever. Will you marry me now?"

She knew the answer but could barely speak. She took a huge breath to steady herself. "Yes, Andor."

Before she could say another word, he engulfed her again in his arms. When he finally released her, she remembered for the first time that they were not alone. All the guests were cheering. As she turned to glance at the crowd, her smile was the brightest thing in the room.

Father Yates began to recite the rite of marriage. The traditional bread and wine were passed to the guests, who ate and drank to mark the beginning of the celebration. The small morsels helped settle the butterflies in Lorien's stomach. Next came the traditional vows. Lorien and Andor said the words sealing themselves together forever.

The joy of being beside Andor made the words feel easy and natural. Lorien had hoped for this for so long that it now felt preordained. As Yates declared them man and wife, Andor pulled her close and touched his lips to hers.

The crowd erupted in cheers. Andor squeezed her hand and nodded, signaling that he would speak to the guests. She turned with him to face the room. Andor raised his hand, holding it high until the room was still again.

"You are good to come, friends. We would not be here without you. Lorien and I owe you our deepest thanks. There is a steep road ahead, but let's take this time to recognize the good work that you all have done, much of it hidden from each other, to bring us to this special moment together."

"We give thanks to Scarlett and the women of her network of inns. They hosted Ravien and me in secret rooms as we made our escape from the mountains to Valemidas."

In the back of the room, three beautiful women in immodest dresses bowed deeply. Lorien had never seen them before. She would not have forgotten women like that.

"We give thanks to Ulysses, Tel, and their knights," Andor continued, "who worked without anyone's knowledge to monitor and keep Lorien safe in Valemidas. They held back Ramzi without inciting a rebellion before it was ready."

Ulysses, Tel, and the men around them beamed in response. Lorien recognized some of their faces as the men who had escorted her visitors in recent weeks.

"We give thanks to Pikeli, who learned who I was and, against his usual manner, kept quiet, and told his squire to do the same."

A slight, average-looking man hopped up and down in the middle of the room. "You hide as well as a giant in a room of ants!" He said loudly to Andor. "And you better take down Ramzi. That man has banned direct inquiries to the prince. How is a talker like me supposed to express himself? And one other thing—"

His squire elbowed him in the side. "You all now see the impressiveness of this man's restraint for me." Andor joked, and the room filled with laughter. Andor held his hand up again.

"We give thanks to Sebastian. He was our spy and our distracting agent. My foe would have known of me much earlier if not for him. He handled Ramzi and brought my bride to me, earning the first part of his reward."

The foreign man nodded grimly. Lorien felt a shiver run down her spine—she was beyond thankful for his help, but he had spoken hardly a word as he rescued her from the palace. He was a man of dangerous power. It made her uneasy that she had no idea what the first, much less second, part of his reward would be.

"You have my word, Sebastian, that I will deliver on my promise." Lorien felt Andor's grip on her hand tighten. Sebastian bowed in response. The expression on his face never changed.

"We give thanks to Selia, who hosted me and then helped Lorien build my support here in Valemidas without detection. The wives of many men have been whispering in their ears of my imminent return."

The bright woman curtsied in the first row. "Anything to stop this mess of laws mandating head-to-toe dark clothes. I need my flare," she laughed and spun. Her yellow and orange dress swirled around her, again leaving Lorien impressed that a woman like her could manage a resistance movement in secrecy. She supposed it was like hiding in plain sight.

"We give thanks to Father Yates. He is a rock of faithfulness in this world. He lives out the divine disciplines better than anyone I know. He nourished me when I was at my lowest, physically, mentally, and spiritually. I would not be here, and I would not be fit to serve you again, if not for him."

The old priest smiled and tears filled his eyes as he spoke in response. "God has blessed us through you, Prince Andor. You have always been great, and now you are learning to be humble. You recognize your need for God and for others, and with that wisdom you will remain a force for the good. You have just started on this long path, and it will not stay straight. But you have sensed despair and felt the touch of light. Continue to seek it, and you will grow. If you grow, we will all be ruled in justice and righteousness."

Yates looked toward Lorien with a grin. "Learning to love your princess better every day is a perfect start."

"Indeed it is!" Andor answered happily. He then turned to look at Wren.

"Last, and very far from least, we give thanks to Wren and Jon. They have been my friends for life, but with a deeper bond now. They stayed loyal when many fell away. They risked everything they had earned to accompany me on the journey. They served their roles like mighty men. Words cannot do justice to their feats."

"Jon could not be with us tonight. You all know him as one who could vanquish any foe but who offers kindness instead. While we celebrate here, he stays close to Tryst, as is his duty. He fought valiantly at Tryst's side in Icaria. He serves on the Knight's Council, but remains loyal to us. I wish he was here now, that he could know of our joy, but his absence is one of our greatest securities, and a key to our victory. When he learns what we plan, I trust that he will understand that it would have endangered too much to have him here."

"Finally, Wren, the shrewd trader, who gave up the business he mastered for me. Your mind cut through to the best plans, and your gold funded it all. For your service and friendship, I am indebted."

"And now to began repaying," Andor announced the crowd, "I give the stage to Wren and Ravien." Lorien saw puzzled looks on the guest's faces, much like her own. "When she and I traveled together," Andor said to Wren, "she told me of your encounters, and how her amusement with a merchant grew into love for a knight. I wish the best for you two."

"Another wedding!" Father Yates announced. The confused murmur in the crowd turned into cheering as Andor led Lorien to Ravien's side, and Wren stepped to the spot where Andor had been. Ravien turned and embraced her sister.

"I wanted to tell you," Ravien said excitedly. "Wren proposed just yesterday. We thought it would be better not to distract you before your own wedding."

"Indeed!" Lorien responded with a smile. "I wish I could say I am surprised that my sister has kept a secret from me." She looked at Wren. "I could not have asked for a better husband for my sister."

Wren beamed back proudly and took Ravien's hands.

Father Yates began the second marriage ceremony. As he spoke the ritual words again, Lorien was filled with joy at the thought of the pair. Ravien was the elusive princess. Wren was the sharp man of the world. She was the dark mystery. He was the trading savant. They were both like assassins, her in royal politics and him in mercantile plotting. The differences in their facades evaporated under the brightness of their focused and powerful souls. Their union was sure to bring excitement.

Over as it began, with cheers and joy, the ceremonies ended as Father Yates declared both couples to be married. He encouraged the guests to celebrate at the Morning Crest, an inn where neither knights nor nobles would be found this night, but still to speak no word of what had happened here. He then led the couples outside, and the guests followed.

"My deepest congratulations to you four. It is a special time when the light shines on two couples such as this. I believe you know your places and your duties this night, so I will take my leave."

He touched each of their foreheads as a blessing, and then urged them on. Lorien and Ravien exchanged a hug before parting.

Andor took Lorien's hand and led her along the River Tine, further away from Valemidas. He beckoned for silence with a finger pressed to her lips. "And now, another surprise for you."

The song of katydids filled the night, and fireflies hovered above the glistening river. They turned to walk down the bank just after a willow that leaned far out over the water. A dark figure rested on a slender boat at the water's edge.

"I see you, Andor."

"You are hidden from my sight as always, Sebastian."

Sebastian smiled in response. "Out of sight, out of mind. All is ready."

He spoke not another word as they boarded and he rowed across the broad river. Once they were half way across, Lorien could see the lights of Valemidas far off, raised up like a torch in the midnight landscape. Not long ago the city had made her shudder; tonight it comforted. The men and women there might soon be released from oppression.

As they drew close to the south shore, Sebastian dragged the boat to land. Andor stepped out, and before she could protest, swept her up into his arms. They both burst into laughter as he climbed up the bank. Sebastian stayed behind on guard.

"Why not start with you in my arms?" Andor asked as he ascended.

"Because I can very well walk myself!" Lorien settled into a relaxed pose as she looked up into his eyes. "But I will let you whisk me away on our wedding night."

Andor carried her uphill to the surface of a large stone looming twenty feet above the river below. A structure the size of a small room sat atop it.

"How did you?" Lorien gasped upon seeing it. It had obviously been hauled up in pieces, and it looked like a mini-castle. Four posts rose from the corners, and stones had been stacked to form low walls around it. Candles burned in nooks along the inside of the walls. A feathered bed formed the floor, and the moon and stars provided the ceiling.

Andor laid her gently on the bed. She looked up into his eyes and pulled his head down to hers. They had been apart for so long, but their bodies felt like home to each other as they united.

Afterwards, they reclined together, still and serene, as if the past months had never happened. Despite the many words that had not yet passed between them, their hearts knew that their love was stronger than ever.

"Hope for this night preserved me while I was away," Andor eventually said as he turned away to look up at the stars.

She took hold of his arm and ran her fingers along the scars. "You still have not told me what happened to you. Yates hinted at things, but he held back much. Andor, please tell me about the Gloaming."

"The memories are painful, my love." Andor sighed uneasily as if his thoughts were drifting to the past. "I feel like I conquered death to get out of there. I was brought to nothing down, resigned to die. Then a man named Lucian died to save me. It somehow helped me glimpse a divine light. The Gloaming is horrific and miserable, crushing and senseless, but Lucian's sacrifice is what it took to make me understand."

Lorien looked at her husband tenderly. She had always respected him, more than any person she had ever met. His newly quiet and calm demeanor made his natural gifts seem all the more powerful. She waited for him to continue speaking.

"I will of course tell you more, but my focus now is on prevailing in this first battle," he said with confidence. "What comes after that is harder."

"What comes next is restoring our city to what it once was. Why is that harder?"

"Restoration is much harder than destruction," Andor turned to look into Lorien's eyes. His voice was measured. "We must restore Tryst. Lorien, I must tell you what I believe will be next. After Tryst falls, we will cast him down to the Gloaming. I will tend to Valemidas in the following days, but soon after I must go down there for him, to try to bring him back."

Lorien could not suppress her surprise but she also could not doubt his sincerity. "I had feared that you would have grown more harsh. I did not expect you to soften toward the man who betrayed you."

"Our love for Tryst, the fallen man that he is, requires that we give him the same opportunity that I had in the Gloaming."

"Love for Tryst?" Lorien asked flatly. "Whatever familial love he had from me is lost. You cannot love him after what he did to you." She traced the outlines of his brow and cheekbones. "It inspires me to hear of your escape, but you cannot sacrifice yourself for him. He is not worth it. I will not have your life traded for his again."

"We both loved Tryst before. He has been corrupted under Ramzi's guidance, but I believe he can be brought back. He would not have rebelled against me if not for Ramzi's poisonous words seeping into his mind. It would be a shame to lose the great man deep down in Tryst."

"What Tryst once was matters less than what we are going to be. The risk will be too high."

"If we are going to be the restorers of our people and servants of the light, then I must do this. Let acceptance be your first act of faith." His face was patient, imploring. "I have come back once from the Gloaming, and I will come back again."

"I might believe you if you were not going down there for Tryst. It will be hard enough to depose him here in Valemidas. If we succeed in that, he will harbor even deeper hate for you. Meeting him in the Gloaming is a death wish."

"He will be weakened down there. After a week of starvation, he will be ready to mend his ways. Ravien assures me that he is open to change. She would not have helped me if she did not believe that, and I would not be here if she had not helped me."

"My sister put you up to this?"

"Your sister is responsible for me being here today, and her only condition was that I not cast away my prior respect for her brother, and yours. If Tryst listens to me, I come back with him. If he does not, I come back alone. Either way, I will return to you."

The words of Lorien's father echoed in her mind. *Love him, and make sure Andor stays close to him.* She believed that her father's son was lost and gone forever, replaced by a backstabbing tyrant, but she could not disregard her father's charge, nor Andor's conviction. The weeks of plotting were ingrained on his face.

She closed her eyes as the truth sank in. She admired his commitment, even if she feared its result. The pain would tear her apart if she lost him again. And yet, she could not stand in the way of his force of being. That was the man who had long inspired her love and had only grown in his strength. Choosing courage in the face of fear, she resolved to support Andor, come what may, and to live fully in this moment.

"If you do not return," she said playfully as she climbed up on his chest, "I will come after you, and you do not want that.

You are mine, and I will not allow you to be lost in a prison cave."

"I will not be lost again." Andor smiled. "I have seen the light, and it has brought me to you."

The touch of their lips silenced the talk. The night was still young.

Chapter 22

The Scale Tips

**"The tree of liberty must be
refreshed from time to time,
With the blood of patriots and tyrants.
It is its natural manure."**

The sky was full of amorphous clouds, the kind that Jon loved to watch. He laid on the grass of the palace grounds, looking for shapes in the soft wonderland above. A breeze rustled leaves in the trees above and played on his skin.

As he enjoyed the dappled light, he caught sight of a large cloud splitting in two. The smaller piece of the cloud seemed to have ripped itself out, as if determined to find its own plot of sky for itself. The breakaway cloud drifted towards another, even larger cloud. The larger cloud looked like it had fingers reaching out to seize the approaching cloud. As the smaller cloud touched the edges of the larger mass, the combination was immediate. The massive fluff had engulfed the assault of the little cloud, as if the separation had never existed at all.

Jon rose to a sitting position, assuring himself that the clouds signaled nothing. Still, he could not shake a growing anxiety. He wished Wren were around. He had hardly seen his brother since their knighting in Albemarle, and not at all since leaving Icaria. Jon thought Wren would probably rather be in their store than lying in the grass. If he were in Jon's position now, Wren would turn his ambition to forecasting every move that Tryst and all the other players might make.

But that was Wren. Jon could not bring himself to overthink his task today. The weather was beautiful. Just as there were divisions in the sky, divisions would soon rip through Valemidas. Rather than worrying about the others, Jon tried to focus on his own duty.

He walked through the grounds, towards the palace's central keep looming above him. Here there was a natural sanctuary of ancient trees within the stone walls. Something about the trees, and the soft grass underneath, helped ease Jon's concerns. As much as the city churned, these grounds remained in balance year after year.

As Jon stepped into the small amphitheater where the Prince and nobles would soon meet, he paused to admire the place. Wedged between the palace grounds' towering trees and the central keep, the meeting site had witnessed much of Valemidas' political history.

It was a small venue for such events, a snug fit for a hundred people. The flat ground gave way to steeply sloping stone benches carved into the earth. The bowl was cut in half by the keep's walls looming almost a hundred feet above, forming the back of the amphitheater. The bottom of the bowl was perhaps ten paces across, and in its center rose a small platform, half as tall as a man.

Everything about the design was simple, functional. Yet the spot gained grandeur from its setting. Stuck between the walls and the trees, the semi-circle felt hidden, submerged in the ground. And usually it was ignored, except when the nobles called upon the Prince. Custom demanded that they do that no more than twice a year, but it was said the nobles never needed to call the best princes for such a formal audience.

A few nobles had begun to gather and take their places on the lower benches. Jon made his way to the platform. Last night the nobles had joined Tryst for a feast to celebrate the victories over Icaria and the renewed allegiance of Albemarle. Jon had been there, and had tried to steady Tryst when he got heavy into the wine.

The prince had been in a rage about his missing sister Lorien, but he had been too proud to announce that she was gone. He probably figured that her flight had something to do with Andor. Jon thought Tryst was probably right, but the prince had been keeping him too close for him to learn what Andor, Wren, and the others were planning.

Tryst's celebration with the nobles had fallen flat. While Tryst was declaring victory, the nobles were complaining about how Valemidas had already changed, and for the worse, since Tryst became prince. Tryst seemed to have been too lost in his anger, vanity, and drink to notice it. Even with Jon's limited knowledge of the nobles' politics, it was clear to him that discontent had been sown among them while Tryst was away.

The witness accounts of Andor's return had fueled that discontent. Some of the nobles had loved Andor and had been grieved upon his disappearance. Jon guessed they would support him now, if he were to return. Certainly the man who raised him, Sir Davosman, would.

Jon watched the nobles as they steadily filled the amphitheater. He stood on the platform, leaning against the stone wall that rose far above him. From that perch, he could see that something was amiss. By the time most nobles had arrived, there was an eager, rebellious tone to their interactions. Jon thought of a pack of hyenas, ready to attack a wounded lion.

The bells of the palace's chapel began to sound midday. The chimes resonated in the amphitheater. The last bell rang and left an echo in the air. Just as the echo faded, the sound of a trumpet boomed into the bowl.

Tryst walked in from the right. His head was lifted, proud, triumphant. He wore his usual black. Striding purposefully, he came to the front of the platform, without gifting anyone with eye contact. He jumped onto the platform and took three steps to stand in front of the lone chair. It was a simple stone block, set in the middle of the platform, with the keep's wall serving as its back. The seat afforded a view of everyone in the amphitheater.

Trailing behind Tryst was the rest of his Knight's Council. Jon realized immediately that he should have walked in with them. Hopefully Tryst would not care. Jon had hardly been a knight for two months, and Tryst had many other things on his mind.

Jon felt out of place as the nine other members of the Council, in full armor, approached in a formal line. They fanned out into positions along Tryst's right and left. Jon went to join them as they fell into rank, becoming the knight furthest to Tryst's left.

While Tryst took his seat, the knights remained standing, poised for action. The nobles settled into their seats with growing unease, casting furtive glances at each other. Silence lingered and the space seemed to shrink, with everyone enclosed within this normally peaceful nook of the palace grounds.

After another eternal minute of watching the nobles fidget, Tryst finally spoke. "This is your show, nobles. You called it, you run it. What do you want of me?" His voice dripped of contemptuous amusement. His body did the same, as he lounged back, relaxing as if he had not the faintest concern. Jon could not imagine how anyone could find comfort in the stone chair, but Tryst seemed more comfortable in his skin than anyone Jon had ever known.

More time passed in silence. There were little movements and occasional whispers among the nobles, but nobody took action. Nobody said a word that could be heard on the platform. Jon began to feel rigid from the inaction and the rising anxiety of it all. Tryst continued to look like this was the most normal thing in the world.

At long last the bells of the chapel rang again, followed by one last ring to announce the first hour of the afternoon. That final bell echoed in the amphitheater. Tryst sprang to his feet, and the nobles jerked up as well. All were standing as the sound of the bell faded.

"You are due another hour here." Tryst took a step forward. The nobles leaned backward. "Why are you wasting my time, the people's time?" The threat in his voice was thinly veiled. As he stepped to the edge of the platform, the nobles pressed back into their seats, trembling. "Answer me. Answer for yourselves."

Silence again. Tryst pulled his sword out and motioned for his knights to advance.

"You have never had an answer for the prince or the people. You are pompous leeches, sucking the life out of our great city. The people do not need you. I have heard their desires. They want order and meaning in their lives. They do not care for your histories and customs. We live for today and the future, not the past. You nobles are a dead people to them." His voice continued to rise, in volume and in intensity.

"This will be the last day you call upon me, the last day you can claim to have power separate from the people. They elected me prince. You are no longer necessary. Kneel and give up your titles now, or you will not leave here alive—"

One of the nobles yelled out before Tryst could say another word. "A prince may never threaten the nobles!"

The response shocked Jon and even seemed to catch Tryst off guard. "Who said that?" The prince demanded. "Men of the Lycurgus emerge!" He called out beyond the amphitheater.

Most of the nobles stayed seated in fear, but a handful stepped forward confidently. Justus Davosman was standing in the front.

The next few seconds splintered around Jon. Soldiers flooded into the amphitheater, charging from the grounds. They looked like men of the Lycurgus. Jon had no idea who was friend or foe, but he knew his duty: to protect the prince.

To his right, the prince's knights broke into fighting among themselves. He thought he saw Ulysses, who had been beside Tryst, dive at the prince and send them tumbling off the platform.

He pulled out his sword and ran towards Tryst. Without pause he leapt off the raised platform and landed in the middle of a group of soldiers. They were advancing in phalanx—their huge shields becoming a wall that encircled the prince. Outside the ring, Jon saw others fighting for their lives. One of Tryst's knights had crossbow bolts pinned into his torso. Around him lay the bodies of several men.

Jon turned again and saw that Tryst had broken the line of men around him.

"Tryst!" Jon yelled as he ran towards the Prince.

Tryst saw him and pointed toward the exit of the amphitheater as he ran up the stairs. Jon caught up as two of Tryst's other knights charged ahead at the next wall of shielded men.

The first knight to reach the phalanx rolled below the wall's protruding spears and slashed upward, throwing a few men back. Tryst, Jon, and the other knight seized the instant and carved into the gap in the shields. They had broken through this line as well, but a group of crossbowmen stood between them and escape. The phalanx continued collapsing around them. Jon focused on deflecting every assault at Tryst.

With Tryst at his side, Jon never lost confidence that they would get out. The Prince's black figure was everywhere, followed by the blur of his sword. Zarathus no longer shone—it was covered in blood.

Tryst darted around the crossbowmen to try to find another way out. More and more men were surrounding them. Jon and Tryst dodged attacks and sliced their way into the onslaught.

Just as they reached the top of the bowl, Jon thought he saw Wren. Then a shout stopped him cold.

"I am the Prince!"

Jon heard the voice come from behind him. The bellow filled the amphitheater. Turning, Jon saw Andor standing before the stone throne. Most of the fighting had ended.

"Stand down, Tryst!"

Jon knelt cautiously for his true prince, but kept his sword at the ready. The men around him had just been trying to kill him.

Tryst stood beside Jon, staring into the bowl at Andor. He turned and looked down into Jon's eyes and clasped his shoulder as if to say thanks for fighting at his side. He then reached up slowly and slid off the crown. His black hair fell flat, moist from the fight and no longer framed in silver. Jon thought he saw a bittersweet light flicker across Tryst's solemn face as he fell to his knees.

"A prince will never threaten the nobles." Andor declared, loudly enough for everyone in the amphitheater to hear. He pointed at the usurper.

"You, Tryst, have violated their trust and your oath to serve. I have returned and stand ready to retake the throne that you stole."

Jon scanned the crowd. The knights loyal to Tryst seemed to have all been cut down. The other soldiers seemed to be obeying Andor. Most of the nobles had fled their seats in apparent shock and terror. Perhaps a dozen stood confidently, gazing at Andor. Six nobles had been bound by soldiers. The standing ones must have set the stage for Andor's return, Jon thought.

There was clearly much plotting that he had missed, just as Tryst had.

*   *   *

Father Yates stood beside Andor with a look of approval. He had counseled Andor that this should not be a revolution. It was important to preserve order and tradition. An uprising or a revolt would be too much. It left a taste in peoples' mouths. Once people had that taste, they remembered it. They could dwell on the possibility of change, if only for change's sake.

Between change and tradition, Father Yates had explained, tradition was the better course. He knew it was a hard lesson for a prince, but that made it all the more important.

Andor had agreed without much debate. He seemed more ready to agree with Father Yates on many more things since his time in the Gloaming. The old priest had not hesitated in blessing this plan of Andor's for returning to the throne. The hardest part was still to come.

As he looked out into the amphitheater, Yates was reminded again why tradition was so vital. There were too many dead bodies here today. Sometimes people would die for the greater good, but that truth did not make it any easier for him to see the losses.

This change had followed custom as closely as it could. It was not a coup; Tryst had forced himself to stand down by his own choices. A prince cannot be prince without the nobles, Father Yates thought somberly as he lifted his arms to announce Andor as prince, for the second time.

Chapter 23

Descent into Darkness

"He has to live in the midst
of the incomprehensible,
which is detestable.
And it has a fascination, too,
which goes to work upon him.
The fascination of the abomination.
Imagine the growing regrets,
the longing to escape,
the powerless disgust,
the surrender, the hate."

I was alone and naked except for tattered trousers, ropes tied to my arms, and honey and feathers layered over my body. It did not matter that familiar faces were staring at me. I ignored them as I stood before a gaping pit in the ground. The Gloaming.

A guard behind me whispered in my ear that he had loosened the ropes, but that I should wait to pull my arms free. He said he was following Andor's orders and was passing along his message: *Stay alive. I will come.*

Andor always wanted to control everything, even my imprisonment. I should have known sooner that he had returned, but how could I when those I trusted turned against me? Once he showed up in Icaria, I knew my control over the Lycurgus was slipping. By then it was too late, but I still had not expected him to move so quickly.

Many knights and soldiers must have felt the vestiges of fealty to him. Word of his return, and his survival against my blade, had fueled their disloyalty against me. The nobles should have stayed on my side, but Ramzi had ruined that while I was away from Valemidas. I had tried to act first, calling my knights to action against the nobles. Andor had set that stage against me.

Thoughts of what I could have done better tormented me. I tried not to think of Ravien's betrayal; it still hurt the worst. Instead, I focused on Wren, Sebastian, and the rest of them—they would die slow deaths at my hand. So would the nobles. They would pay for humiliating me, parading me around the main square covered in honey so the incited people could throw feathers and whatever else at me. Ramzi had fared worse, as only his head on a pike was given the honor and parading.

Sycophants turned torturers, the nobles had confirmed that I was right to try to eliminate their authority. Andor feigned kindness to intervene on my behalf to stop the nobles and my humiliation before the people. I would comply with Andor's suggestion of staying alive, but only so that I could kill him. If he had managed to escape this place, then I would too.

That thirst for revenge gave me focus as the guard pushed me into the pit. I slid down a pitch-black tube and landed in a metal box. The floor gave way moments later and I crashed down onto a pile of rot and bones.

The smell of death and decay hit me immediately. The light was barely more than night, like the moment when the last of the sun's warmth retreats. I had just gotten my feet under me and the ropes off my arms when dozens of figures emerged from the darkness.

Kneeling, expectant, I wished the feathers on my back could take the form of wings. I was the fallen angel, awaiting the demons. A group of men began to circle me like feverish rats. Each one was gaunt and gray, with a ravenous look in his eyes and a wariness of everyone around him.

The first few men came straight at me. I grabbed a bone from the pile. It was the length of my thigh and rivaled some of the others' crude bludgeons. I picked up a second, shorter bone in my left hand, for good measure.

Moving off the rotting mound, I spun away from the first assailant and swung the longer bone into the back of his head. I always marveled at the fanaticism of a first attacker. It took guts to be the first to die.

Two more men closed on me. I rolled under their reckless attacks. A swiping blow to the back of one's knees brought him down. I punched upward as I stood, smashing the shorter weapon into the other man's head.

By the time I had caught a breath, an instinct of fear hit me for the first time. No matter how weak they were individually, a large enough mob would swallow me. Mobs are like mindless swamps. If you force them to flow in a narrow channel, you can steer them clear of the oaks.

In this swamp, danger was coming from every direction at once. The circling figures were closing in on me, rushing at me. At first, some of the men stood back until they saw a weakness. Now they seemed to be charging in unison.

I moved into spinning attacks and landed many blows before anyone touched me. I swung at faces, legs, and arms. I found a flow within the dimness. Each figure became like a straw training man to me. If I moved fast enough, they were not moving. The onslaught continued and danced around the open square.

Men kept coming relentlessly, and I felt the first tinges of fatigue. It had been many hours since my last food and drink. Each man I fought drained strength, and they came without end. I had taken out at least ten before they began to swarm over me.

Instead of attacking, they seemed to be trying to bite and lick at me. I had thought they were trying to kill me because of who I am, but their motive was becoming clear. They were starving, and I was covered in food. My desperation swelled at the grotesqueness.

I pushed forward in one direction, towards a gap between two of the taller buildings around the square. Defense was not going to keep me alive if these men were so crazed. Throwing all of my energy into the push, I jumped and slammed my blunt weapons down on the heads of two men in front of me.

They fell but four men behind them pressed on me. One man connected with a jab at my side, knocking me off balance. The next hit was a fist to the side of my head. Ears ringing, I tried to roll to the side, but was kicked down by another man.

Before I could rise, they were diving onto me. I wrestled along the ground, fighting to get to my feet. The only thing that kept me alive was that they wanted the honey more than anything. They did not seem to care whether I lived or not. Also, once they had me pressed down, they began ripping at each other. A disgusting face tried to gnaw at my arm, only to be kicked away by another man. As soon as that feeder was swept away, another would fight for the place. It felt like giant ants were crawling over my body.

I writhed and twisted, but gained mere inches. My legs could not move. I could barely breathe, with the weight of the men crushing me into the ground. My failed movements converted into fury. My body weakened, but my soul blazed.

How could this happen? This was not my end. This could not be. I am the Prince. I am the greatest thing our world has seen, and here I am under a pile of ragged, sweaty humanity. Mankind deserves to die, if it is to treat me like this.

My thoughts drifted to no avail. Intense rage, passion, and even defeat clouded my mind. I was lost to my body, my eyes closed. My emotions seared away revealing a clear vision of light beaming from a throne. It was like a brilliant beacon that burns a hole through the darkest, most ominous cloud. I felt pitiful under that light. I felt broken and insufficient, which gave way to sorrow and an odd peace beyond my understanding.

In that moment my muscles eased. I no longer fought. As if wrapped in a cocoon of man's worst, my lips drew into a smile as the chaos stormed over and around me. This was not man's worst. This was not man. Man is only man when he has that light, but I turned away from it. I resolved to be more than just a man.

Suddenly I pulled in a large breath. My lungs had found a moment without pressure. I opened my eyes and saw gaps in the pile of men on top of me.

They were still over me, striking viciously at each other, but they were clearing themselves out. A few were biting at my skin, but they had cleaned off much of the honey. It gave me the opportunity I needed.

In a quick, fluid move, I summoned every muscle to action. It took only a couple swift kicks to clear my legs enough for me to rock backwards and bounce to my feet. The men looked up at me with surprise and terror. Perhaps they had thought me dead.

I seized that moment to unsheathe another weapon—my voice. I sucked in as much air as my lungs would hold, opened my mouth, and released.

"You need me!" The sound of my shout sliced through the men and brought stillness.

Yelling again, I gave my first command: "Obey me or die." Stillness continued, and I did too. "Kneel now. Do not move. If you follow my orders, you will have better than this. I will be your light."

I am not sure if I expected them to obey, but they did.

Chapter 24

Return to the Gloaming

**"Nothing makes a prince
so much esteemed as to
carry on great enterprises and
to give rare examples of himself."**

My father had taught me that there was no virtue in a man doing what he wants to do. It takes a great man to do what he should. As usual, in his teachings to me, Father Yates had intensified that simple moral. He believed that doing what one should did not mean anything unless it was done for God and for the love of fellow man.

As I was lowered into the Gloaming, I could not think of a greater form of love than returning to this pit of despair to save a wretched, fallen man. When I had said as much to Yates, he gave one of his rare, approving smiles. He was the only one, other than Ravien, who had not tried to convince me that this was a terrible idea.

Whatever the others said, I knew this had to be done. For Tryst, and for me.

Besides, this time was different. I was not being dropped out of a cage, already in a state of decay. I was healed, fed, armed, and with backup ready to follow me. After much negotiating, Wren and Jon had consented to wait two days before they came with others to find me, but only after I agreed to let them be stationed in the box hanging above the Gloaming. It would be enough time. Tryst had already been down there a week.

The lights above began to dim and then darkened completely. I could see nothing in the pipe, and I felt the cool underground air closing around me.

Breathing deliberately, I fought the urge to panic. This time was different, I repeated in my mind. I was not a conquered man. I was the conqueror, coming to declare my victory over this place. I kept telling myself that while I broke out into a cold sweat.

After a long slide I landed in the box. The metal under my feet was smooth and thin, ready to give way. The smell was debilitating.

I tried not to think about the piles of men and trash that had sat in this very spot over the past months, ready to fall and die. The prison guards had assured me that they had sent men and food scraps down just hours ago. No one experienced in the Gloaming would expect another dropping this soon. And, if all went according to plan, I would be the last person to make this journey.

I began flexing my legs, practicing the landing. All I had to do was land on my feet and run. I thought I could track down Tryst in a few hours.

My confidence felt surreal, but I held fast to it. I had survived here before. I had to do it again, and better. I owed it to Lorien.

I had to find Tryst, convince him to see the light, and get out in one piece. The difference this time was my shift in focus. Survival was not the goal; it was simply a necessary step.

Standing straight, steeling myself with another deep breath—and nearly gagging on the air—I yanked hard on the rope three times. A moment later, the floor fell open as I had expected.

The ground rushed up to meet me. I was shocked to see it cleared. The pile of bones was gone, and men encircled the landing area. I rolled as my feet hit the hard surface, softening the force of the fall. My eyes adjusted to the dimness, and shouts filled the air around me.

There were six men, each armed and rigid, glaring at me.

"Down on your face! Hands out! Down now!"

They yelled together, repeating the words and stepping closer to me.

"Who are you?" I yelled back.

They hardly registered the question as they continued shouting commands. It seemed there would be no talking my way out.

They froze when I drew my sword. Zarathus was enough to make any man pause. I charged the man in front of me, who dove out of the way and opened a path out of the square.

My legs pounded hard, each muscle tensing as I ran at a full sprint. I heard men chasing close behind me.

A single huge guard blocked my way out of the square. He held up a blunt club and braced for my impact. I reached his swinging range running at full speed. Just as he pulled back to swing, I sprang up high to his right and stabbed my blade straight down through his shoulder. I landed behind him and did not turn back.

The streets were empty as I had remembered them, and I sprinted on without hesitation. After several quick turns, I found the nearly pitch-black alley I was looking for. No noises followed, and I ducked into the open door of a stone, two-story building, breathing heavily.

This had been my home once before. The building was suited for hiding, because it had only the one door on the alley, and a tight staircase led to the small room upstairs. It would be hard for anyone to stumble into this place. If they did, I would hear them before they made it to the second floor. Fortunately, my quick survey revealed that I had the building to myself.

I leaned against the sole window in the upstairs room. It was almost my height, with no glass, open to the air and fifteen feet above the ground. The smooth stone around its edges was cool to the touch.

The Gloaming had the same eerie quiet. In the silence, my heart relaxed its pounding, and my thoughts turned to those men in the square. They had the same viciousness I remembered, but not the same desperation. They looked beaten down as before, but their movements were ordered. They could not have attacked me like that unless they were united somehow.

At first I rejected the idea. It was impossible. I had lived in this place. I had weathered months that felt like eternity here. There were too many bodies, not enough food. Most men were murderers and thieves. Groups never held together. It was every man for himself. Anyone who tried to impose order was conspired against. The Gloaming turned men into animals. It would take a devastating tyranny to hold any sort of social fabric together in this dark city.

Tryst, if anyone, could rule like that. He had to be behind this order. Maybe he had extracted oaths from men he could have killed, and then armed them as their small group grew in power. If so, it was an impressive yet tragic accomplishment. Brutal force could bind a small group only for a short time.

My rival had always harbored a devastating power inside him. He softened its edges as much as was necessary for him to rule in Valemidas, but a will to control had been in his nature since childhood. He created the rules, and if someone broke them, he would mete out punishment. He was never able to tolerate disobedience. He used to be harder on himself than he was on others. It seemed that had changed as he gained power.

I considered escaping now, if I even could. Why try to save the man? He had proven himself a threat to freedom. If his tyranny worked here, why not let it? Why subject the world above to the risk of him returning? How could he do here what I had failed to do?

A familiar voice spoke in my mind. *Do not go if not for love. If you are trying to set yourself above him, if you still have pride, you will fail. God will not bless the effort. You have faced your punishment and been redeemed. You know now that you need the divine light. You have to show Tryst that. If he sees and accepts your change, bring him back. It is his choice, and he knows the stakes. If he does not see the light, he cannot rise again.* I could almost hear Father Yates' solemn voice.

Love could be a tough master. Yates said you must love your enemies. Whatever Tryst was, he was at least an enemy. He was a challenger, a traitor, but he had once been like a brother—an exceptionally strong and occasionally demented brother. I would face him again, give him a chance of redemption. Maybe I could persuade him, if I could restrain him from killing me, and me from killing him, in the process.

At the very least, he would hear my invitation to leave this place on my terms. I had been given Lucian, who showed me there was something greater at work and inspired my escape. I would do the same for Tryst. I must not second-guess myself.

I leapt from the window to the empty street below. I began walking toward the heart of the Gloaming. Tryst would have selected a place near there to set up his rule. He was probably in the tallest warehouse I called the ladder. He would want to look down on his surroundings.

As I drew closer, two men began to walk together at a distance behind me. They were silent, and obviously following me. The opening to the square came into view, guarded as before. Sensing the trap, I turned and faced the followers.

"Where is Tryst?" I demanded.

They stopped, unable to hide. I drew Zarathus and walked towards them. They stood their ground, cowering like mice facing a lion.

Anger surged as I thought about the terrible things I had faced in this place. I had been forced to endure solitude among decaying men for months. And now these pathetic men were standing in a clump, unable to fend for themselves to save their lives. They would not have made it out of the heart of the Gloaming, not when I was here.

"He's been looking for you." A ragged whisper came from beside me.

Turning, I saw the familiar shaved head and glaring eyes of Granville. He looked more beaten down than I had ever seen him. His blacksmith muscles had thinned to nothing, suggesting he had not eaten in many days.

"I had feared that I would see you here, my friend. But I am relieved that you live. What happened?" A glance back confirmed that the other men were keeping their distance as Granville crept closer to me. I held my blade at the ready.

"After that fight up in Icaria," he began timidly, "I joined the march back to Valemidas. Many soldiers began to declare support for you. I helped spread the news, having been a witness to your return. Tryst must have learned of it, because as soon as we reached Valemidas, he had me thrown into the dungeon in chains. A dark little man named Ramzi put me to the question."

The large blacksmith shivered. "He tortured me, over and over. The pain—well—it still hurts." He bit his lip and looked down at his feet. "It probably always will. But still, I told him more than I should have—and, um, some of it was about you."

I clasped his shoulder. The man's cowed look was a poor fit on his stern face and frame. It was like Ramzi had bottled up fear and forced the man to drink it. Sympathy welled up within me.

"Have you seen Tryst down here?" I asked gently.

"No, I would not dare let him catch me. He has set himself up like a king of the underworld. He's a terror around here; everyone's afraid. We call him the prince of death. Men whisper that he has many minions. I can't trust anyone."

He looked at me in the eyes for the first time, wearing a plea on his face. "He must know that you're here by now, my prince. Please stay with me and hide away from him." He looked down again. "He'll hurt you, Andor. The world needs you up there. It's just darkness down here. You've got to get out and take me with you. Please."

"You have always been stronger than a forge, Granville." I tried to build him back up.

Granville stared blankly at my arm on his shoulder. He seemed to look closer at my sleeve, and then spoke in a warmer tone. "You're wearing the armor I made. The light leather suit, without a helm." A smile touched his face for the first time.

"Absolutely, Granville. This armor is a beautiful piece of work, mostly because it is so hard to detect. It served me well in Icaria, and it may do so again today." The blacksmith smiled wider, although his eyes still wore fatigue and despair. "I expect you to make more like it someday soon."

I took a step towards the central square and pulled Granville along. "Come, show me where rumors say Tryst is. If he knows I am here, there's no use hiding or escaping. I must see him."

As we walked to the square, still being followed, Granville quietly explained more. It was said that Tryst had forced ten men to bend the knee when he landed in the Gloaming. He had taken an iron bar from one of them, and then sent the men in groups of two to search for more weapons and compliant men.

He had waited in the central square for them to return, opening himself to anyone who would attack. Apparently some of the first ten men had never come back, either because they fled or died. But a handful did return, and they brought more men and crude arms. One of his men had returned with a rusted sword, and Tryst had struck him down and taken it on the spot. It made him practically invulnerable in one-on-one combat. He let anyone challenge his rule by fighting to the death at any time. It sounded like Tryst had finished with an armed group of about twelve, which he kept in order by killing anyone who disobeyed, and feeding those who followed them.

Granville confirmed that Tryst and his men controlled the ladder, as I had suspected, and they kept constant guard over the central square. The rest of the city remained in anarchy. Men could still make it out of the square with a crumb of food in the midst of the chaos that always follows a new falling. It seemed that even the greatest tyrant could have only limited power here, and I doubted that his rule would last long.

We approached the central square from the same street that I had escaped on. The guard I had leapt over lay in a pool of blood at the entrance. I kept Zarathus held high as I stepped into the square. Granville stopped at the entrance and pointed.

"Up there, my prince."

Following his arm, my eyes went to the building, which stood well above the other buildings of the square. Of course Tryst would claim this tower. Its walls gaped open from years of decay.

"Thank you, Granville. You have been a great help to me, as always. Now you should hide and watch the central square. When you see me there, come quickly. We will get out of here together."

Emotion flooded his face, bringing back more life than I had seen in him yet. I smiled at the hope of his fire returning, clasped his arm, and turned for the tower.

Two men stood at the front door to the building. They looked more like hideous decorations than guards. Confident that I was the only one with a sword, I strode through the huge doors without pause. The men did not budge to stop me.

The ground floor was as I remembered it—dark, musty, and miserably compressed under the weight of tower. Tryst had to be at the top. I walked straight to the central stairs.

The first four floors were unremarkable, except for the restraint showed by the few men whom I saw along the way. They seemed starved and feverish, like men always did in the Gloaming. Yet they held back their aggression from each other and from me. They just stared around nervously.

The whole place seemed to be teetering toward a breakdown. The unifying force was fear. When I had been in the Gloaming, there was always fear, but it was not targeted. Everyone feared death or losing the will to survive. Now, it seemed they all feared Tryst more than death.

As I climbed the stairs of the fifth floor, things became different. Three men were talking at the base of the final flight of stairs. This seemed to be Tryst's inner sanctum of sorts. The talking ceased as I came to face them. They looked ready to attack, and to carry it off well.

The largest man stepped down from the stairs above, pulling out a pole that looked a lot like the one I had once wielded. He pointed it a few feet from my face.

"You're Andor." It was not a question. He had greasy close-cut hair and a face covered in scars. He looked like he had been on the losing end of a glass diving contest. His face was familiar, and it was not one easily forgotten. He was the first man I had ever sentenced to life in the dungeons, for rape and murder. I had no idea how he had come to this place.

I opened my mouth to answer, but he cut me off.

"Shut up, pretty boy. I don't care what you're going to say. The Lord wants to see you, so get on up there. This'll probably be the end for you. Want any kind of last meal?" He burst out into crude laughter, and the other men joined in.

Emotion and instinct urged me to attack. I could take down this man and seize the high ground on the stairs. Others might come for me from below, but I could take them, to make sure of a clean exit. If it got too risky, I knew that I could jump out of the tower and land on the roof of the next building a story below.

My legs and arms tensed. My hand clenched the pommel of Zarathus.

The laughing stopped and the men grew restless in the quiet.

"Out of my way." I uttered the words through clenched teeth, fighting to restrain myself.

The ogre laughed again. "Pretty boy's mad." He took a small step to the side, leaving a foot for me to pass through. "Better hurry boy. You've got a date with a painful death up there."

I bridled my tongue and slipped past him. Their laughter followed me as I climbed the stairs to the room above. I shut it out and tried to think of Father Yates.

I was here to help Tryst, for love, not justice. The Gloaming was beneath me now. It had to be. It, and all the sins carried with it. I had been forgiven. Being here seemed to summon back a dormant savagery, but my soul could not afford another outburst. Enough men had died by my hand, and I would not let Tryst be added to the tally.

I stepped through a hatch at the top of the stairs and slammed it below me, cutting off the sounds of laughter. I stood silent in the cavernous top room. I had been here only once before.

There were no walls on three sides of the room; just bare wooden beams arching above. Six old iron chandeliers hung above. They dipped down to just above my head. Without any candles, they seemed to put out darkness instead of light. The floor was an inky black. I began to walk slowly towards the far side of the room with a wall. Each step was difficult.

I was half way across the room when I heard him move. He emerged from the darkness ten feet before me, wearing only black trousers and a sword. His face had the same sharp lines, the same blue eyes. But through the grime, he had a different look than I remembered. It was more sinister and open at the same time.

We each held our ground, eyes locked, swords drawn, bodies coiled. It was the kind of moment that could have stretched on into eternity.

Chapter 25

Light on the Fallen

**"No one after lighting a lamp
puts it in a cellar or under a basket,
But on a stand, so that
those who enter may see the light."**

Andor fought to stay calm. Tryst broke the silence in a clear, penetrating voice.

"I did not think you had it in you, Andor. You had me within reach three times before, but you were too weak to face me like a man. First you disguised yourself like a lowly knight, then you ran away with my sister, and last you let the nobles and soldiers seize me. Now you come *here* to taste death by my hand? I admit it is an unexpected relief. Cowardice does not sit well on you." He spread his arms as if in welcome. "The Gloaming is a fine place to end this."

"I am not here to fight you, Tryst." Andor's voice was soft but firm. "I came to bring you out."

Tryst began to move slowly around Andor, like a vulture circling above a wounded animal. "If you will not fight, then you will die easily."

"And then what? You stay here, a fallen tyrant in the dark?" Andor tried to maintain his distance from the predator. "You and I know you were meant for more than this."

"Your eyes adjust to the Gloaming. I am making something of this place, which apparently you never could. Order and obedience are replacing chaos's reign. I will be god here."

"You would be satisfied to rule this pitiful kingdom, dependent on the waste of our city above?"

"Admit it, you failed here," Tryst taunted as he circled closer to Andor.

"Everyone fails here. You cannot measure yourself against other men. Success is judged by something greater. I escaped from this form of death, and how I compare to those around me does not matter anymore. I want to enable every man to reach his best potential, including you."

"Your vanity has always come up short, Andor. What you and I want is the same, but Yates has made you think you do not crave the power that we cannot help but seek. Other men can never achieve the greatness we can. You let them hold you back. That is why I will be the only one left in this room alive."

"I invite you to join me when I leave, but you have to accept my help. I am not asking you to come because you deserve it. The world can march along without you."

"You are here to try to prove yourself." Tryst punctuated the sentence with a jab of his sword at Andor, who deflected it and hopped back out of reach. The clash of their blades echoed through the room. Tryst was beginning to close Andor into a corner.

"Tryst, listen to me. This is not a competition, and it is not about me. I have come because of what I learned while I decayed here. Yes, we are alike, but I was wrong to think that the arc of history had to be shaped by me. We are all flawed inside, so no man's will should prevail over the lives of others. Men need something apart from and greater than us. If you can accept that as I have, then we can return to Valemidas together."

"That sounds like a tired sermon from Father Yates. Ramzi taught me better, despite his flaws. The church's drivel drags you down into the dismal throng of humanity. The insidious teaching of men like Yates has stomped out the brightest souls for generations. I reject it. It is a shame that you, of all people, would believe their lies."

Tryst had come within arm's reach with his sword raised. He stared into his foe's eyes and held his position. "I expected more from you, Andor. Not long ago we shared similar promise. Ramzi recognized my greatness and helped me take the throne. I could have killed you then, but I exiled you here hoping you would come back and join me someday, on my terms. Instead you returned the favor, the usurped turning usurper."

"I would almost respect you for it, if not for your groveling. Ramzi explained what it means when great ones like you cave to the philosophy of servitude. You become a threat to world-historical souls. You become a traitor to your own kind. The few men born like us must push man's spirit to a new consciousness of freedom. You are no longer willing to see men sacrificed to develop a stronger and higher being of man."

Andor stepped back, a look of disappointment plain on his face.

Tryst's lips curved into a smile. "Now you have run out of time, and we cannot coexist."

He swiftly thrust his blade at Andor's stomach. Andor deflected it and slid to the side. Tryst struck again, and faster, slashing his sword down at Andor's head. Andor rolled away but caught a glancing blow to his left shoulder. It drew blood, but Granville's armor had stopped the full force.

Tryst pressed closer with a flurry of blows. Andor parried most of them with Zarathus, but he took a few more grazes through the armor and a cut on his cheek.

The men circled each other, metal ringing as they clashed. Tryst was relentless and strong, but Andor had the better sword and the stamina for patience. Both were breathing heavily when Tryst charged and, after blocking an attack, surprised Andor with a punch to the face.

As Andor reeled back, Tryst swung his sword at Andor's sword-bearing arm. The blade bounced off the armor, but the force was enough to knock Zarathus out of Andor's hand.

They both dove for the blade and grappled on the floor. Andor managed to pin Tryst down. In an instant he pulled a dagger from his boot and pressed it to Tryst's throat. Zarathus was just out of reach.

Sweat and blood dripped from Andor's face onto Tryst's. Their muscles quivered as Andor struggled to hold him down. One slice of his blade and Tryst would die.

"This is your last chance, Tryst," Andor breathed out. "We are only human, not divine. Serve the light, not yourself."

"I am the light, Andor. God is dead."

"You are dead, if you do not come with me."

Tryst's body relaxed, but Andor kept his dagger at his neck. He fought every temptation to kill the man who had betrayed him and sent him to the Gloaming to rot.

"Leave this place with me, Tryst. If change is what you want, I promise it will come. I will put an end to the Gloaming. No man should face this punishment. I will bury Zarathus here. It is a relic of a twisted past that corrupts men who worship the will to power. You could be prince again, because starting with me, no man will be prince for life. I will serve several more years and then step down. The nobles will no longer hold their positions by name and title. They will be elected and allowed no more than twenty years of service."

Tryst lay quiet and still, his face blank. Andor continued to speak, hoping his words landed in fertile soil.

"You and Ramzi were right about man's depravity, but you were mistaken in trying to control it solely through the force of laws. We must empower the people to lead themselves, to take more responsibility and realize their potential. Only with such obligations can a mature and lasting happiness prevail for generations. Men may join the Lycurgus if they please, but it cannot be forced on mere boys. Valemidas has grown decadent and weak, it is true. Maybe someday you will again lead the Lycurgus if you come with me. Build the traditions that military requires, and raise up leaders of stature and spirit."

"I prayed that this place would show you the truth about yourself. We must be stripped and broken down, especially when we have constructed delusions about our own grandeur. That is what happened to me. You sent a man named Lucian here. When Lucian fell, I was worse than death, but something about him inspired me. He died saving me. He helped me see the light in the Gloaming. I believe you will come to see it, too. You will leave the Gloaming reborn, as I did."

"Are you finished?" Tryst asked casually, as if they were drinking in a tavern.

"One more thing." Andor answered, not noticing the ounce of tension that had faded from his hand holding the dagger. "You should know that I am not here just for myself. More than anyone, Ravien insisted that I come for you. She loves you, Tryst, and she hopes for your return on these terms. She had grown to fear what you were becoming, and so had Lorien. But they would welcome you back."

Tryst stared levelly at Andor and spoke with contempt. "I would rather be god of the Gloaming than your puppet. Enough of your weakness and lies."

Like a coiled snake striking, Tryst spat and then slammed his forehead into Andor's face. As Andor reeled back, Tryst planted his free hand on the ground and thrust his sword at Andor's chest. "Your death is my—"

Tryst's words ended in a writhing scream. Andor, while rolling away from attack, had stabbed his dagger through Tryst's hand, pinning it into the wooden floor. As Tryst dropped his sword and reached frantically to pull out the dagger, Andor slammed his boot into Tryst's side and kicked away the dropped sword. He dashed to pick up Zarathus and then looked back.

"How you have fallen!" Adrenalin coursed through Andor. "You leave me no choice but to abandon you in this pit, lost to the light. You could have been so much more."

The prince sprinted to the room's nearest open side. He dropped to the ground and began to slide off the edge as he gripped the ledge firmly. He used his swinging momentum to land on the floor below. From there he leapt to the nearest building's roof. He found its stairs and sprinted to the bottom. He ran out a door and toward the center of the square.

Six men were standing under the black box. Before he reached them, Andor pulled a bag of round stones from his pocket. He threw three of them consecutively at the box as he ran. The sound of their thump against the metal was lost in the frenzy of men yelling on all sides, but it was heard inside the box.

This time the men in the square did not attempt to stop Andor. Their faces wore confusion and fear as they stepped back. Suddenly the doors of the box dropped open and a rope fell from the dark space. Andor grabbed it and began to rise when he turned and saw Granville running toward him. Three men blocked Granville's path.

He could not leave him.

Dropping the rope, Andor yelled and charged with Zarathus held high. Behind Granville, he saw Tryst and his group of men flooding out of the building. Time was running short. The three nearest men turned to stop Andor.

Andor stabbed his blade into the gut of one man as he ducked under the swing of an iron pole. He spun as he pulled Zarathus out and severed the arm that had been holding the pole. The third man ran as the other two lay screaming on the ground.

Granville reached for Andor's outstretched hand but fell to his knees. The hilt of a crude dagger stuck out of his back. Tryst was holding another dagger, ready to throw.

"Go!" Granville yelled as Andor tried to lift him. "Leave me!" He screamed as the second dagger plunged into his back.

Andor looked up and saw Tryst pulling out another blade to throw. At least ten men were with him. Andor nodded farewell to Granville, turned away, and sprinted the short distance to the rope.

He grabbed it just as a blade flew into his shoulder, knocking Zarathus out of his hand. He held fast to the rope and tried to ignore the pain.

He lifted quickly off the ground to the box above. He looked up and grabbed the hand reaching for him.

"Stop him! No!" Tryst's voice shouted from below, full of desperation.

Sorrow and anger and relief swept over Andor as he watched Tryst pick up Zarathus and reach out toward him with his other, bleeding hand.

The doors of the box slammed shut, snapping Andor's mind back to the present. A lantern's light filled the small space, and Jon and Wren sat before him.

They had followed his orders and stayed stationed in the box until the three stones struck it. The brothers wore harnesses tied to a rope leading to the dungeons above, which had allowed them to lift him up after the doors opened.

"It is finished, my friends." Andor winced as he spoke. "I could not have done it without you."

"Thanks to your inspiration, my prince." Jon answered somberly. Andor glanced down, thinking of the man lost below.

"You look better than the last time you left this place, my prince," Wren said with a grin.

"I would hope so. This time I return to the position where I belong. We lost Granville. It will take a long time for these wounds to heal." Andor rose to his feet, and the brothers sprang up to help him when he staggered.

"You will not be feeling better at all, if we do not get you mended soon. Can you keep a hold on the rope?" Jon asked.

Andor nodded and gave the rope two hard pulls. "Let's go."

After they were lifted to the dungeons above, Andor led them out to the palace grounds. He walked to the top of the stairs overlooking the city. He had promised Lorien he would go there first.

She and Ravien were waiting. Lorien let out a cry of relief and ran to Andor's arms.

As Lorien tended his wounds, Andor briefly explained about the fight, and Tryst's refusal to join him. He steered his mind, and the conversation, to focus on the future.

"We have much to do to make things right again." He turned from the city to look at Lorien, Ravien, Wren, and Jon. They watched him with respect. "I hope one of you will have a turn at the throne after me, but do not let the power go to your head. You have seen what that did to Tryst and to me."

"What we have seen, my prince, is that you died and came back to us with more wisdom and strength." Wren spoke. "It seems the same is not to be for Tryst. He can live and reign in the underworld." Ravien said nothing but her countenance darkened.

Andor did not respond at first, his gaze moving from the city to the ocean and storm clouds to the east.

"As long as he is down in the Gloaming," he said distantly, "a piece of me will be there too. Maybe he was right that we cannot coexist, but we meet in the shadows left by this world's light. Tryst can remain below."

The prince looked back at Lorien and the others. "My place is here, with you. We cannot rid ourselves of darkness, but we can choose to walk in the light."

Epilogue

**"By its light will the nations walk,
and the kings of the earth
will bring their glory into it."**

Two men and a woman sat in the high tower of an old noble house. The candles in the room had nearly burned down, but the first morning light was shining on the parchment before them.

They had negotiated over the words through the night. It had been mostly cordial, thanks in part to the wine, but a few threats and bribes had been necessary to find agreement on the stickier points. Now they were done, and each had applied their seals in blood.

Ravien stood with her hands planted on the table, staring down at the inked words. She had not wanted it to come to this. Andor was supposed to bring her brother back, but her brother was a proud man. He had been wrong to entrust Ramzi with power and wrong to try to dismantle the nobles. Still, Valemidas needed him to lead its army against the coming threat. At least her brother was last seen alive, and this agreement was the best chance of bringing him back. Mailyn had told only her that she carried Tryst's child. Walking to the window, she looked out over the ocean to the east of Valemidas. The view brought some peace, because it reminded her that she and Wren would be sailing away from this place for a while.

The old noble, Justus Davosman, paced around the table and the parchment. He had long feared that this day would come. The Lycurgus had been a step in the right direction, a return to the old ways of discipline and fortitude. Valemidas had grown too soft, and a city like that could never stand long against another people hungry for power. This agreement meant it was soon time to spread the news that only the three in this room knew. If Andor had the courage, that news could save Valemidas. Davosman alone knew Andor's parents and their lineage, which gave him hope in the restored prince.

Sebastian leaned back in his chair with a smile. His people, the Sunans, could not lose with this agreement. Either they conquer or they walk away with chests full of this city's treasures. The infighting of their princes had left them vulnerable, as had generations of peace before Tryst. If his people conquered, no one would be in a better position to be prince than he. This agreement saw to that.

Made in the USA
Charleston, SC
07 October 2013